BACK O

D. G. Compton was born in 1930 and lives in London. His many critically acclaimed novels include *The Steel Crocodile*, *Chronocules*, *The Continuous Katherine Mortenhoe*, *Ascendancies* and *Nomansland*. *Justice City*, the first Alec Duncan mystery, is also published in Vista.

Also by D. G. Compton in Vista

JUSTICE CITY

D.G.COMPTON

Back of Town Blues

An Alec Duncan Mystery

First published in Great Britain 1996
by Victor Gollancz

This Vista edition published 1997
Vista is an imprint of the Cassell Group
Wellington House, 125 Strand, London WC2R 0BB

A catalogue record for this book is available from the British Library.

ISBN 0 575 60131 0

Printed and bound in Great Britain
by Cox & Wyman Ltd, Reading, Berks

97 98 99 10 9 8 7 6 5 4 3 2 1

1

Night. The sound of water lapping. Light shines down from a street lamp in a steep cone on to a wide paved walk, and at the light's edge a woman leans on a heavy black wrought-iron rail, staring out into the darkness. Behind her, on the far side of the walk, trees in full leaf are outlined faintly against a cloudless, moonlit sky, bright with stars.

The woman stands so exactly at the edge of the cone of light that, while her legs and body are brightly lit, her head and the top of her shoulders are in shadow. Her hands, also in shadow, rest on the rail in front of her, one of them holding a plastic Safeway carrier bag, apparently empty. Her ankles are bare beneath shin-length flowered tights, and she has grubby white trainers on her feet. Her weight is on one foot, the other is lifted and hooked behind it. She wears a dark woollen jumper down to her thighs, with an Aztec-patterned knitted waistcoat hanging open over it, and a shabby fringed felt shoulder bag.

Her hands fidget on the rail. They are chapped, their knuckles are swollen, and her thick ankles are webbed with veins. Her style of dressing may be that of a youngish woman but these details suggest that she probably adopted it a good few years back, twenty or thirty, and has not thought about it since. Her life, these details suggest, has been poor; badly organized; not easy.

The rail on which she is leaning guards a ten-foot drop, a wall marked with greasy tide marks, down to a narrow shingle beach. Little choppy waves break on it softly. The street lamp is the last in a long line of identical lamps, a mile of them or more, curving away to her right beneath a skyline of dark city roofs and tower blocks. To her left the paved waterfront walk ends in blackness: trees, dimly seen, and a rusty footbridge across swampland.

The woman has been looking out across the grey moonlit water, at far distant cranes and warehouses silhouetted against the night sky. Clearly this expanse of water is part of a wide estuary or coastal inlet, heavily industrialized. Now the woman's attention is distracted by lights moving slowly by on the water: the ship itself is invisible but its lights, masthead and starboard, and living quarters aft, are bright. She watches them until they are gone, then looks away, down at her wristwatch, and lifts her arm up sideways to see her watch more clearly in the light from the street lamp. When she sees what the time is she shows no reaction, no surprise, no impatience, just returns her hand to the rail and her gaze to the opposite shore.

This movement, her leaning sideways to peer at the watch, brought her face into the light from the street lamp. Its harsh white glare did her face no favours: black eye sockets above wide flat cheeks, an over-lipsticked mouth, a curiously child-like nose that cast a small, chubby shadow, pale hair in thin permed curls. She is wearing little daisy earrings. Once perhaps, forty pounds lighter, she was fluffy and pretty. Now, through neglect, and hard work, and the passage of years, she is fluffy and pretty no longer.

Up between the trees behind the woman, a flight of paved steps joins the waterfront to a gravelled turn-around at the end of an unlit road leading back along the coast, towards the city's tower blocks. The road, and the wide newly mowed grass verges on either side of it, are deserted. Nothing moves.

Faint traffic noises, intermittent, as of individual vehicles, passing rapidly, can be heard from a main thoroughfare somewhere. The hour is clearly late. This is an improbable place for a rendezvous, and the woman an improbable lover or conspirator, yet she is here, and alone, and apparently waiting, so she must surely have in mind some manner of private encounter.

She straightens her back, eases it wearily, walks slowly to the other side of the cone of light, and leans again on the rail. Having moved, she is once more still, accepting without surprise or impatience the lateness of the hour. Only her hands are unrestful, fidgeting as before with the Safeway plastic carrier bag. Something weighs it down very slightly. It looked empty at first sight but now it seems not to be.

It is impossible to tell exactly when the sound of the approaching car becomes audible. The silence here, the rustling water and the night city all around, rings in the ears. The woman does not help: she gives no sign when she begins to hear the car. Almost no sign – perhaps, in the darkness under her brows, her eyelids close. Certainly they are closed by the time the sound of the car has become unmistakable, and they stay closed as the car's headlights scan the road behind her, as the car itself comes into sight, a rusty mustard-yellow Nissan, at the top of the steps. It stops there and the driver opens the door, revealing himself in the interior light. Thirtyish, with meagre hair and scraped, ungenerous features, he wears a light-coloured duffel coat, narrow jeans, and expensive black tasselled loafers over white socks. He gets out of the car and trots down the steps very quickly and neatly, a foot to each step, leaving the car's engine running, its radio playing, its headlights on, its door open.

The woman takes a deep breath, opens her eyes, visibly gathers her life force together. She turns from the water as the man approaches.

'I'd given you up.'

'I know.' He joins her in the light from the street lamp. 'Couldn't get away. Then the soddin' motor wouldn't start.'

'You said midnight.'

'I told you, lady.' His cheek twitches. It might be a wink. 'Couldn't get away.'

She turns back to the water. Her accent is Liverpool, his from somewhere nearer London. She fusses resentfully with the strap of the fringed bag on her shoulder.

'I've been here since midnight.'

'Go down on me soddin' knees, shall I?'

'Business is business. I don't like being messed around. I was daft once. I'm not any more. Have you brung it?'

His cheek twitches again. 'Don't you trust me?'

'If there's money for you in it, I do.' She looks him up and down. 'You said bullets. When we talked, you said bullets. So where are they?'

He pats his duffel coat pocket. 'Old dependable, that's me.' The cheek twitch is clearly habitual. A tic. He does a nervy little sideways shuffle. 'Didn't your Trev tell you?'

'Thing is, Mr Drew, my Trev's not around so much these days.' There is a beat of silence between them. A point made. 'So show us what you got.'

He bounces back. 'Thing is, Mrs B, bloke like me, first of all I like to see the readies.'

A small protective movement away from him suggests that the money is in the plastic carrier bag. It suggests also that Mrs B is more afraid of Mr Drew than she pretends.

She folds her arms. 'Hundred and ten.'

'Hundred and fifty.'

'That's what you said.'

'That's what I meant.'

'It's too much. I can't raise it.'

He does not believe her and she does not expect him to. This is ritual.

'Of course you can raise it. Don't mess me around. That paper paid you thousands.'

She looks away, frowns, hitches her shoulder bag, not answering. This is different: he has raised a bitter memory.

'That paper—' She stops, thinks better of it, bows her head.

He gives himself a little hug. 'Thousands,' he says again. '*Thousands* . . .'

He walks to the lamp post, two steps and a chassé, and swings from it on one arm, watching her. In his car, up on the road, music is still playing. The beat is clear, but no tune, just a faint tinny background jangle.

His cheek twitches. 'Not that anybody's blamin' you. They'd of done the same in your place. Anyone would.' He swings further, a complete circle round the lamp post, still watching her. She ignores him and he clears his throat to attract her attention. 'Thing is, lady, I don't think you got much option. Sad but true. You want the shooter, I got the shooter. Sad but true.'

She lifts her head. 'Nine thousand, if you really want to know. Nine thousand pounds. Hardly a fortune. And then all the bloody reporter woman does is—'

'It's the middle of the night, lady. Tomorrow we go somewhere nice and I buy you a cup of coffee and you tell me your troubles. Tonight we—'

He is boring her now and she stops him. 'You said bullets.'

'Thrown in. Two clips. Ammunition. Not bullets, Mrs B. *Ammunition* . . . Bullets is naff.'

'I can see why they bloody call you Dancer.'

He stops swinging, steps away from the pole, and reaches inside his duffel coat. 'Ex-copper. Biggish, but you won't be carrying it around.' The automatic pistol he produces from his duffel coat looks huge. 'No holster, but you won't need one. Not around the flat. Hard to come by, holsters. All them straps and buckles.' He offers her the gun. 'Like I said, ex-copper. Lovely job – the latest lightweight carbon fibre. Only the best for the filth, these days. I don't reckon he parted with it easy.'

She hesitates, then opens her carrier bag and brings out two bundles of banknotes, one still tied together with a bank's blue paper strip. In view of all her haggling she handles the money surprisingly casually.

The sight of it brightens his eyes and sets off a barrage of twitches.

'You got a good deal here, lady. You won't regret it. Don't care who they are on the estate, the fuckers'll leave your place alone with this.' He cocks the automatic, points it out into the darkness, and pulls the trigger. '*Pow* . . .' The firing pin clicks on an empty chamber. He lowers the barrel. 'Peace of mind, Mrs B. Cheap at the price.'

She hangs the carrier bag over one wrist and gives him the money. He gives her the gun. She takes it in both hands, finds it is lighter than she expected. She swings it round, pointing at things, then holds it out to him again.

'Show me what to do.'

The banknotes have disappeared, uncounted, into his coat. Its side pocket yields two ammunition clips. He takes the gun back from her, slides one clip up into its butt, slaps it home.

'Ten shots,' he says. 'Do a lot of damage, ten shots will. And they won't never jam, I loaded them myself. And this here's the safety catch.' He shows her. 'Pushed forward like this, forward against the stop, it's ready. Pulled back here, lying down, it's safe. Think you've got that?'

'Not like for a woman.'

'You what?'

'For a woman, lying down's dangerous.' She does not smile and he sees that no joke is intended.

'You've got it. And the clip's retained with this . . . So that's it, then.' He gives her the gun again, and the spare ammunition clip, which she drops into her carrier bag. 'Always happy to do business with a lady. Any other little thing, you know where to find us.'

She is examining the gun, using both hands as she pushes the safety catch back and forth with her thumbs, her head bent over it. She does not answer him and after a few seconds he sees that he has been dismissed. Even so, something is bothering him. Possibly he has only just been struck by the incongruity between this dull old woman in her dull, once-trendy clothes, and the formidable police issue carbon fibre automatic she is holding.

'Sure that's everything?' He's clearly reluctant to leave her. 'A gun like that kicks. You'll be surprised . . . And what about reloading? Reloading's a doddle. No problem. No problem at all. The spring there that holds the clip – all you does is—'

'I won't be reloading.' She does not raise her head. 'Ten bullets is a lot. Ten bullets is plenty. Why should I be reloading?'

'No reason.' He shrugs. 'I just thought . . . I mean, well, the day may come, you know. I mean, you can never tell, lady – stranger things have happened . . .' He tails off and does one of his little dancing shuffles. 'I just thought . . .'

But she does not respond and he gives up, shrugs, walks away, fastening the toggles on his duffel coat as he goes. At the edge of the pool of light she stops him.

'Dancer Drew?'

He turns to face her. 'That's me. Dancer by name and dancer by nature . . .'

She waits a moment. Then, 'You killed him.'

'I never.' The denial is automatic. 'Killed who?'

'My son. Trevor. My son.'

'Come on, missis. He's not dead.'

'He's worse.'

There are three paces between them. She lifts the gun in both her hands, just to be sure, and points it at his chest and fires. She fires three times, quickly, her hands and arms jerking, her face screwed up against the noise. The bullets all hit him, hit his upper body, and he staggers.

He stares at her, amazed. 'You're crazy. You fucking bitch, you're—'

The noise has been so loud that she is almost certainly temporarily deafened and does not hear him. In any case, she takes a step forward and fires again. This fourth impact flings him back and he falls on the paving stones. She waits for a moment, her face still screwed up, then relaxes it, lowers the gun, now in her right hand only, and walks stiffly away to the rail. Standing very straight, she looks out across the water. Then her back weakens, seems to break, and she falls forward against the wrought-iron rail, shuddering. Moonlight picks out the small ripples breaking on the beach below her.

Dancer Drew moves and groans. He moves again, heaves himself on his elbows into the light. At the rail Mrs B is easing her neck, rotating her head to uncramp the muscles. His progress into the light catches her attention. She winces at the sight of him, and looks away. He is moving less, but still groaning. Wearily shaking her head, Mrs B reaches into her shoulder bag and brings out a wad of paper tissue on which she wipes her eyes. She drops the tissue over the rail, down on to the muddy beach. Eventually she walks back to where Dancer is lying. Against his pale duffel coat the fresh red blood from four exit wounds is brownish-grey in the light from the street lamp. He sees her and lies very still, no longer groaning. She points the gun in her right hand down at him, its muzzle now no more than two feet from the side of his head, and looks away, up past the lamp at the sky. Her left arm is held out to the side almost horizontally, one finger raised, as if asking for silence. She fires again, just once.

After this shot a lot of time seems to pass. Only her eyes move, flicking sideways and sideways, until at last she can force them to be still.

She looks down.

Having seen that Dancer Drew is dead, that this fifth bullet has spread his blood and brains and bone splinters across the brightly lit paving stones, she steps carefully forward over his body, avoiding the blood and brains and splinters, and walks away, out of the light from the street lamp, and keeps on walking. She doesn't look back. She seems hardly to see where she is going, yet she walks away purposefully, out into the moonlit darkness. Behind her, on the paving stones, Dancer Drew lies quietly, without pain. At the top of the flight of steps, the door to his car hangs open, the radio plays, the engine runs, and the lights still shine.

She walks away across the rusty footbridge. A short distance along the rough path on the other side she pauses, unhooks the plastic carrier bag from her wrist, and drops the gun into it. It chinks against the loaded ammunition clip already there. She walks on along the path, the light of the street lamp left behind and the moon bright enough to see by. She is very tired now but she walks steadily, the path winding away from the water, uphill between tussocks of long grass and scrubby bushes. These merge into the beginnings of a narrow lane, three wooden posts stopping cars from getting too close to the water. Beyond them a fence looms out of the darkness on her left, and then double gates across a tarmac drive. She comes to houses, quite classy, not her style at all, set back from the road behind rockeries and banks of flowering shrubs, their blank windows catching the moonlight. She goes on past them. The lane curves, and at a junction between high stone garden walls she turns left.

The lane opens out into parking spaces and pathways between areas of worn grass around the bases of small square tower blocks. A sign announces *Riverview Heights: Liverpool Housing Action Trust.* Many of the cars in the parking spaces are derelict, vandalized, burnt out, and the pathways are littered with cans and wrappers. Broken tricycles and plastic toys lie about on the grass, the moonlight leaching out the stridency of their colours.

Mrs B pauses as two small dark figures appear at the corner of a row of lock-up garages. Whispering together, and laughing softly, and shushing each other, they jump up on to a low boundary wall and run along it, balancing theatrically, arms outstretched. One flings himself off, down on to the grass, and the other follows him and they roll about together, still laughing. Mrs B walks on past them and they stop their tussling to watch her.

She goes up a path to a tower block entrance. The heavy door stands open, off its hinges, its coded electronic lock system smashed, its video surveillance camera stolen. Curiously, the exterior light here has survived, and illuminates the step and the nearest downstairs windows. Mrs B goes inside. The two children scramble to their feet and run off, chasing each other. A few moments later, on the other side of the block, there is movement in one of the ground floor flats. A door opens out on to a small oblong balcony that, like all the other ground floor balconies, has had its protective steel grid ripped away, and for a while Mrs B stands just inside the unlit room, looking out. Faintly, in another block, raised voices are heard and a series of crashes, probably the sound of breaking furniture. Mrs B steps back from her balcony door, and slowly closes it.

2

Earlier that night, around eleven o'clock, Alec Duncan was taking a break between sets. There'd been nobody on the tiny dance floor when he quit, the applause had been scattered and there wasn't exactly a queue of punters waiting to buy him drinks. Life wasn't all bad, though: so far there hadn't been the funny man with the bad Bogart accent who called him Sam and asked him to play it again, while his mates pissed their pants at the bar. Several times a night, some nights. It was difficult enough, playing bar piano. Being black as well put the lid on it.

There *was* one drink though, a glass containing what looked like a double whisky, standing on his pile of sheet music. Charlie had brought it over while Alec was winding up the set's final number, a stride version of 'Million Dollar Baby'. Charlie'd nodded in the direction of his fan, but Alec had been too busy to look. 'Baby' was a new arrangement, very sharp and spacey, and the left hand needed his full attention. Now he picked up the whisky, sniffed it and raised his eyebrows, smelling Charlie's one and only single malt, kept on the top shelf for special customers. He glanced across the tiny dance floor. A man sitting alone in a booth under an art deco Craven A advertisement caught his eye and raised his glass. Alec returned the toast warmly. Not only was the man free with his money, he'd taken the trouble to find out from Charlie the way to Alec's heart.

It was a thin night in Tony's. Mondays always were. A handful of cloth-ears propping up the bar and most of the booths empty. Liverpool's dinks – those who weren't out on vigilante duty – were recovering from the weekend, catching up on their beauty sleep. Tony had hoped that a twenties theme pub would pull in all ages but it was mostly the young who went for it. Cocktails, chromium bar stools, Charlie with a bow tie and bands on his shirtsleeves, jazz on a white grand piano – it was natural yuppieland. Crumblies preferred the sixties that they could just about remember. Elvis, for God's sake. There were sixties theme pubs all over town.

Alec leaned his elbows on the piano keys and inhaled his whisky, warming it in his hands. He had a fan. Life for a single, black, forty-plus, out-of-work Scotsman in Scouseville was looking up. Forty quid a night and tips. His name, on a board surrounded with dancing semi-quavers, was on an easel by the piano: *Alec Duncan, King of Swing.* And now a fan. The snappy caption was Tony's idea, who thought he'd made it up. He'd probably never even heard of the original King, Benny Goodman, whose coat-tails Alec didn't aspire to touch. Still, the job paid the food bills and left a bit over. *Ah, fuck it* . . . Last week there'd been a piece on him in the *Merseyside Gazette*. They'd spelled him *Alick* as in smart, but he didn't complain. Five nights a week at Tony's, and volunteer portering in the hospital . . . it passed the time. He had money in the bank, savings, plenty to tide him over.

His sister disapproved. Once a social worker always a social worker, she said he wasn't going anywhere and he couldn't argue with that. He wasn't going anywhere, he was fine where he was. Occasionally, like tonight, a punter noticed.

Alec raised his glass again to his fan, and emptied it. He put it down, stretched his hands and played a preparatory chord. Tony didn't like long silences. He wasn't around tonight but it was amazing how the word got back. Alec wandered through the keys, then settled in E flat and launched into Cole's 'Easy

Listenin' Blues'. It was one his fingers knew and he could leave them to it. His fan puzzled him – he'd noticed the man come in and he was wrong for Tony's, not the right generation (late forties) and not the right get-up. Alec eyed him covertly: not a get-up at all. Nothing so vulgar. The suit was hugely expensive, very well cut, and utterly discreet; the shirt too was unexceptionable, plain white and probably made to measure, with a modest collar, and the tie looked military. The face also, even when it smiled, revealed impressively little. Such restraint suggested a fairly senior job in the Ministry of Education. Decidedly wrong for Tony's.

The man was on his own but the glass in his hand was only his second so he wasn't a drinker. He'd brought a folded newspaper with him yet he'd been in the booth for an hour or more and it was still folded. And now the whisky. So what was the attraction?

Alec didn't flatter himself it could be his playing, not at the price Charlie asked for his single malt. A gay pick-up? Possible. But Tony's wasn't that sort of pub. Hungry singles, of whatever persuasion, did their hunting elswhere. So if it wasn't Alec's playing, and it wasn't a pick-up, then what was it?

Alec's fingers reached the end of the Cole. He glanced up at the clock as he sorted through his pile of music for ideas. He had another half-hour to go and the few remaining punters were dozing off. Better wake them up, and himself, with something acerbic. He straightened his back, assaulted the keyboard in an Errol Garner-style intro, and set out at a driving bebop pace to murder 'How High The Moon'. Such post-war violations of the twenties theme never worried Tony: Alec had a feeling that anything played on a white piano was twenties to Tony.

Did bebop sell more drinks? The findings that Monday night in Tony's were equivocal. Of the five punters at the bar, two drifted out on to the dance floor and sidled through a couple of half-hearted jive sequences, while the other three slightly shifted their elbows on the bartop and reordered. The two dancers missed good drinking time, but sweated and may have made up for it later, while the man in the booth remained attentive, nodded inaccurately to the faster beat, and nursed his original glass. Alec did all the repeats, then segued into 'Stardust' at a similar lick. It was hardly the night of the big spenders.

As midnight approached Alec wound this final set down. 'Deep Purple', 'Moonlight over Miami' . . . he spared himself 'The Last Waltz' (the place wasn't full enough or drunk enough), and quit on 'These Foolish Things'. The dancers were back at the bar and only the man in the booth noticed when the music ended: he applauded silently, hands above the table. Alec realized that he'd been putting more of himself out on the final numbers. Payment for the single malt? It seemed a bit tradesman's entrance. He closed the lid on the piano keys, stood, and went over to the booth.

'Thanks for the whisky.' He paused. 'I've a feeling, though – and you'll correct me if I'm wrong – I've a feeling my sort of music's no really your style. In the normal course of events, I mean.'

The man inclined his head. 'I can take it or leave it. Sit down, Mr Duncan.' The name, Alec realized, might have come from the easel by the piano. 'What can I get you?'

Alec hesitated. 'Am I missing something? Have we two met?'

'No.'

'And you don't like my music. So why the generosity?'

'A word. Just a moment of your serious attention.' He looked across at Charlie and clicked his fingers. 'Barman?'

'You're from a paper.'

'Not at all. After nine months? You flatter yourself.'

Alec sat down across the table from him. Nine months? Was it really so long? But the man's directness appealed. It was like no gay come-on he could imagine.

'The name's Hardcastle.' Alec expected a hand to be offered, or a card – from the breast pocket of that discreet expensive suit a discreet expensive card – but neither came. 'You have partly to thank Sergeant Grove for this intrusion. He told me where to find you.'

Alec felt easier. Frank knew the people he could bear to talk to just at the moment, and the people he couldn't. But it was still odd – Frank had the Sefton Park address, so why send this Hardcastle to Tony's?

Charlie arrived at the table. Hardcastle looked across at Alec. 'Same again?'

Alec shook his head. 'Perrier. I'm driving.'

'There speaks a policeman. An ex-policeman.' He turned to Charlie. 'Make that two Perriers. With such an example, what else can I say?'

Alec put a hand on Charlie's arm and pointed back at the bar. 'And one of yon poor wee sandwiches.' He'd just remembered that he hadn't eaten since lunch, and the refrigerator at home was almost certainly empty. Charlie went away. To Hardcastle Alec said, 'You know a lot about me.'

'A bit. And you know nothing about me. Point taken.' Hardcastle emptied his glass. He gestured round the bar. 'It's not enough,' he said. 'Playing these . . . *gigs* , it's not enough.'

Alec prickled. Directness could be taken too far. 'Enough? What sort of word's *enough*?'

'I'm sure you understand me. Enough for a man of your abilities.'

'That's my business.'

'It could be mine. The people I work for's.'

Suddenly the expensive suit made sense. And its wearer's evasiveness. Alec laughed. 'Am I being head-hunted?'

Hardcastle considered him thoughtfully. 'You're in no hurry, Mr Duncan. You're taking your time and I can understand that. But for how much longer can you afford to?'

'You're buying me a sandwich, Mr Hardcastle. You're no buying access to my bank statement.'

'I wasn't referring to money. I think you know that.'

'Then it was bloody impertinent.'

'Agreed. But you're still listening.'

That stopped him. He was still listening. The fact was, he had no interest in a job, no interest in the sort of job Hardcastle could offer him, no interest in a *job* job at all, so it had to be what he had seen so far of Hardcastle's MO that was keeping him. As a cop, as an ex-cop, he was still listening because he was interested in the man from the ministry's modus operandi.

Also he had an empty flat to go home to, and the sandwich would lie like lead, and he probably wouldn't get to sleep before dawn.

'You know a lot about me. How much do you know about me?'

Hardcastle raised a reassuring hand. 'Only what was in the papers. Your sergeant was admirably reticent. I have other contacts, naturally, but for once they failed me.'

Thank Christ for that. 'So what was in the papers?'

Charlie returned with the two Perriers and the sandwich. Glasses were arranged, and a plate and knife. The sandwich was four tiny equilateral wholemeal triangles stuffed with something pink under a sprig of parsley. Hardcastle paid, checking the amount and the tip carefully, holding Charlie's dim pencil-marks close up under the fake Lalique lamp on the table, and Charlie went away.

'I know,' Hardcastle said, 'that you were the youngest black detective chief inspector on the Force.'

Wrong. He'd been the *only* black DCI on the Force.

'I know also,' Hardcastle went on, 'that you were entrusted with a very delicate inquiry in one of Her Majesty's prisons.'

Wrong again. In one of Her Majesty's Punishment and Protection Centres. Where had Hardcastle been since the vocabulary of the New Enlightenment?

'And I know that you resigned from the Force in the middle of that inquiry, following an assault upon a female suspect during interrogation.'

Wrong again. He'd resigned because jails (by whatever name) were the principal beneficiaries of a policeman's work, and he'd seriously lost faith in them.

'You were spared prosecution on compassionate grounds. You were overwrought. You'd suffered that very same day a deep personal bereavement.'

And wrong yet again. He'd been spared prosecution because the woman had refused to press charges. She'd been too ashamed. She'd pushed him beyond all endurance and she'd known it.

'And you haven't worked since.'

Right. Unless you called Tony's *work* . . .

Not bad. One fact right, out of five. Twenty per cent. As newspaper reports went, not a bad success rate.

But Hardcastle hadn't finished. 'Furthermore, your sergeant has suffered with you. Not so much, but significantly. Sergeant Grove has been at the Bridewell ever since, and he'll be there till he retires.'

Aha. The coup de grâce. Alec's shame, the one act he regretted.

Poor old Frank, loyal old Frank, banished to serve in the main Bridewell on Liverpool's Cheapside, police housing for prisoners on remand or waiting to go to court, its staff a dumping ground for the lame and lazy. Poor loyal old Frank who was neither lame nor lazy, who should have been cruising in to his retirement on the crest of the CID wave, working out his time instead as nursemaid to two hundred-odd remand men, Liverpool's finest, trainee villains, innocent until they were proved guilty.

Alec's shame. He was prepared to bet Hardcastle hadn't got *that* from the newspapers. His other sources? Not that it mattered a damn, but—

Hardcastle shot a gleaming cuff and looked at his watch. 'Remarkable. The pub clock seems to be right. How's the sandwich?'

Alec hadn't got round to the sandwich. He'd had other things on his mind. For one, Hardcastle's modus operandi. He thought it, for a head-hunter, unusually forthright. No arse-kissing. First, get the client down on the ground, then kick him. Anything, rather than appear ingratiating. Let alone agreeable.

'Don't fuck me about, Mr Hardcastle. What's the deal? There *is* a deal, I imagine.'

'You have already turned down one of our competitors. That's why I'm being so elusive. The point is, ours is a much better offer. At the level we're talking about here, you could—'

Already turned down? Of course. He should have guessed. Not the Min of Ed, but close. 'Security. The job's in Security.'

'We're talking policy-making. At boardroom level. Social engineering, if you like. The formation of—'

'I'm no interested.'

'I was discussing the matter with your sister this morning and she—'

'First Frank Grove and now Morag. You're a busy man, Mr Hardcastle. You've been up in bloody Edinburgh too, mebbe, taking tea with my mother. *Discussing the matter* . . .'

'Your sister suggested that your interests now might lie in the direction of crime prevention. I'd just like to point out that ours do too.'

'I'm still no interested.'

At last the wallet was removed from the breast pocket and the card was passed across the table: *Aiken Hardcastle – Personnel – Guardians Plc.* Discreet indeed. You couldn't get much more discreet than that.

'What sort of bloody name's *Aiken*?'

'You have a great deal to offer to our organization, Mr Duncan. Our work is wide-ranging. You could virtually write your own job specification.'

'I'm still no interested.'

'You really ought to think about it. There are more people these days in security than in the police. But we lack accountability. And we get things wrong. We need someone who can—'

'It doesna worry you, Aiken, that I assault witnesses? That I beat them half to death? Or mebbe it's a recommendation. A useful qualification. Look well in the brochure, would it?'

'Your record indicates that it was hardly typical behaviour.'

'Advantageous, though. To be borne in mind. Useful in an emergency.'

'I'd say you had more valuable skills.'

Alec leaned forward across the table. 'Are you aware, Aiken, of how close I've come this evening to assaulting *you*?'

Hardcastle met his gaze. 'Very close. You still are. On the other hand, I'm fitter than I look. It wouldn't be entirely one-sided.'

Alec laughed. He had to, the man was hard to credit.

'Whose idea was it for you to meet me here? Morag's?'

'Not at all. It was mine. I wanted to look you over. I also wanted an open situation, one in which there wasn't a front door to be shut in my face.'

Alec stood up. Eventually the directness joke wore thin. 'But there bloody was, Mr Aiken Hardcastle. There bloody is. And it's just bloody shut.'

He walked away. He'd touched neither sandwich nor

Perrier. The bar was deserted. They were the last two in the place, Hardcastle and he, and Charlie was packing up.

Alec paused by the chrome-and-glass bead curtain at the end of the bar. He looked back. 'You never mentioned money.'

Hardcastle hadn't moved. He turned to face him and said, 'Money.'

Alec waited for him to go on, taking longer than he should have to recognize this variation on the directness joke. He'd been wrong-footed yet again. Aiken Hardcastle was never going to waste his time talking financial inducements. Clients like Alec could sneer at financial inducements. Financial inducements weren't the point.

Alec left the pub, the bead curtain jangling wildly behind him, and went on round the corner to his car. Hand on its door, he remembered that he usually closed the piano and brought his music with him. *Ah, fuck it*... he wasn't going back. Just for once it'd do the cleaner no harm in the morning to tidy up after him.

Tony's was a modern pub in a classy new residential development on the waterfront, wooden dormer windows, pre-weathered brickwork and cobbled roads, not half a mile from the city centre. After midnight the gates were closed and Alec had to show his card to the security man. As a regular, he got no hassle. Another black, even with a card, would expect a car search at the least. Cards meant nothing – these days they were available for any office block or estate in the city, if you knew where to go.

Alec drove off the cobbles and out under the carbon steel bar. The city centre was deserted, its hard bright surfaces stretched to breaking point by lights and emptiness. The men who moved in it, or stood to watch him go by, were empty too, slow and unreal, without shadows. At that hour of the morning there wasn't any of the traffic congestion that usually afflicted this once-derelict area, where the bright new juvenile

Punishment and Protection Centre was now going up. Alec turned right along Chaloner Street, then left up to Park Road. He was going home and he drove on automatic pilot. The irony of jail-building as inner city urban renewal had long ago stopped amusing him. Tonight, in any case, Hardcastle's words haunted him: *How much longer can you afford?* He didn't have an answer.

3

Iain and Morag McKinley lived to the north of the city, in Blundellsands. Stray German bombs back during the war had left gaps in the sooty Victorian rows and one of these, two houses wide, had been filled in the fifties with a rather grander detached replacement. Festival of Britain contemporary, in brown brick with a flat-pitched roof, its upper storey unsuitably hung with green pantiles, it did nothing for the street, but its double garden had sold it to the newly married couple when Iain came down from Edinburgh to take up his job at Manor High School, just up the road. He and Morag bought very reasonably, in the nineties trough of the housing market. They had Jamie now, and the garden was his wilderness playground.

Alec knew he'd find Morag home on a Tuesday afternoon: weekday mornings she worked in the office at the Alexandra Park family clinic, but the only afternoon she gave them was Friday. Jamie was five now, and had graduated from nursery school to Crosby Primary, so there were pressures on her to put in longer hours at the clinic, pressures of money and of residual Scottish Presbyterianism, but she was holding out against them. She'd been a social worker before Jamie, straight from college, family counselling on the estates, working every hour God gave, and her free afternoons still felt special.

So Alec had left his visit until the afternoon, when he had

the best chance of finding her at home, busy around the house somewhere. He parked the car in the drive and went round the back, leaned in at the kitchen door and gave the family whistle. A shout from upstairs drew him inside, and he went through into the hall.

'Where are you?'

'Come up. I'm tiling the bathroom.' He climbed a couple of steps. 'Second thoughts, Alec. Make some tea and bring it with you. I'm parched.'

He went back into the kitchen, filled the kettle and put it on the gas. Morag drank tea at any hour of the day or night that offered an excuse. He seldom touched the stuff, other than when he came here. Tea was Morag, and Morag's house, and that untidy, lived-in, cared-for feeling that he thought life was all about but had never quite managed. Iain's name was on the house deeds too, but the feeling was all Morag's. Iain didn't get round to things, let them slide, and then worried. Morag was happy with her priorities.

Alec made the tea and went upstairs with mugs and milk on a tray. The bathroom was a mess, cluttered with empty tile boxes and tubs of grout, Iain's folding work bench, disconnected towel rails, numerous shampoo and bath cleaner bottles. Morag, in her socks, was standing in the bath, scuffling aside bits of broken tile as she squinted at a spirit level.

'They're leaning,' she told him. 'The whole bloody panel's going downhill . . .'

Alec put the tray on the stool. The medicine cabinet door was open and he caught a passing glimpse of his face in its mirror. It reminded him of what he had known all his life but sometimes genuinely forgot: he and Morag were different. He and just about everyone else he knew were different. They were white, while he, like his father, his mother's first lover, was not. There was a photo of his father's band in the family album, cut from an Edinburgh Festival programme, and, not to put too fine a point upon it, his father had been black.

She tilted her head. 'D'you think it'll show, love?' She talked posher than him, too. The time down south at college had ironed her out. 'It won't show, will it?'

He stared at the tiles. 'A mile off.'

'Thanks for nothing.'

'It's only the top couple of rows. You can cheat with the grouting.'

'It's the whole panel. I must get them off before they dry.'

'They'll have dried. Come and drink your tea. You'll only smash them.'

He was right so she fixed the top two rows and cheated with the grouting. Then she sat beside him on the edge of the bath, one arm round his waist, and drank her tea.

'You'll see it,' he told her. 'No one else will.'

She hugged him. 'That's what Iain always says . . . So why the visit?'

'Does there have to be a reason?'

'It's been a week or two. And I nag. You might be staying away. I was afraid I was getting to sound like Mam.'

'I'd no thought of it like that.' He did now. 'Mebbe you do. It's a nice sort of nagging, though . . . Thing is, I had a visitor last night. At Tony's. Name of Hardcastle. He bought me a single malt. A double.'

'I'm impressed. Still, if this is the man I think it is, I'm sure he could afford it.'

'You sent him?'

'I did no such thing. He was here in the afternoon and I sent him packing.'

'That's no the impression he gave.'

'He wouldn't, would he? Don't you believe me?'

'He mentioned crime prevention. That's one of your notions.'

'I said it just to put him off. *Then* I sent him packing.'

'I'd rather you didn't discuss me. In future, I mean. For God's sake, I don't even know what crime prevention is.'

'In future? Are there going to be other Hardcastles?'

He shrugged. It wasn't vanity – retired policemen (for whatever reason) were desirable in certain circles. He got up off the edge of the bath. He'd been unfairly sharp with her.

'He went to see Frank too. It'll be Frank who told him where to find me.'

She accepted the apology. 'How *is* Frank?'

'How d'you think? . . . *There's* the man Hardcastle should offer his bloody job to.' He started collecting up empty tile boxes, flattening them, and stuffing them into the plastic rubbish bag by the door.

Morag watched him. 'You still see Frank, don't you? You haven't cut yourself off?'

'This bag's full.' He leaned on it, squashing its contents. 'I'll just be away down to the kitchen for—'

'Because of what you did to him, Alec? You haven't let that get in the way?'

Alec tied a knot, very carefully, in the bag's top. Like no one else, a sister pinned you down. 'He didn't allow me, Mor. You know Frank.'

In the weeks immediately after May's death and his resignation from the Force he'd been impossible – angry, wretched, ashamed, resentful, guilty. Frank had refused to be turned away.

He looked up. 'The man's a saint. He pretends I've done him a favour. Like, the Bridewell suits him fine. Wardering suits him fine. He's glad of the regular hours.'

'Perhaps he is. People are, you know.'

'But no like that. It's humiliating.' Alec thought about it. Maybe humiliation, like beauty, was in the eye of the beholder. 'His Doris isn't well these days . . . Mebbe you're right. Mebbe the regular hours aren't so bad.' It was a new idea, the possibility that Frank wasn't just being noble.

'You can go and get that bag now.' Morag stood up, climbed back into the bath. 'And take the tray with you. I'm bound to kick it over.'

The box of new bags was under the kitchen sink. He pulled out two and went back upstairs with them. Morag had marked a tile and was cutting it on the work bench.

He'd been thinking on the stairs. About why he'd come. About Morag's nagging. 'There are other ways to live,' he said. 'People don't have to be always at it. I've been at it non-stop, ever since school. There are times for waiting to see what happens.'

'Who's arguing?' She pressed down and the tile snapped neatly along her line.

'You are. Be fair, Mor. You never stop. Not in words, mebbe, but . . . You think I've been moping around too long. May died in January and now it's September. You think I should be getting on with . . . things.'

The cut tile fitted perfectly. She aligned it with plastic spacers. 'I think all that?'

'That's why you sent Hardcastle round.'

'I did not—'

'That's why you told him I was interested in crime prevention.' He was becoming indignant. Outraged. 'What the hell *is* crime prevention? Fitting locks and alarms and bullet-proof glass? Persuading more fathers to stay at home with their kids? Better rehab? Legalized crack? Giving people jobs? Giving them Jesus? More bobbies on the beat? More bobbies on the beat with assault weapons? Bringing back the birch? What the hell *is* crime prevention? I wish you'd tell me.'

'I wish I knew.' She was smoothing in grout with her thumb. 'There's a damp sponge somewhere, Alec. Could you—?'

'I could not. That's your "handling Alec" voice. I'm serious and I want an answer.'

'You want an argument.' She found the sponge herself. 'You want a row.'

Yes. Yes, he did want a row.

No . . .

Staring at her, he realized suddenly that what he wanted most of all was to be clean. *Clean.* It was something a row could never accomplish. And she was absolutely right – a row *was* what he'd come for. All this way across the Liverpool traffic for a row. A terrible night, and a worse morning, and all he'd had to cling to was the thought that she was responsible for Hardcastle. He could have purged Harcastle's visit with a row. If she'd let him, if he'd let himself, he also could have purged his shame at being so long idle, at being so long unmanned by his double bereavement. (May and his job, both dead and gone. A terrible thing, but way back in January, and January to September was nine months. Far too many.) He could have purged all this with a row, and Morag the natural victim, but not his sense of the unclean.

'I don't want a row,' he said. Unclean? In what way, for heaven's sake, was he *unclean*? 'Rows are a disgrace. Mebbe I should call Hardcastle.'

'I doubt he's your sort.' She ran water into the basin and squeezed out the sponge. 'You could always try him, Alec, but I doubt he's your sort.'

'He's their personnel man. Chances are, once I got the job, I'd never see him again.' He blew into one of the plastic bags to open it. 'You're hard to please, Mor.'

She stopped fiddling with bits of equipment and confronted him. Standing in the bath, she was exactly his height. 'Just any job won't do, Alec. You've got to be ready. That's what I nag you about. Not being ready.'

'It's after three. Go and get Jamie, shall I?'

'No. We're talking.'

'I've stopped. You're a mess, the bathroom's a mess, and someone has to go and get Jamie.'

It was his right, stopping when he'd had enough. No it wasn't – setting boundaries was a luxury, a luxury Morag would allow him because she was his sister. They went back, she and he. They knew each other well enough for there to be no dishonesty in walking round, stepping aside, simply not insisting.

She leaned forward, knelt on the edge of the bath and gave him another hug. 'You go. I'd like to get finished here. We've had the tiles for ages. It's finding the time that's the problem.' She corrected herself. 'Finding the will.'

Jamie's school was in walking distance. Taking the car and sitting in it once he'd got there would save Alec from the waiting mothers, but he walked. He'd been to the school a good few times back in the summer term (being unemployed did wonders for nephew/uncle relations) so the mothers were used to him. They hadn't exactly talked to him yet, but towards the end of the term they were smiling in his general direction.

He waited just inside the school gates. The day was warmish and sunny, and swept away his mind's clutter. Harcastle? Who was he? Rows, purges, shame? *Uncleanliness?* Jamie came out on the dot of three-thirty, dozens of him, like puffed wheat shot from a gun, in anoraks and woolly hats, while the bell was still ringing. He flung himself up at Alec, his lunch box over his shoulder, arms wide. Alec caught him and they hugged.

'Oof!'

Clearly none of the kids was giving him a hard time yet for having a big black uncle.

'Where's Mum?'

'Busy. Back at home. She's tiling the bathroom.'

'I got a star.'

'Good for you. Gold or silver?'

'Silver. For my picture. Noola got the gold one.'

'Noola?'

'Over there.' He pointed vaguely. 'Her lunch box has a real lock and key. Where's my present?'

'I haven't brought one. I'm not a present machine.'

'Put me down. I'll go and get my picture.'

He wriggled away, and disappeared into the school. Alec waited while children streamed round his knees and the sun shone. Hardcastle? Who was he?

'It was on the board. Mrs Troop said I could have it.'

Alec saw some smudgy black aeroplanes machine-gunning each other in front of a roundish sun with uneven rays sticking out of it. The picture seemed to him hardly silver star material.

'We call her Mrs Poop.'

'You would.'

'No.' Jamie corrected himself, remembering. 'Poopface . . . We call her Mrs Poopface.'

'And what does she call you?'

'Don't know. Nothing much. Come along. I want to show Mum my picture.'

Alec let himself be pulled away. He was amazed at how kids operated. He hadn't said a word about the picture, and they'd talked ever since about more risqué matters, but even so Jamie knew his uncle wasn't keen on it. He didn't hold this against him (there was always his mum), but he'd picked up the vibes . . . And if kids did it, then how much more so villains? In the interrogation room, picking up the vibes, making allowances, rewriting the story. Was he really so transparent?

Alec checked himself. Villains, like interrogation rooms, were last year's business. And it was fine to be transparent.

'It's a good idea, Uncle, having a lunch box with a real lock and key.'

'I expect you're right.' A campaign was in the making here. Alec changed the subject. 'Shall I take that picture? Your grubby paws are wrecking it.'

Jamie handed it over and Alec rolled it up carefully.

'That way, Uncle, no one half-inches your Mars bar.' He didn't give up easy. 'Half-inches means pinches. Did you know that?'

'Sort of. What happens if you lose the key?'

'Noola's is on a string round her neck. It's only a little one. I think lunch boxes with real locks and keys are a good idea. Don't you?'

Alec side-stepped. It was something grown-ups were good at. 'I didn't know your mother let you have Mars bars. Aren't they supposed to be bad for your teeth?'

'Mum doesn't mind.' Jamie hesitated, fighting his natural honesty. 'She lets me sometimes . . .' Honesty won. 'She might, Uncle. She really might . . . Noola's lets her.'

'Lucky wee Noola. Mars bars *and* a fancy lunch box.'

They walked on. Jamie knew better than to suggest it wasn't fair, Noola being so lucky. He'd heard Alec on the subject of 'fair' before. He tried another approach.

'Uncle – how long is it till my birthday?'

'Ages. October, November, December, January, February, March. Ages.' Alec squeezed his hand. 'Christmas is sooner, laddie. I reckon Father Christmas does a good line in fancy lunch boxes . . .'

Back at the house Morag had Jamie's tea ready on the kitchen table. His picture was admired, not excessively, and stuck on the refrigerator door with magnets. Alec stayed for tea and helped Morag clear up the bathroom afterwards. The wall above the basin still needed tiling. He wondered if he should offer to come and see to it tomorrow, but he wasn't handy, and anyway Morag had her pride. She'd see to it herself when she was ready.

He messed around in the kitchen with Jamie, playing squiggles, until Iain got in from Manor High, then they chatted for a while. Iain and Morag had offered to put him up in the spare room when May had died, for as long as he wanted, and it might have worked. Leaving out the terrible cheap wine Iain bought, he and Alec saw eye to eye on most things. Especially since Alec had left the Force. And in any case, Alec bought no wine at all these days, now that a chief inspector's salary wasn't coming in. But he hadn't taken them up on their offer. He had his own mistakes to make, and May's Sefton Park flat to make them in. He and May hadn't been married, and they'd had their ups and downs, but she'd left him everything. Her big Steinway in the living room. Everything.

He left around six, turning down dinner because he had food waiting back home, because he had to shower and change for Tony's, because he had to look over a couple of new arrangements, because he'd been there since three and too much family living wasn't good for him.

Morag saw him to the door.

'I'm sorry I nagged.'

'I'm sorry I got so ratty.'

'You don't want Hardcastle.'

'I know.'

She stood on her toes and kissed his cheek. 'Come again soon, Alec. Weekend, mebbe. I'm at the clinic now till then. One of the others is sick.'

'I'll give you a call.'

He went down the path, got into his car, drove off. They'd have her full time at the clinic if she wasn't careful.

The traffic around Lime Street station was terrible, the main access route temporarily blocked by a huge articulated lorry that was delivering steel plates for the new Punishment and Protection Centre. Construction inside the hoardings was going well, and in places the black riveted walls were already two storeys high, a significant landmark. Alec didn't get out to Sefton Park till nearly seven. Dusk was falling, the cloudless sky a perfect opal. As he turned into his road, the park on one side and big Victorian houses on the other, divided into flats, he saw the night's vigilante group gathering on the corner.

He'd been invited to join the rota but he'd pleaded his job at Tony's. He had only two nights free and he claimed he needed them. In fact he had the British copper's distrust of vigilantes. More guns on the street they did not need.

He slowed the car and stared at them: three young men jostling each other and fooling around, two older men with clipboards. They were a new idea on Sefton Park. Up until last January, when May had died, the Sefton Parkers had thought they weren't needed. There were druggies in the park itself, but mostly they weren't a bother.

One had been, though. In January one had been a bother.

It had been May's death, ironically, that had changed the minds of the Sefton Parkers. *Solicitor dies in drug-related stabbing*. May's death. Her murder. Her mutilated body. Her unheard screams. Her blood on the hall carpet and out on the gravelled drive. Her pain. Her many wounds. Her unheard screams. Her pain.

May hadn't died quickly or easily.

Alec stopped the car. His hands were shaking and there were tears on his cheeks. Convulsively he reversed back to the corner, the car lurching, almost out of control. He lowered the window and leaned out.

'Bastards,' he shouted. 'Where were you? Bastards. Where were you then?' He pounded the car door with his fist. '*Where were you then?*'

The men on the pavement stared across the road at him. He leaned his forehead on the door frame and closed his eyes. 'Where were you then?' he whispered.

One of the men walked towards him. 'You all right, mate?'

Alec raised the car window, faced the front, drove off. He couldn't answer the man. He was ashamed. Astonished. He drove off round the park. The house where he lived, in May's ground floor flat, was far enough round the corner for the men not to be able to see him turn in through the high stone gate pillars. He stopped on the mossy gravel, switched off the engine, and sat gripping the steering wheel, his knuckles white. He wondered if any of the men had recognized him. Presumably he and they belonged to the same residents' association and went to the same meetings.

Christ. What did it matter? What the hell did it matter? Of course they'd recognized him. It didn't matter. He had this habit of worrying about things that didn't matter. It was something people called a displacement activity. No, not *people* - psychiatrists. Psychiatrists called it a displacement activity. He was a mess. May was dead, murdered, and nine months later he was still a mess. He hadn't dealt with it. Psychiatrists would say he hadn't dealt with it.

His hands were still shaking. He found his handkerchief, wiped his eyes, blew his nose, got out of the car, went into May's flat. No. No, May was dead, murdered. He went into his flat.

In the kitchen he put a frozen lasagne in the microwave and had a quick shower while it was being zapped. He changed into his King of Swing suit for Tony's, then opened a bottle of wine from the diminishing store he and May had assembled, and drank half of it with his lasagne. His hands were better now but his head wasn't. He could go on like this but it wasn't a good idea. He had to do something.

Alec joined the M62 just outside West Derby, going east. He was doing something. The time was just before noon, the day was fine, a white autumn sun in a hazy, cloudless sky, and he was on his way to Justice City, the big Punishment and Protection Centre recently built on the moors beyond Manchester. His cell interview with Trevor Bladon was scheduled for two, so he had to hurry. It had taken him far longer to set up than he'd expected. His old boy contacts proved to be useless. Where letting him talk to the young man who had murdered May was concerned, they didn't want to know.

Mebbe they didn't trust him. Mebbe they were remembering the day he'd resigned from the Force.

He settled himself behind the Rover's wheel, glanced in the rearview mirror, and swung out to overtake. Ironically it was the government's new Victim Support Agency that had helped him. They didn't know about his record: to them he was simply Mr Alexander Duncan, acknowledged cohabitant of the deceased. As such the VSA charter said he had a right to apply for an interview with her murderer, providing the individual in question was properly convicted, sentenced and incarcerated. The individual in question was not obliged to agree to any interview, but official pressures could be brought to bear. In the government's opinion these meetings were often mutually beneficial. Restitutions were made. Guilts and hatreds, on both sides, were laid to rest.

Alec despised the government. He despised its opinions and its policies, but he was prepared to make use of both. He sought no restitutions and felt no guilts or hates. Trevor Bladon's guilts and hates and restitutions were his own affair.

He said none of this to the VSA. He simply told them he wanted to talk to Trevor Bladon. Now. Today. As soon as possible. Could they fix it?

They said they could – always assuming that Bladon was willing or could be officially pressured. Which, and without official pressures, it seemed he was. Boredom? Nothing better on the telly? Alec could think of no other reason for Trevor to be willing to talk to his victim's acknowledged cohabitant.

The day before May's murder Alec had seen him in the street near her flat. He was in bad shape, a drug addict, his leg was bleeding, and Alec had helped him. He'd taken Bladon into May's kitchen, sat him at her table, bandaged his leg, given him coffee, and thirty quid . . . The following evening Bladon had returned, waited with a knife in the dark in May's drive for her to get in from work. All he'd wanted was money – how else could he buy tomorrow's fix? – but May wasn't like that. She'd fought him, and one thing had led to another, and eventually she'd died.

Catching Trevor Bladon had been a snip. He left dozens of fingerprints, Alec provided a description, and Merseyside's A Division found May's blood on his clothes when they picked him up the following afternoon. He hadn't left the city. He said he hadn't dared to, but he probably hadn't even thought of it. He was an addict, he couldn't risk his supply.

Alec drove fast, low nineties, watching the mirror. There were radar checks, but he chose to chance them. The VSA had advised him to be prompt: if a prisoner in a PPC was reluctant for some reason, lateness gave him an excuse to cancel. Alec could have left the whole thing till tomorrow morning, but he wanted to get it over with, and to get what came next started.

His rage against Bladon had quickly faded. Violence happened. He knew about violence. The day he'd heard about May's murder, a few hours later, for the first time in his life, he'd assaulted a suspect. There'd been reasons, fine, but he'd beaten her up. Seriously. He knew about violence. It was in people. It didn't have to show itself in bashing or punch-ups, and it wasn't the same as cruelty. He couldn't understand cruelty at all. But *violence* . . . the way he was driving now was violent. He had an excuse, an appointment to keep, but today he'd have driven like this if he'd had all the time in the world. Certainly he'd have wanted to. He needed it. Letting rip like this at ninety-plus was stupid, self-indulgent, criminal, but those were civilized abstractions. Violence was older. It was flesh and blood.

So Alec's rage against Bladon for May's death, for his bereavement, had been reasoned away. Violence happened. It was flesh and blood. And in any case, Bladon the addict, uncensored, primeval, was near-as-dammit innocent. A hungry habit, like a standing prick, hath no conscience.

And now, thanks to A Division, and counsels and judge and

jury, Bladon too was suffering a bereavement. He had lost the centre of his life, an unimaginable thirty-five years of sun and rain and lechery taken away from him, and no remission. So mebbe you could say the two of them had a lot in common. If you were that sort of reasonable.

Alec's rage against life, against the God he didn't believe in, was less easily dealt with. Nine months on, it was still destroying him. Morag saw it. He needed to move on and he wasn't ready. She said it and he knew it. Hence this violent journey to a violent reunion. No bashing or punch-ups planned. It was just that Trev and he had unfinished business.

Alec eased his foot on the accelerator pedal. His speed dropped to eighty and he tucked his Rover in behind a silver BMW. He had no idea, realistically, what to expect from this meeting. *Unfinished business* was a grand sort of phrase but it didn't mean much. He was looking for a punctuation mark, a full stop and a line drawn under it. He wanted the book closed. May's death had been so outrageous, such a careless deployment of suffering. It seemed to him the worst possible circumstance, the most disgusting and degrading. It seemed to him simply that the God he didn't believe in hadn't been paying attention.

He smiled grimly. How did you close the book on that? More to the point, to this moment's point, how could Trevor Bladon, of all people, help him?

Mebbe he could help him because he *was* May's death. He was the word made flesh. Mebbe if Alec could shake his hand – *shake his hand?* - and say hello and then later goodbye, and leave the prison, and drive back along this road, then mebbe May's death would—

Goodbye, May . . . Alec swung his car into the outside lane again, blared his horn, left the silver BMW standing. He blasted a path along the motorway. It was a messy way to die. A messy way to live, also. Which was why he was going to visit Trevor Bladon.

Government cuts in police funding (presented as area reorganizations) had reduced the number of patrol cars on the Manchester–Huddersfield motorway. Alec made it to the prison turn-off alive and unapprehended, with fifteen minutes to spare. Justice City, set into the bracken hillside high above him, was a forbidding presence. Eight years old now, and the government's flagship PPC, its black riveted steel walls had been politically so successful (voters were reassured by them) that they'd become a feature of the nationwide prison-building programme. They were also, as a bonus, difficult to escape over.

Alec had often been here, professionally, but this was his first time as a mere member of the public and today the black steel gates in the black steel wall at the end of the approach road stayed closed to him. Surveillance cameras surveyed him and found him wanting. He parked the Rover near the gates, on the broad gravel turn-around. Up there on the moor the sunlight felt cold on his face, chilled by the wind. Three sheep watched him, chewing anxiously, as he walked to the small black steel visitors' gate.

A grille opened before he could ring the bell. 'You the VSA guy?'

'Yes. Yes, that's right.' He'd nearly called the man *sir*. It was what these gates and this door and this grille did to you. 'My name's Duncan.'

'ID?'

He held it up. It was officially a driving licence, but it had photograph and DNA coding, and a smart computer chip, and it was far more than that.

The prison officer might have demanded the card through the grille. Instead, as a concession to Alec's personable, though black, appearance, he opened the door and took the card from his hand. He swiped it along his machine and no warning bells rang.

'Come in, Mr Duncan. Your interviewee is expecting you.'

'Thank you.' Alec warmed his hands at such glowing approval.

The officer took him past the guard room and across the granite-walled inner courtyard to Reception. 'Nice weather we're having for the time of year, Mr Duncan.'

'We are that.'

'A proper Indian summer.'

'Aye.'

The reception area, with its token rubber plant and vase of seasonal flowers, chrysanthemums today, looked the way it always did, a cross between the Liverpool nick and a funeral parlour. Haircuts were short and faces were long. Jocularity, in front of visitors, didn't happen. This was the prison's public face. Inmates were lucky: they went straight across the courtyard to Inductions, and never saw it.

The officer delivered Alec to the desk. 'Alexander Duncan. Cell interview with 7765 Bladon.'

'Fine. Thank you, Harry. Good afternoon, Mr Duncan. I've got all your VSA papers. Are you familiar with our procedures?'

Alec nodded. 'I've been here before.' There seemed to be no harm in admitting it. They hadn't recognized his name or face and that was salutary: one of his hang-ups was that everybody knew him, and what he had done, and pointed him out.

'No harm in a recap, Mr Duncan . . . As a visitor, you get a lapel badge you must wear at all times. It gets you through no security gates. These are operated by coded electronic cards that are carried only by authorized staff members. An escort will take you where you need to go. He or she will wait for you and bring you back. There are many security gates and you will be unable to get through any of them on your own. Visits longer than half an hour are permitted only in exceptional circumstances. Finally you must understand that, while we aim to take good care of you while you're here, you visit an inmate entirely at your own risk, and you are required to sign a liability waiver before you enter. Have I made myself clear, Mr Duncan?'

'Aye. Very clear.' The welcome had cooled, post-Harry.

He stuck on the self-adhesive lapel badge and signed the liability waiver. A young woman prison officer approached him.

'I'm Officer Danby, sir. I'm to take you to 7765 Bladon.'

'I'm much obliged, Officer Danby.' So the public got to know names. It wanted prisons to be cold and unrelenting, but not towards itself when it came visiting.

Danby took him to the barred gate at the rear of the reception area. It led through into the prison proper. 'After you, sir.'

He went through on his own. In the door frame there was a metal and explosives detector. Also, as a final identity check, a scanner that read all the plastic cards he had with him. By the time he reached 7765 Bladon, prison security would know for certain not only who he was but his credit rating, who carried his health insurance, and the size of his shirt collar.

Danby followed him out and the gate slid shut behind them with worrying finality. She caught his backward glance. 'When you're in, you're in, Mr Duncan. I always tell visitors, even if they sock me one and steal my gate cards, they won't know the codes that go with them.'

How nice. A tactful way of saying, *Don't bother, mister*.

They walked down a short corridor lined with closed doors, out through another sliding gate, into one corner of a grid of covered walkways. Alec knew it well. Ahead, across a square rioting with dusty pink roses, was the Punishments Building. To the left, past a couple more gates, were Justice City's Long Term Incarceration blocks. 7765 Bladon's home from home.

Alec let Danby show him the way. He'd have turned into LTI Admissions, which was where he'd always gone when he was calling on a matey in the line of duty, but she led him past. Members of the public got plusher treatment.

'Wait here, please.'

A carpet, Van Gogh cornfields, modular seating, a TV set tuned to the shopping channel. Every modern convenience.

Danby returned with his three minders. 'These officers will look after you.'

For security reasons no cell door was opened without three officers present. 'Cell' was a misnomer. 'Suite' would have been more apt. The elaborateness of the accommodation was supposed to console inmates for virtually never leaving it. Sports, workshops, free association, all were casualties of low staffing levels: they couldn't be securely supervised and anyway they encouraged intimidation, violence, sex, drugs. These were LTI men. You didn't mess with LTI men.

Alec followed his minders past yet another gate. The LTI blocks were a fortress within a fortress. 7765 Bladon was in the third block along, on the ground floor. The three officers walked briskly along a silent, rubber-floored corridor. No matter how many times Alec came here, the contrast with other jails was always remarkable. The violence here was different.

They stopped by a door. One of the officers checked the monitor screen in the wall beside it, then switched on the intercom. 'Bladon? Your visitor's here.'

In the monitor Alec saw an empty living room, the standard issue upholstered chair, upright chair, desk chair, table, computer, TV set. 7765 Bladon went in for books. He'd made himself shelves above the table.

'Bladon? Let's be having you.' The officer consulted his clipboard. 'Your visitor's name is Alexander Duncan. You don't have to see him, but you told the VSA you would and if you change your mind now that he's come all this way I'll personally piss in your tea for a week.'

'*Coming*. . . Tell him I'm changing my shirt in his honour.'

Alec turned away. The voice was hard to bear. He hadn't attended Bladon's trial. This was the first time he'd heard his voice since the morning in May's kitchen. His face was familiar from local front pages and the TV news. His voice was hard to bear.

'We're coming in.'

The prison officer tapped in the day's lock code and the door opened. He and his two companions stood back for Alec to enter.

'Half an hour, sir. Bladon's never given trouble. He's a good lad. But we'll be outside if you need us.'

Alec went in and the door closed behind him. Sounds of movement came from the prison officer's good lad in his sleeping annexe. A drawer slid shut. Alec waited, appalled by the situation he'd got himself into. These meetings were supposed to be therapeutic. He'd got nothing to say to this young man. Nothing.

Trevor Bladon came round the edge of the partition, buttoning his shirt cuffs. Alec forced himself to look. He had to admit it – LTI had worked wonders. At the time of Bladon's trial the media had used pictures taken shortly after his arrest, harsh mug shots, suitably degenerate, with sunken eyes, pasty grey heroin complexion, beat-up teeth, sparse ginger beard: images that matched Alec's recollections of the addict he'd scraped up off the Sefton Park pavement. Today's Bladon, nine months later, was clean-shaven, plump, bright-eyed, his smile showing quantities of expensive prison service dental work. His skin was still greyish, but a different grey, from his indoor life, and without the spots and sore places. He was a good lad.

'Mr Duncan. Nice to see yer. Park yer bum.'

Alec chose the upright chair by the table. He didn't, after all, offer to shake hands.

Bladon smiled at him. 'This is a funny one, isn't it?'

Alec cleared his throat. 'I must begin by thanking you for agreeing to this visit.'

'Balls to that. I owe yer, Mr Duncan.' He sat in the desk chair, crossed his legs. 'You can't think a lot of me.'

'No.'

'And it won't be much comfort that I don't think a lot of myself.'

'No.'

Bladon uncrossed his legs, crossed them the other way. 'You want to know what happened?'

'No. I already do.' Clearly young Bladon had decided in advance that he needed to take control. Alec wondered if it mattered, if he should let him, and decided that it did and he shouldn't. 'I saw the police blow-ups,' he said, regarding Bladon squarely. 'I read the reports.'

Bladon met his gaze. 'I was heroin dependent, Mr Duncan. My drug of choice was heroin.'

'And that's an excuse?' Alec hadn't expected to lose his temper. Not as quickly as this. 'And that's an *excuse*?'

Bladon's control held. He eased the crease in his trousers over his upper knee, but his hand was shaking. He saw it and held it firmly down on his thigh with the other.

'I've been putting things together since the VSA called, Mr Duncan. The authorities really loused yer up.' He indicated the VDU on the table. 'I've been accessing the newspaper files. I saw the papers at the time of course, but it didn't register. I was a mess. You mostly read the stuff about yerself at times like that. It's understandable.'

Alec winced at the complacency. 'You're an understanding man.'

Curiously, the sarcasm hurt. Bladon struggled. 'I've had to get here from there.' He paused. 'So have you. It hasn't been easy.'

His voice broke on the final word but Alec was past caring. 'I didn't come here for your fucking sympathy.'

It was only then that he realized what was strangest about 7765 Bladon. Nine months ago his every other word had been *fucking*. It had been a part of his speech rhythms. An admission of weakness then, it was just the same from Alec now.

If Bladon noticed it, he too was past caring. He spun his chair away. 'You don't want information. You don't want sympathy . . . What *did* you come here for?' He swung back again, leaned forward. His eyes were bright with tears. 'To cheer yerself up, looking at the animals in the zoo?'

He'd needed his control. That was why he had judged his behaviour nine months ago to be 'understandable'. That was why heroin had been his 'drug of choice'. He was speaking of someone else. He'd made the shift, but only barely, from there to here, and staying in control was necessary. Alec was his test, and he'd failed it. He'd lost his control and he was back with the animals in the zoo.

Alec got up slowly, went to the armoured glass window, looked out at the grass and the blank wall of the next block. The window was sealed, the cell air-conditioned. Claustrophobic, but no great cause for pity: it was only what many quite expensive office workers had to put up with.

Even so. *Even so* . . . Even so, with his Sefton Park flat and his Rover at ninety on the motorway, what did he know? He turned back to Bladon. Reached out. 'You got from there to here,' he said gently. It was more than he had managed, with his Sefton Park flat and his Rover at ninety on the motorway. 'I'd like to hear how.'

Silence lay heavily in the contained air as Bladon thought about it. Then he laughed. He got out a handkerchief and blew his nose. He was putting himself together again. 'You need to know where *there* was, first,' he said.

Alec shrugged. 'I've nicked pushers. I've been on dependency seminars. Courses on prevention.'

'They lied to yer, mate. Not the pushers – the courses. It

begins in the schools. It's like sex – they're afraid that if they tell yer about it, you'll do it.' He laughed again. 'You do it. You do it all wrong because yer ignorant – and because they've filled yer up with fear, you don't want to know. You believe all the lies about how terrible drugs are, and you don't want to know.'

Alec returned to his chair. This wasn't what he'd reached out for. Not for a lecture on drugs education in schools.

'The courses they send yer on do the same thing, mate. They tell yer, one snort and yer hooked. Ten snorts and yer dead. They don't tell yer the drugs, taken right, never kill. Look – the place is full of functioning addicts. Ten, fifteen, twenty years . . . then they grow up, or whatever, and come off them, and if they're pop stars they get to talk about it on the telly.'

Alec couldn't let that pass. He pointed out, 'They're the lucky ones.'

'Yer right. Lucky because they're rich. Lucky because they've always been able to afford good reliable stuff. Doctors who didn't treat them like moral degenerates. Gays know all about it. Anyone who's different. Look at yerself – blacks know it too. But I tell yer, mate, users have it tougher. There's laws against users. It's laws that do the damage. Dirty needles, cut drugs, silly prices, the whole criminal bit.' He leaned forward. 'I tell yer something else, mate. Even then, it's the dealers that die mostly. And the police, of course. You know something? Last year, in the UK, fourteen people died of illegal substance abuse, only fourteen, and ten of those was kids under twelve sniffing glue.'

Alec glanced at the books on the shelf beside him. He thought he'd recognized the signs – a lot of long-stay prisoners made themselves experts in what had put them there. The books confirmed his guess. *Heroin, AIDS and Society* caught his eye. *Living with Heroin* was another. There were folders of cuttings too, and social services booklets. He felt depressed. For a moment there might have been contact. Now Bladon was back behind a performance. He himself too: the sober authority figure.

He tried again. 'You were going to tell me how it was.'

'How it was? You mean, when I was doing the business?'

He nodded. This was another Trevor Bladon. Perky. The boy who'd twisted social workers round his little finger.

'Thing is, Mr Duncan, it kept me pretty busy. I reckon that's how it started. They lost me, last year at Toxteth Grammar. All that school crap, not going anywhere. *Boring*. . . My mother had a new bloke then, too, so I didn't go home much. No job, of course. All my mates were doing stuff so I did it too. Kept me busy. People talk about pushers but that's nonsense. Nobody pushes. Nobody needs to. It's yer mates get yer going. Peer pressure.'

7765 Bladon had dropped into his patter. Alec glanced at his watch.

'Whatever doing stuff is, Mr Duncan, it isn't boring. It's all go. Thing is, you wake up most mornings feeling pretty rough. Yer on a mate's floor or sofa or whatever, and it doesn't matter how much stuff you had the day before, you wake up feeling pretty rough. It's time to get dressed, just whizz out, head for the nearest shopping area, lift what you can. Then sell it, go and score, smoke what you've scored, shoot it up, whatever, then get back to the shops. Plus trips to yer social worker, court hearings and that. Yer never bored, Mr Duncan.'

Alec was, though. Bored stiff. 'Sounds marvellous. I'd say you were more than "pretty rough", though, the day we met.'

'Couple of bad trips. Dirty stuff. You know the way it goes. I reckon the bastard was cutting it with toilet cleaner. Mostly I scored with a guy called Dancer, Dancer Drew, but the fuzz pulled him in for a couple of days. Dancer looked after me. He was pricey but you could count on his stuff. Dancer and me went back a long way.'

Alec nodded absently. Everybody on the Merseyside force knew Dancer Drew. The most they'd ever been able to get him for was possession of two ounces and a suspended sentence, but it wasn't for want of trying. Dancer was nimble. Quick on his feet. Dancer by name and Dancer by nature.

'If I'd stuck with Dancer I'd of been fine. This picture people have of the junkie OD-ing in a dirty toilet, needle hanging from his arm – they need it, it's the excuse for their laws. It happens, sure, but so it does with winos. You see them in the gutter, drowning in their spew, but you don't rush off and close all the pubs and lock up all the barmaids. I tell yer, it's harder to get off booze than it is off horse. All you ever hear about is the horrors of detox, so you never think it's possible, and it's all lies. I quit, cold turkey, the day I got nicked. Had to. And a bad cold's worse. They never tell yer that in school – they want to frighten yer.'

Alec sighed. This was the man, the chatty campaigner, who had murdered May. He'd found God. He'd got here from there by finding books called *Heroin, AIDS and Society*. He was all new. A good lad. He'd read up on his old self's failures and the reasons for them, and he'd put them behind him. In theory Alec disapproved of guilt as an emotion. In practice, today, here in this cell, he thought a little guilt would be a bloody good thing.

He went to the door. His half-hour wasn't up, but his patience was. His patience with himself. He'd come here hoping somehow to tidy up the mess of his life, to draw lines, to close books, to say hello to 7765 Bladon and goodbye, and the idea was sentimental rubbish. Pathetic. He'd let himself plead. His one consolation was that Bladon was too blinkered to have noticed.

He was looking up into one of the surveillance cameras, about to ask a guard to open the door, when Bladon stopped him.

'Would you do something for me, Mr Duncan?'

Alec turned, stared at him coldly.

'Now that yer here, sir. I mean, I could ask social services, but they take for ever and my mind's not easy, and now that yer here—'

'What is it?' The man was amazing. Truly amazing.

'It's my mum. My mother. I've been calling her for a couple of days now and she doesn't answer. If you could—'

'If I know you lot, she hasn't paid the phone bill.'

'She isn't short, Mr Duncan. She told me that newspaper paid her plenty. Besides, I checked with the operator.'

'Couldn't she just have gone away? Friends? Relations? Some bloke?'

'She'd have told me. I call her regular. Find out how she's doing. She knows that.'

Alec had helped him once before. It hadn't turned out well. 'So what do you want me to do?'

'Pop round. Won't take a minute. Talk to the neighbours, you know the sort of thing. She didn't answer on Monday evening and she hasn't answered since. I called at ten and she's always in by then. Today's Wednesday and she still hasn't answered. My mind's not easy.'

'Don't you have any family?'

'Do me a favour. Dad snuffed it years back. Mum's bloke pushed off too, the sod. There's my cousin Evie, but her and me aren't talking. Aunt Kate's down in—'

'What about where she works?'

'She doesn't. Used to have a decent little Tesco checkout number. Not any more.'

It sounded like the beginning of an explanation, but none came. Alec sighed, went to the table, found pen and paper. 'Toxteth, you said?'

'Not any more. The council moved her. The newspaper helped. She's over in Riverview Heights now. After what I did . . . after what I did like, well, the Toxteth people weren't too friendly.'

After what I did . . . Alec could imagine it. Graffiti. Dogshit through the letter box. Broken windows. Abuse in the street. Kids copying their elders. The Tesco job had probably gone the same way. The terrible righteousness of the poor and simple. Bladon gave him his mother's address and he wrote it down.

'I'll do what I can.' He would. One visit, nothing more. Generous, but not excessively so. He could live with that. He moved from the table, eager now to be off, but Bladon was standing between him and the door.

'What I did, Mr Duncan—' The phrase had refused to go away. He tried it differently. 'What got me put in here, Mr Duncan – we haven't talked about it.'

Alec didn't answer, ground him down with his silence.

But Bladon was unconscionable. 'It's just that I'm sorry.'

Alec stared at him, his face blank. 'Aye, lad,' he said very clearly. 'So am I.'

The words were meaningless. He had wanted them to be, intending no comfort. He waited, then looked past Bladon, up at the camera.

'I'll be on my way out now, officer, if you don't mind.'

The lock clicked and the door opened. As Alec started forward Bladon called after him, 'I wasn't going to tell yer this, Mr Duncan—'

Then don't, laddie. Alec increased his pace.

'I wasn't going to tell yer this, but—'

The door was closing between them.

'They told me when they banged me away. I'm HIV positive.'

Alec tapped his foot impatiently as one of the waiting officers relocked the door. He glanced at his watch. He didn't want to know what Bladon had just told him. He couldn't bear the jolt of pleasure the news had given him.

4

Riverview Heights, the council flats in Wood End Park where Mrs Bladon now lived, were less upmarket than the name suggested. Alec knew them well, too well, from his days as a copper. The area was damp and low-lying, the heights were a couple of mini-tower blocks, and the river view from them was of distant muddy water and the Bromborough oil storage depot on the far side of the Mersey. The estate had been nice enough once, a well-meant low-cost housing development back in the socialist days of the Liverpool Housing Action Trust, but those days were long gone. It was the dump now for the council's undesirables. Toxteth, where Mrs Bladon had moved from, had the bad media reputation, but Riverview Heights gave the police more trouble.

Coming into town along the M62 from the north-east, Alec got caught up in roadworks and missed the Oak Vale exit down to Aigburth and Wood End Park. He wasn't paying attention and found himself in Wavertree. A further chance turning, intended to get him back on course, placed him outside the Funrama Videodrome, directly in front of which stood an unoccupied parking meter with fifty minutes still unspent. Alec stood on the brakes. Parking spaces hereabouts were like gold dust, and the Funrama Videodrome was where, in the late afternoon on an ordinary working day, one was most likely to find everybody's friendly neighbourhood drug dealer, Dancer Drew. Someone up there was trying to tell him something.

Alec hadn't planned to look up Dancer, and had nothing much to say to him if he did, but clearly some things were meant. He reversed neatly into the space, ignoring the distress of a driver on the other side of the road who had been waiting patiently to get across to it. He hadn't seen Dancer in over a year. Hadn't given him a thought, till Trevor Bladon mentioned him. Mebbe Dancer would like to hear how one of his most valued one-time customers was getting along, banged up in LTI for the rest of his natural. Not that this was Dancer's fault, of course – he deplored violence as much as the next man. A drug dealer only sold the stuff – it was up to the buyers what they did with it.

Alec felt cheered. The last time Dancer Drew had given him that story, Alec had been in the Force. This time round, having nothing to lose, he might feel less inhibited. It was every gun dealer's story too, he only sold the things, and the corpses he wasn't responsible for would stretch from here to Dallas, Texas, and back.

He left his car and went into the Videodrome. Pitch dark, with circling laser beams, and tacky, and inhumanly noisy, techno-rock beating against his face like blood, it was his idea of hell. He checked, while his senses adjusted. His eyes managed it first – the darkness in fact was illusory, a matter of black walls and floor and ceiling, flickering VDU screens and brilliant lasers. The management liked their heavy in the change kiosk to be able to see what was going on. At the far end of the cavernous space, two steps led up to a raised area and the classier, two-quid video games. It was there that Dancer would be found holding court. He never had stuff on him, but sent customers to a drop for it after taking their money. A lot of their money. He could work that way because customers trusted him. He'd been around a long time.

He wasn't around today. Alec moved further in, down the

central aisle, to make sure. The place was almost deserted, three greasy teenaged lads squashed into one game booth, fighting over a comic book and ignoring the Kung Fu sales pitch on the screen. Dancer wasn't up on the higher level, or at any of the other games that Alec could see. At the end of the aisle a boy with bleached white hair, twelve years old or so, was sweeping round with a wide broom, pushing at cigarette ends and crisp packets. Alec cornered him by a Gladiator Android game and stooped to make himself heard.

'Mebbe you can help me. I'm looking for—'

'Piss off. I don't do fuck-all with spades.'

Alec leaned closer. 'You what, lad?'

'You heard me. Black cocks aren't my scene, darlin'.'

Alec grabbed the front of his T-shirt, lifted him against the side of the booth. Then he reconsidered, took a deep breath, lowered the boy and stepped back.

'A lad like you could get himself into real trouble. You know that? Real bad trouble—'

The boy, looking past him down the aisle, didn't seem bothered. Alec remembered the heavy in the change kiosk, and understood why. He turned in time to face the man as he arrived. They sized each other up.

'Out.' The man jerked his shaved head in the direction of the street. '*Out* . . .'

Alec stayed watchful, his hands away from his sides. 'When I'm ready.'

'Not true. When I say so. And that's fucking now. Out.'

'I'm looking for wee Dancer.'

'Another of them. Dancer isn't here. Out.'

'In a minute. I'm interested.' The policeman in him was. 'Is he taking a piss or has he moved his business to other premises?'

'Who wants him?'

'I do.'

'Who's that, then?'

Alec was painfully aware of the boy, leaning on his broom, watching. 'Dancer and I go back a long way.'

'I don't care if you go back to fucking Methuselah. Out.'

'Or what?'

'Or I give the fucking fuzz a bell. Yer was feeling Jacko up. Indecent assault on a fucking minor. I fucking saw yer.'

Alec thought about that. He grinned. 'You've got me there,' he said. With the history Jacko must have, the threat was a farce, but he preferred not to test it. He tousled the boy's hair, then moved towards the door. 'Tell Dancer I'll be back.'

He ambled off, careful not to hurry. He'd made his point – the bruiser had the weight, and impressive tattoos, but he hadn't dared to use them. He'd invoked the fuzz instead.

Alec crossed the pavement, opened the Rover's door, leaned on it. He closed his eyes. Was that what he'd been doing? Making his point? Proving his manhood, for God's sake? Defending his race? For whose benefit? His own? *Jacko's?* He got into the car and drove off. Grow up, he told himself. Grow up.

Behind him, in the car mirror, he saw the Videodrome heavy out on the pavement, watching him go. He wondered, briefly, where Dancer had got to on a good trading afternoon.

Riverview Heights, even on a sunny September evening, were everything he remembered. The grass was bald and dusty, the paint was peeling, the concrete was cracked. Stained foam mattresses leaned against the snapped-off stumps of little once-ornamental trees and plastic trucks and broken tricycles littered the paths. Open windows relayed competing mega-decibels reminiscent of the Videodrome. Alec parked the Rover, locked it carefully, and referred to Trevor Bladon's piece of paper for his mother's flat number. The estate consisted of a grid of long four-storey blocks and two towers. If Mrs Bladon's place was seriously out of sight of his car he'd give it a miss. The Rover wasn't new, and had already lost hub caps and three sets of wiper blades, but he'd rather not have its bonnet drawn on with a brick or its boot prised open. Mebbe he'd park up on the busy Aigburth Road and walk down.

The Bladon residence turned out to be on the ground floor of the nearest tower. Its door was in past a vandalized entrance security system and down a short corridor, and he could come back out quickly for a look if Mrs Bladon took time answering. He pressed the bell push, heard a chime inside.

Nothing moved. He looked back over his shoulder, then rang again. The door was set in a frame with heavy obscured glass panels. He cupped his hands round his eyes and peered in, but saw nothing. He rang again, then returned to the entrance. A shaggy brown dog peed against the Rover's offside front tyre and kids were gathering. Trevor's mum appeared not to be at home.

'Hey.' He called to the kids and pointed back at the flat. 'The woman who lives there – any of you lot seen her? Today, I mean? Mebbe yesterday?'

The older kids grinned sideways at each other and hitched up their jeans.

'I'm serious. I need to talk to her.'

They sniggered and one of them mocked his accent. '*I need tae talk tae her*. Hoots, mon.'

Laughter burst out of them, blowing snot with it, and he turned away. Kids of that age didn't register grown-ups' comings and goings – he'd been foolish to try. He went round the side of the block. All the ground floor windows were barred. Mrs Bladon's were on the corner, a kitchen with venetian blinds facing east, then a bathroom facing south, a bedroom, and a tiny balcony with a door that had once been glass but was now filled in with blockboard, opening presumably into a living room. The bathroom had obscured glass and the bedroom and living room curtains were drawn. Like the other ground floor balconies, Mrs Bladon's had been covered with heavy protective wire mesh and, like the other protective wire meshes, hers was useless, bent up and wrenched away from the wall. On the other side of it Alec saw that the balcony door into her flat had a scarred frame and wasn't properly closed.

Several of the kids had followed him round. Alec didn't like the silence in Mrs Bladon's flat, or the drawn curtains, and he didn't like the signs of a forced entry, but if he went in to investigate the kids would either cry blue murder or else crowd in with him and get their sticky little fingers into everything before he could stop them. This was a job for the police, of which he was no longer a member.

He returned to his car, called up the public emergency number, and asked for the local Allerton nick on Rose Lane. When the desk sergeant came on the line he explained the situation.

'There's milk bottles going sour,' he lied, needing to be taken seriously. 'The mail's piling up. She hasn't answered her phone for days and her family's worried.'

'Families usually do, sir. And your name?'

'Alexander Duncan.' He didn't want to be recognized over the phone, and that was less likely if he was Alexander. 'I'm a . . . friend.'

'And you just happened to be passing, Mr Duncan?'

'No. No, I came round specially. Mrs Bladon's son asked me to. He couldn't get away.'

The desk sergeant was silent, possibly making criminal connections, possibly just keying in the information.

Eventually, 'If you would kindly stay at the address, Mr Duncan, I'll get a car round as soon as I can.'

'Of course. Thank you.'

He could easily push off but he was curious. More than that, he was concerned. Bugger Trev, he was concerned for Trev's mum. A woman living on her own in Riverview Heights wasn't a good bet. Why the hell had the council given her a ground floor flat?

Kids were staring in through the Rover's windows as if they had never before seen someone use a mobile phone. He and they were developing a beautiful relationship. Mebbe something could be made of it. He got out of the car again and leant against the wing.

'Why aren't you lot at home watching telly?'

Sidelong glances. Then, from the brassiest, previously the Scots mimic, 'Telly's boring.'

Inevitably the brassiest had a rival. 'Videos aren't boring. My dad's got porno. Shelves of it. It's class.'

Suggestive hoots were followed with tussling and chatter. The general opinion was that class, too, was boring. Alec couldn't be sure if this was genuine, or a sophistication laid on to impress him.

'So what *isn't* boring? What *do* you lot do with your time?'

Their answer took thought. It was an effort to remember. 'Hang around. Go climbing. Us've got a tree house. Go to football. Chase tarts. Nick things.'

'Chase tarts? Whatever for?'

''Cause they're fucking stupid.'

'Anyone you know ever nicked anything from Mrs Bladon?'

Nobody recognized the name.

'Hasn't been here long. Moved into that ground floor flat there.'

'Fat old tart in a Red Indian jacket?'

Alec didn't recall having seen Trevor's mother. 'Could be. Have you seen her today?'

'That's Mrs Brown. Saw her a couple of nights ago. Late. Me and Del was—'

A white Merseyside armoured panda car with its windscreen mesh raised came round the corner and the children scattered. It stopped and Alec went over to it. The driver wound down his window.

Alec said, 'That's very prompt.'

'We were in the area.' The driver referred to his notebook. 'You'll be Mr Duncan.'

Alec nodded. He'd never worked with this constable and saw no reason to elaborate. Members of the Merseyside force who knew him had taken sides – there were those who thought his resignation had got him unfairly off the hook.

'Mrs Bladon's flat is just over there, officer. Ground floor. I think it's been broken into.'

The driver's companion got out of the car and introduced himself as PC Baynes. Harry. Bulky in his body armour, gun holster clanking, but Harry. Part of the latest friendly police/populace interface. Alec took him into the tower block. He didn't comment on the lack of milk bottles outside Mrs Bladon's door. He probably hadn't been told about them. He rang her doorbell, knocked, then thumped his shoulder against the door. It held.

'You say there's been a break-in?'

'From the balcony. Round the corner outside. I looked.'

Harry looked too. He lifted the protective mesh experimentally. 'Waste of council money,' he said. 'On estates like this nothing keeps the bastards out.'

Them and us. Clearly Alec's clothes and car and manner, if not his colour, had marked him as a cut above Riverview Heights.

He nodded wisely. 'I suppose the council has to show willing.'

Constable Harry Baynes wasn't so sure. He turned back to the balcony, peered at the door into the flat. There was a gap of an inch or so between it and the jamb on the handle side and gouge marks were visible. He hesitated, needing justification before he could break and enter.

'You say the family's worried?'

'It's been four days now.' Probably two and a half, but members of the public always exaggerated. 'Not a word. And she isn't answering her phone.'

Harry went to the living room window, tried for a gap in the curtains, found none. He stepped back. 'Come with me, sir, please.'

They returned to the panda car and Alec stood at a tactful distance while the two policemen conferred, radioed in, came to a decision. Constable Baynes emerged with a jemmy.

'I'm going in, sir. Would you kindly be present?'

'Of course.' Alec approved. It was sound procedure to go in at the front and leave the damaged door untouched, in case forensics were needed.

Back at the front door Harry Baynes knocked and rang again, and called Mrs Bladon's name, to continuing silence, then inserted the jemmy. The door opened easily and wasn't on a chain. Alec was relieved – Merseyside's annual making good costs stirred up the regional finance office more than almost anything else. The door swung open over junk mail and a freebie newspaper, into a small dark hall with bare vinyl tiles, the living room straight ahead, shadowed by drawn curtains. The furniture was minimal: a greasy sofa on a worn carpet square, a metal kitchen chair tucked under the flap of an open drop-fronted desk, empty save for a pad and some envelopes and what looked like a rent book, a wooden standard lamp with a bare bulb and no shade, and in front of the sofa a matt black stand for a TV set. A square dustless area on the stand suggested that a TV set had been there until recently.

'Mrs Bladon? *Mrs Bladon . . .?*'

The constable's words bounced tinnily off bare floors and walls. The place sounded terminally empty and Alec had one of his feelings. Up to this moment he'd have said Trevor's mum had done a flit, but now. . .

Baynes put a hand on his arm. 'Stay here please, Mr Duncan.'

He left Alec, looked round the living room, behind the open door, then returned. A second door from the hall led into the bedroom. As he opened the door Alec saw past him: this room, too, was pathetically bare, the bed unmade. Mrs Bladon was hardly more than camping here. The council might have relocated her at short notice, on compassionate grounds, but their compassion hadn't stretched to much in the way of home comforts.

Next round the hall was a coat cupboard, empty in Baynes's torch beam, then a short corridor, presumably to the bathroom and kitchen. Baynes examined the bathroom, most of which was out of Alec's line of sight, without comment. Opening the kitchen door, though, raised an ominous buzzing of flies. Alec glimpsed an upset metal table and a chair the twin of the chair at the desk in the living room, and a woman's body, brown Aztec-patterned knitted waistcoat, legs in flowered tights, lying on the vinyl floor tiles. He couldn't see her head, the greasy neon tube on the ceiling wasn't switched on, and closed venetian blinds at the window made the room very gloomy, but the flies, and now the smell on this warm September evening, left little doubt that the woman was dead.

Harry Baynes stooped over her briefly, picked up a felt shoulder bag from the floor beside her, looked around, then backed hastily out of the kitchen, closed the door, and released the breath he'd been holding. Out in the hall he reached for the light switch, then reconsidered. He shepherded Alec out of the flat, wedging the front door shut behind them with a folded Balti take-away voucher off the mat.

'One woman's shoulder bag, sir.' He showed it to Alec and outside in the daylight he opened it and brought out a purse. The purse had two ten-pound notes in it, some change, postage stamps, a packet of condoms and a Social Security card. Baynes, who had seen the dead woman's face, looked at the name on the card, and the photograph. 'I'm afraid your Mrs Bladon's dead, sir.'

Alec was unsurprised. 'Beaten up?'

The constable shook his head. 'There was a struggle, but

not much. The bastard shot her. Close quarters. Nasty mess.' He put Mrs Bladon's purse back in her shoulder bag. It was cheap felt, with a scraggly fringe. 'I'm sorry, sir. That was unnecessary. I—'

'It's all right.' The constable was young enough, new enough, nice enough, to have been upset by what he'd seen. 'I'm not a relative. I didn't even know her. I was doing her son a favour, coming here. He's in prison, y'see, in LTI, and—'

'He'll have to be told . . .' Baynes looked at his watch. 'I'll need to call in now, sir. Perhaps you'll be good enough to wait in your car. There'll be questions . . .'

'Of course.' They hurried down the cracked concrete path. It was time to own up – later would look odd. 'I know the drill. I was a policeman once.'

Baynes kept going. 'The name rang a bell. Wasn't there a bit of a . . . ?'

'There was.' They reached the panda. 'I'll be in my car when you need me.'

Alec settled himself in the Rover, stared out at the tower block, at its windows and balconies. A poor wretched woman, quite ordinary, shot to death in her kitchen. Well, that was Riverview Heights . . . What the hell had the killer hoped to get? Breaking and entering with a gun, armed robbery, it was all so heavy. A woman like that, a flat like that, it didn't make sense. The woman was dead now, and all for what? A telly? He hadn't even taken her purse, her Social Security card. In through the balcony door, after dark probably quite late, surprised to find the occupier awake and in her kitchen, panicked, did the business. What was he expecting to find? Mebbe he found it. Mebbe the telly was an afterthought. A blind. In any case, out with it through the front door, and away . . .

The gunshot? Constable Baynes hadn't said how many. Wouldn't matter much, in Riverview Heights. House-to-house needed: someone might have heard, might have gone to a window, but the chances were they'd have minded their own business. Chances were they'd mind their own business now, too. Villains had friends, these days. It didn't do to have seen things.

Alec glanced at the clock. The time was after six and he'd be here for quite a while yet. Luckily Wednesday was one of his nights off from Tony's. He turned on the radio – Classic FM, Mozart by the sound of it, some symphony's rumpety-tumpety final movement – and wondered who Rose Lane's chief superintendent would send. Faces changed all the time and in any case he was nine months out of date. He realized he felt very excited.

Incident rooms, SOC people, exhibit bags, team briefings, press releases, the whole amazing roadshow that was a serious crime investigation – he'd been missing it. Of course he had. Why not? It had been his life, once, a game he'd been good at . . . But it was pretty pathetic to imagine that his present role as The Man Who Had Alerted The Police would somehow give all that back to him. Ten minutes of the inspector's sergeant's time was what he'd get. If he was lucky.

Suddenly he was appalled. The inspector and the sergeant. The game they played, picking over the bones of someone else's tragedy, which it was their job to ameliorate with the sad, ugly gift of retribution. Alec sweated. Was that what he was missing? The tricks of the interrogation room? The pressures available against reluctant witnesses, the shaping of statements to suit the investigating officer, the advantage cleverness had over stupidity, experience over innocence, training over insecurity and fear? The ruthless search for evidence of guilt – not for the truth, leave that to the philosophers, laddie – for evidence of guilt that would stand up in the face of everything a crafty defence could throw at it? The entire elaborate game coppers played on behalf of a vengeful society? Was that what he was missing? And then the booze-up when the job was done? Drinks all round, and a bar-room song or two, knowing that some poor bugger – poor bugger, deserving bugger, did it matter? – was well on his way to being banged up for life? All the stuff, in fact, that had made him pack it in, was that what he was missing?

There were other sides to policing. Of course there were. Or there had been once. These days P & P – Punishment and Protection – were squeezing them out. Certainly, in the days since he'd progressed above detective sergeant, he'd seen precious little of them.

Then again, coming back to the present case, in his role as The Man Who Had Alerted The Police, there'd be the inspector's sergeant's questions, and to the most obvious of them his admission that he was there because he'd chosen for some odd reason, for some sick reason, to help out Trevor Bladon, to do the man who'd stabbed May to death a favour. The inspector's sergeant wouldn't like that. It wasn't his place to like it or not, but he wouldn't like it. Alec couldn't blame him. He himself, now, didn't like it.

Alec fixed his seatbelt, turned off the radio, and started the engine. He was buggering off. The inspector's sergeant's questions had made up his mind for him. He didn't need them. He refused to sit around, waiting to be humiliated. He'd done enough, reporting the crime. Why the hell did Mrs Bladon have to get herself murdered? She'd no fucking right. His hands were shaking. He released the handbrake and looked in the rearview mirror.

Constable Baynes tapped on his windscreen. 'No need to move her, sir. You're in nobody's way.'

Alec took a breath. He was losing his mind. He reset the handbrake and wound down the window. 'I—'

'On second thoughts, Mr Duncan, you can push off if you like. You've been very helpful and we're grateful. If I could just have one or two details, address, phone number, that sort of thing, then you can push off. Even when the inspector gets here it'll be ages before he gets to you. So if you don't mind, sir, just one or two details . . . We'll be in touch again later.'

Alec gathered himself. It was sympathetic policing. It was what often got lost behind all the games and the body armour. He gave the details Constable Baynes asked for.

'Like I said, sir, we're very grateful. And you can leave the rest to us. We'll inform the next of kin. You don't have to worry.'

Alec didn't. The next of kin was Trev, and Trev was in good hands. Governor Ransome, over in Justice City, was a man of massive sensitivity. He'd do a great job. '7765 Bladon? I expect you're wondering why I've sent for you. I'm afraid I've got bad news. Stand up straight, man. Your mother's been murdered.'

Alec drove away. It was just his joke. Telling Trev wouldn't be like that at all. Justice City, like everywhere else, had social workers. Bereavement counsellors. Trev would like that.

5

Poor Trev. Life was tough. Long Term Incarceration, HIV, and now his mum gone. Poor Trev . . . No, that was flip. Shame on you. Once more, with feeling: *Poor Trev.*

Alec drove back to Sefton Park on auto-pilot. By the look of things Trevor's mum, like Alec himself, hadn't made much of the last nine months. No job, a dump in Riverview Heights, a sofa and a big TV. And now she was dead. Her murder bothered him. What had attracted the robber? Mebbe he'd taken other things as well as the telly, but from that particular woman in that particular flat it was hard to imagine what. Stolen silver candlesticks she was looking after for a friend? Her life savings in a cardboard box under the bed? Stranger things happened.

In any case, perhaps such deaths weren't unusual in Riverview Heights, and for even humbler loot. If you were poor enough, or angry enough, you took what you could get.

Trevor had called his mum at ten on Monday evening and she hadn't answered. He said she was always in by then, so had she already been dead? Had her killer stood by the phone and watched it ring? After such a time gap – Monday night till now – no doctor would let himself be tied down to a particular hour. It would be useful if her watch had stopped at the moment of her death, but watches only did that in the books. He caught himself wishing he was the investigating officer, with access to such information, and was ashamed. It hadn't taken long, only ten minutes, and he was back wanting to be part of the game.

The game . . . When Constable Baynes had apologized for being tactless about the shooting, he'd said it was all right – he didn't know the woman. Lucky him. Other people weren't so fortunate. They knew the woman. Her son Trevor knew her. Her niece Evie, who lived locally, knew her, and so did her sister Kate, down in London. It wasn't all right for them. The mess a bullet, or mebbe two or three, had made of Joan Bladon wasn't all right for them. For them the game was less attractive.

It had to be played, of course, and played well, and therefore played with enthusiasm. Enjoyment even. But not by him. He was off home to some grub and the telly. He'd done his duty by Joan Bladon's son and the matter was closed. He felt sorry for the lad, but life was tough all over.

Alec drove round Sefton Park, turned in between the worn stone gate posts, and parked on the gravel at the side of the house. The ground floor flat in which he lived used the original kitchen entrance. A metallic grey Mercedes was there ahead of him, with two large men in suits standing by it.

Something about the two men's largeness and their suits suggested to him that he might sensibly reverse and drive straight back out again, but he decided that would be an over-reaction. They couldn't help being large and their suits might be selling insurance. He got out of the car. This was Sefton Park, for God's sake. In broad daylight.

'Alexander Duncan?'

'Aye. What can I do for you?'

One of the men produced a silenced handgun. 'Turn round, please. Hands on the roof of the car.'

He sounded professional. Alec hesitated. He hated guns. Their weight, shape, feel, smell, purpose, everything about them. The baggage they'd collected as male symbols didn't say much for men. 'If you're CID, then mebbe I can—'

'Just do it.'

Alec did it. Since when had the CID used metallic grey Mercedes or silencers?

The second man wandered across the drive, blocking the view of possible passers-by as the first man searched Alec for a weapon. They weren't CID and he'd helped them with the angle at which he'd parked the Rover. In any case, Sefton Parkers were car users. The time was after five, too late for school children to be about and too early for that night's vigilantes.

'This way please, *Mr* Duncan. Into the car.'

His emphasis on the *Mr* was carefully offensive. The other man moved neatly into position, opening the rear door of the Mercedes as Alec approached it.

Alec baulked. 'I'm not going.'

'You're going. With or without a round in your leg, you're going.'

The silenced gun would make no more noise than a champagne cork, but would do more damage. He got into the car and the man with the gun got in with him. He was allowed to try the far door of the car and find it locked. Childproof locks were a great invention. The other man slid in behind the wheel, started the car, and they drove away. Grub and the telly retreated. How easy abduction was.

What next? Alec tried to think of a reason for someone to want him dead, and was cheered when he couldn't. 'Who are you taking me to?'

Neither man answered.

'I'll know eventually. Why not now?'

The Mercedes turned left off Aigburth Drive, making for the city centre. Men like this had their orders, no talking, and stuck to them. They represented money power, as did the car. Big money power, therefore sex, drugs, or gambling, or probably all three combined, with protection thrown in. Perhaps – a gloomy thought – they believed he was a policeman and he was going into a ransom situation. The Chief Constable would love that – deals were made that never reached the media, but only for policemen. For members of the public the rule was strict: if one gave in to kidnappers it only encouraged them to do it again.

Alec wondered how quickly he'd be missed. The earliest was tomorrow night, at Tony's. He was expected at his hospital portering job in the morning but if volunteers like him didn't turn up it was days before anyone asked questions. Tony would ring the Sefton Park flat, leave a message on the answerphone, and hire another piano player two days later. As for Morag, he'd told her yesterday, *I'll give you a call.* That could mean weeks.

The Mercedes drove unimpressed past the growing bulk of the new prison, its contractors' safety hoardings thickly spray-painted with ferocious fuck-based graffiti, and stopped sooner than Alec had expected, waiting in the middle of a busy street in Princes Park to turn right down an alley beside a scabby bingo hall, a converted chapel. The indicator warning ticked patiently and Alec looked out at the passing traffic. Would he really be shot if he banged on the window, attacked the driver, created a scene of some kind? Perhaps not. Even if he wasn't, his minder not wanting to mess up the car's interior, he'd certainly be severely clobbered – and in any case the likelihood was that no one in Princes Park would choose to notice . . . Alec folded his hands in his lap. It was wonderful, he thought, the way common sense could be deployed in support of cowardly inaction.

A gap in the traffic arrived and the Mercedes took it. The alley was narrow and dustbin-lined, with a rusty fire escape to complicate access, but the driver had been there before. He glided in over the cobbles, riding on expensive hydraulics, inches to spare, and stopped with Alec's door unopenably close against the wall. The two men got out on their side and motioned him to follow. Choices, choices . . . He followed.

The alley stank of dustbins and cat pee, and the narrow door into the building had rotted and was held together with rusting sheet metal. Alec, emerging from the hushed, leather-scented Mercedes, wasn't thrown by the contrast – real money power, criminal money power, seldom bothered with front-of-house glitz. It had much to prove, but did so in its own way. He couldn't see the surveillance cameras, for instance, yet the door opened exactly as they approached it, revealing yet another suited heavy. Alec recognized no faces, and the bingo hall was after his time, but he totted up its owner's wage bill so far, and factored in the lease and insurance on the Mercedes. The result was only tip-of-the-iceberg stuff, but laundering the profits it represented would need more than just the odd Princes Park bingo hall. A gallery of leading Merseyside villains flashed before his eyes. An old habit, and in this case unnecessary – another couple of minutes and he'd know.

The doorkeeper reached for his internal phone as they went up narrow uncarpeted stairs, Alec the ham in the sandwich, and across a poky landing to the boss's door. It had to be the boss's door: it was the only new door on the landing, flush sapele veneer, its handle B & Q Byzantine gilt. Matters of taste, Alec reminded himself, had no bearing on the present situation. B & Q deaths were as terminal as any other brand.

One heavy went into the boss's room with Alec, the other stayed outside. The boss, behind his government surplus desk, turned out to be an old friend. An old enemy. Alec wasn't cheered – Stan Falco was big money power at its worst, sex, drugs and gambling, all three combined, with protection thrown in and council corruption too, and Alec had pursued him, principally on the drugs side of things, vainly but relentlessly, ever since he'd made chief inspector. Falco's desk might be government surplus but the electronic hardware on it wouldn't have shamed an airline booking office. He owned clubs in Liverpool, Manchester and Leeds, exemplary establishments, taxes paid, licences in order, fire regulations observed, clean food, quiet on the street after midnight, good working conditions, choice of paper in the toilets . . . but he owned much else besides, casinos, construction companies, all Merseyside's sex and drugs, and he had a reputation for rigorously defending his property. People who so much as looked it over, died. Alec could make an informed guess now at why he, at why an unfamiliar black called Alexander Duncan, a stranger in the area, asking after Dancer Drew, had been sent for.

Falco, too, instantly recognized an old acquaintance. He put his hand-stitched brogues up on the desk, and laughed far more than the joke seemed worth. Stan Falco was famous for his sense of humour.

Alec took a chair from beside the door, moved it forward in front of the desk and sat in it, waiting dourly for Falco to be done. This prolonged the laughter. Falco pulled man-size tissues from a box by his computer terminal and mopped his brow. He was in his shirtsleeves, his broad-striped shirt gaping over his belly to reveal a hairy navel. Sharp-eyed, with angular features and receding grey hair, he was an intellectual who'd missed out on school and got into bad company and done well for himself. Eventually he pulled himself together, heaved his feet down off his desk, made a ball of the damp tissues and threw them in the bin.

'Oh dear, oh dear . . . Sorry, love. *Sorree* . . . it's just that I was—'

'You were expecting another Alexander Duncan.'

'*Alexander*. . .' The name produced another attack. He controlled it. 'I have to say, old dear, I never thought of you as a fucking Alexander. I've called you many things, but never that.'

'History, Falco. Dead and gone. I suggest you get Sunshine here to take me home.'

'That's not like you, Alexander. Aren't you curious?'

'What about? Your bouncer out at the Videodrome got on the blower. Right? He said some spade was asking after Dancer. He said I didn't behave like trade and he thought I might be looking to deal a bit. Mebbe for you and mebbe on my own account. Right? You thought he might have something and sent round Sunshine. You got my name and where I live from the Videodrome's card scanner. Right?'

'Wrong. The fucking thing's on the blink, old dear. We got you from your car registration.'

'That was bad luck. The scanner would have given former profession. Even so, you were dumb. You should have wondered about some nigger hopeful who turned out to live in Sefton Park . . . I'll go away home now.'

'Hey. *Hey* . . .' Falco stood up. He was a big man, well-built save for a slight excess of belly. 'Joke over, old dear. You're retired these days, they tell me, but I'm surprised you haven't heard.'

'Heard?' *Retired* was a nice way of putting it. 'What haven't I heard?'

'Young Dancer. Dead, poor dear. Unnecessary quantities of lead . . . So was I so dumb? Dancer shot down and a black sniffing round, new to the area, asking questions and maybe knowing all the fucking answers? Was I so dumb? Wouldn't *you* have . . .' he gestured broadly '. . . have put out feelers?'

Alec thought about it. Mrs Bladon dead, and now Dancer. At least, in Dancer's case it was unsurprising. Guys in Dancer's line of business were poor insurance risks. 'Was he one of yours?'

'So they tell me. I don't do all the hiring . . . So what's your interest?'

Alec ducked that one. He didn't have an answer. 'When was this?'

'Late Monday night. The police were called early Tuesday morning. Otterspool, along at the east end, down by the water. A jogger found the body.'

'Territorial? Was the killing a matter of territory?'

'Not as far as I know, old dear.'

'Don't give me that, Falco. You know. Knowing is how you stay in business. Was it opposition or wasn't it?'

'Alexander. *Alexander*...' Falco went to the window, looked out at the leprous brick wall ten feet away across the alley. 'There is no opposition. Where've you been? There is no opposition.'

Which was a way of saying he'd blasted it, slashed it, garrotted it, terrorized it out of existence. Beside Stan Falco, Trevor Bladon was a Sunday school teacher. Falco brought order, though, which Trevor did not. A minimum of civic disruption. He didn't play by the Chief Constable's rules, admittedly, but it can't entirely have been manpower cuts that saved him from major investigation. Some people suggested that money changed hands, but Alec didn't think so. The Chief Constable was wily, and had a very rich wife.

None of this stopped Alec from being shamed by his own powerlessness. In another screenplay, with a different director, now that he was out of the police force he'd rid the world of Stan Falco with his bare hands, blood all the way up the wall, join Stan Falco in the violence shit, sacrifice the eternal soul he didn't believe he had for the sake of a society he didn't believe was worth it.

Ah, fuck it . . .

Falco was asking where he'd been? Not in the Chief Constable's confidence, for one. Clearly not reading the papers either.

'So who killed him?'

Falco turned back from the window. 'Does it matter? I doubt if Dancer Drews have mothers.'

'Don't give me that. Of course it matters. If he was yours,

it matters. You care about your people. You care about you. That's why I'm here – you thought mysterious Mr Alexander Duncan might be able to help you in your inquiries. To coin a phrase.'

'How cynical you are. I could have been planning to offer you a job.'

'That too. After you'd nailed me and everybody knew it.'

'Do you blame me for reeling you in?' A telephone sounded on Falco's desk, two and a half beeps only. Somewhere in this terrible building a secretary was fielding his calls. 'Your people – your ex-people, that is – won't find him. Won't try to, old dear. Filed under *gangland killing*. No public pressure. Two lines in the local rag. Do you blame me?'

Alec shrugged. He realized that Mrs Bladon's death must have occurred on the same Monday night, and wondered what his ex-people would be filing it under: *Riverview at it again*?

Falco returned to his desk and sat down. 'But you haven't told me your interest.'

'That's right.' Alec realized, further, that Riverview Heights were only a stone's throw from the east end of Otterspool Park. Mrs Bladon and Dancer, the same night, the same fate, virtually the same place. Stranger things happened, certainly, but with Trevor shared between them the coincidence grew harder to swallow. 'It's time you took me away to my home, Falco.'

Falco considered, then nodded to the heavy waiting by the door. 'Put ex-Detective Chief Inspector Duncan back where you found him, Ken.' Alec stood up and turned to go. Falco raised a finger. 'No. Wait on, old dear. Tell me – what are you up to these days?'

Alec kept on walking. 'I'm taking myself away home.' For some, but not for him, Falco's finger was God. 'You can stuff your fucking limo.'

'I could be serious about that job.'

The joke was Alec's now – first Hardcastle and now Stan

Falco. Two sides of the same coin. 'I wouldn't take a job from you, friend, if I was starving in the gutter.'

'Tut. You wouldn't be offered it, old dear . . . Still, I get your message.'

Alec went to the door and opened it. Ken the heavy didn't try to stop him. As he went across the landing and down the stairs Falco had followed him to the door. He called after him, 'I tell you one thing, old dear. Them as killed young Dancer, they're already dead.'

A promise? A statement? In either case, vainglory. The guard on the outside door took a lead from his boss at the head of the stairs and let Alec through. The alley was unattractive, the street it led into hardly less so. Alec started walking, keeping an eye out for a taxi. Spotting one was only the first step. Getting it to stop for him, unless the driver was black too, was another matter.

He'd probably end up walking. Grand dramatic gestures cost, but sometimes – and this was one of those times – they were worth it.

The telephone was ringing. Alec fumbled with his key, got it in the lock, opened the door, expected the telephone to stop just as he reached it.

He'd paid off the taxi out on the road. His journey back from Princes Park had gone well, thanks to a taxi driver, a woman would you believe, who'd known enough discrimination not to practise it. Even so, dusk was falling as he walked up the mossy gravel drive and heard the distant telephone. It continued to ring as he entered the flat and hurried through to the sitting room. He lifted the receiver.

'Chief? Sorry – did I wake you?'

'Frank?' Dozing off in the afternoon? Was that what his former sergeant thought he'd come down to? 'No – I've only just got in.'

'Makes sense. Called earlier and you weren't in then either.

Thing is, it's the night you're not at Tony's, and I'm on days this month, and me and Doris thought you'd like a bite to eat.'

A bite to eat . . . Alec stood in the shadowed sitting room and listened to the silence. Chairs, tables, shelves, pictures, ornaments, books, May's grand piano in the big bay window, the high-ceilinged room ached with emptiness. The whole flat ached with emptiness.

'Chief? Are you still there?'

Alec smiled. Frank was his friend. 'I'm still here, Frank. And I'd love to.'

'Dandy. Any time, then. Any time you can make it.'

'See you.' Alec lowered the receiver, then had a thought. 'Frank? You still there? Do me a favour, will you? Find out what you can about a shooting. Monday night, down in Otterspool. Petty crook name of Dancer Drew.'

'Sounds familiar. Is he dead?'

'Stan Falco says he is.'

Frank whistled. 'You move in fancy circles.'

'I'll tell you about it. A shower then, and I'm on my way.'

He rang off. Tonight was not a night for fighting things. The flat's undesirable emptiness, his own undesirable professional curiosity, tonight was a night for giving in to both. With Trevor Bladon shared between Dancer and Mrs Bladon, and the two of them shot dead, same night, same place, the coincidence was hard to swallow. And Frank and Doris were mebbe lonely too.

He showered quickly and changed. Nakedness reminded him of sex, and of his troublesome celibacy, and he never lingered. Masturbation left him sad and lonely. He left the flat and drove to Frank's terraced house in Anfield, stopping off at the off-licence on Lark Lane to buy beer. It was Wednesday, training night at the football club, and floodlights lit the sky eerily behind Frank's altered roofline – he'd put a room up in his loft for the grandchildren when they visited, and built a big dormer.

Doris let Alec in. Rich smells of roast beef filled the narrow hallway. The Groves didn't believe in mad cows, for all the TV pictures. Frank was talking on the phone by the stairs as Doris led Alec through to the conservatory, and pressed himself against the wall to let them pass. The conservatory was another of Frank's DIY additions, used for extra living space rather than plants, and taking up most of the tiny garden area out at the back. Frank's hours before he'd ended up at the Bridewell hadn't left much time for lawns and flowerbeds.

Alec perched sideways on the wicker lounger, trying to hear what Frank was saying on the telephone out in the hall. Doris stood over him, hands clasped against her apron.

'That's not the way, man,' she told him, as Betws-y-coed as ever. 'Frank'll be out in a minute. Sit you back now and put your feet up.'

She was concerned for him, for his life and his worries. If he hadn't once been her husband's boss she'd have touched his shoulder, patted him, hugged him better. For once her concern made him pay attention. Looking up, paying attention, he saw her, actually saw her, and was shocked.

Ashamed too.

You could visit someone's home every week for months and see the place and not the person. Then, one night, for no particular reason, you saw the person and not the place. You saw her without her furniture and fittings, without past visits, you saw her as she was, as she really was, and her concern for you was shaming. She deserved your concern far more. A plump rosy woman was suddenly thin and grey. Her smile was as young as ever, and her welcome as bright, but she was wasting away. Her cheeks had withered till the teeth underneath them showed, and the skin round her eyes had sagged and sallowed, and her double chins were empty bags, and there was room for two of her body inside her familiar same old clothes. She was dying. Was she dying?

He'd told Morag, *Doris isn't well these days.* The words were Frank's, a husband's, necessarily minimal, a comfortable substitution for any observation Alec himself might have made. Doris was wasting away, dying. He hadn't noticed.

He lay back on the lounger as she'd asked. She said, 'I'll bring you a glass for that beer, then?' and he nodded, closing his eyes. She wouldn't agree to resting, sitting down, non-employment. He waited while she went away, returned with a glass, opened one of the cans he'd brought, poured it skilfully and gave it to him.

'There's nice,' she said, and left him.

He held his glass of beer and stared up at the reflection of himself in the sloping roof of the conservatory. Was she dying? Just then Frank rang off and came in from the hall.

'There isn't much,' he said. 'Do I get told why you're asking?'

Alec changed mental gear, explained about Stan Falco, and Trevor Bladon and his mum. Frank opened a beer can, drank from it, then guiltily fetched himself a glass. His Doris didn't like men drinking out of cans.

He sat down by Alec. 'Falco's evil,' he said.

'I know it, Frank. And yet, face to face, he's so – what's the word now? – so bloody *clubbable* . . . Would you believe it, Frank, he offered me a job?'

Frank grunted and drank his beer.

'I wasn't flattered. I tell you, he makes my skin crawl.'

Frank got back to the point. 'Can't see him involved in killing off the old woman, though – too large a hammer for such a small nail.'

'Me neither.'

'So what about the family – wasn't there a second husband?'

'Common law, I think the phrase is. They never married.' Alec knew lots about Trevor Bladon. He was an authority on everything to do with Trevor Bladon. He'd avoided Trevor Bladon's trial because going every day to watch and listen would have been too much of a public act, and in any case prurient. Instead he'd spent the time reading everything A Division had – post mortem, forensics, statements from the neighbours, the man upstairs who had found the body and the others who, incredibly, had seen and heard nothing, evidence summaries, case assessments, the accused's family background, his psychiatric social worker's report, everything Frank could get hold of. He knew it all by heart. 'And not for a while. He pushed off four years ago. Seems he didn't get along with wee Trev. Jack Fisher, his name was.'

Frank sighed. 'Doesn't sound too promising. It's just that ninety per cent—'

'—of all murders,' Alec finished for him, 'are domestic. Not this one, Frank – looks like a straight robbery with. But in any case, we'll have to wait a while – I only phoned it in a couple of hours ago. Allerton's Rose Lane won't have much yet.'

'Not much better on Dancer Drew.'

'Didn't get yourself into trouble, I hope. What excuse did you give for asking?'

'Old time's sake. Drew and me go back, Chief. I remember him well – nicked him often enough, back when he was a juvenile. Not that it did me much good. Couldn't touch him. Didn't do young Drew much good neither.'

Alec wondered what *would* have done young Drew good. Him and young Trev and all the others like them. Today's juvenile PPCs taught violence as a way of life.

'Any road,' Frank went on, 'Otterspool's in Allerton's patch so I got on to Harry, told him the tale. How I had this fatherly interest. He passed me on to A Division – they're treating the case as a gangland killing and handling it from there.'

'Sitting on it till it dies of suffocation, more like.' Alec had expected this. 'So tell me – you have a Harry in A Division too?'

'Thirty years on the Merseyside force, Chief. It'd be a scandal if I didn't.'

'And what does A Division's Harry say?'

'His name's Phil. He says Drew was shot around one, Tuesday morning. Three times at six or seven feet, then a clincher point blank above the right ear.'

Alec winced. This was hands-on stuff. Someone didn't mind seeing the mess he made. 'They weren't taking any chances.'

'Large calibre, too. Right for being police issue. We've lost a handgun or two, these last few—'

Doris put her head round the door. 'Five minutes,' she said. 'If you're wanting to wash your hands?'

She went back to the kitchen. Alec asked, 'No weapon found, of course?'

Frank shook his head. 'Clearly a set-up. Drew's car was up on the road, ignition on, lights, battery flat, empty tank so he probably left it running. Door open too, but he wasn't dragged out. Only his prints on the handle.'

Alec narrowed his eyes, visualizing the scene. So he'd been lured there. Mebbe a drug drop. He hadn't expected to stay.

'Beats me why he went, Chief. Middle of the night, miles from anywhere, doesn't sound like our Dancer.'

'He had his living to earn. Mebbe the deal was too good to turn up.' Alec drank his beer. It was possible that Dancer'd gone because he'd trusted whoever he was meeting. Possible, but hardly likely. Dancer's life hadn't made him a trusting person. 'No footprints? No signs of a struggle? No convenient fibres under his finger nails?'

'They're waiting on forensics but it doesn't look like it. And it was a fine night . . . One odd thing, Chief – tissue on the beach below the sea wall. Small, and traces that might be blue eye make-up, so it's probably a woman's, but there's no saying. Has to have been dropped around the time of the crime, or the tide would've taken it. Pritchard's on the case and he's sent it for analysis.'

'I worked with Inspector Pritchard once. He did a sloppy job . . . So if it might be a woman, why the gangland label?'

Frank gave him an old-fashioned look and he laughed.

'Sorry, Frank. Stupid question.' Resources were finite, Dancer Drews were dispensable, and the gangland label saved everyone a lot of bother. As far as the public was concerned, the more the crooks killed each other the better it was pleased. Hence Pritchard, who would simply go through the motions. 'Is that all, then?'

'It's all Phil knows about. Drew had a lover. Bloke he lived with, Jackie Patterson, up by the racecourse . . . Phil got me his address. He's a good lad. Had to phone me back. Pritchard was—'

'You men, now.' Doris was back. 'Dinner's ready.'

Alec stood up. 'I'd better go and wash my hands.'

She looked at him. 'Tell me you're winding me up.'

'I'm winding you up.'

'That's all right, then. Wash 'em if you must. Take all day. See me care if the food's stone cold.'

He went through to the kitchen with his glass and the other four cans of beer, and sat down at the table. The dining room was for fine company and he'd long ago progressed beyond that. He was family. The kitchen was cramped, with plastic-fronted cabinets and drawers, but there was friendly clutter and a handsome old oblong American clock with a waterfall and pine trees painted on the glass below the face.

Doris's beef was perfect, crisp brown on the outside, pink in the middle, resting on Yorkshire pudding red with pan juices. Another dish held sizzling roast potatoes and parsnips. Then there were the sprouts and the horseradish sauce, and fresh fruit salad (in deference to Frank's waistline) to follow. Doris had a rural contempt for what she termed 'messed about food', but on the basics she was unbeatable.

She and Frank had invited Alec because that morning they had received a letter from their daughter: their son-in-law was contemplating a job change and they wanted Alec's advice. The change was from selling office stationery to managing a carpets and floor coverings store, neither of which Alec knew anything about, but they expected him to have an opinion so he had one. The shop would keep Steve at home more, he said, and give him more time with the kids, and he knew that Dilys had been feeling lonely and put-upon, so he thought the move would be a good idea. Doris had her doubts, a man had to do what he was good at and Steve had shown himself good at selling stationery, but Frank said Steve would be good at anything he put his hand to.

Doris carved and served and chatted, and fetched the latest snaps of Dilys and the kids, and poured the men's beer, and offered second helpings, and briskly cleared the dishes, and none of it hid from Alec the fact that she ate next to nothing. Frank must have seen it too, and said nothing, so Alec said nothing too.

When washing up time came, for the first time in Alec's experience Frank announced that the men would do it, and there wasn't an argument. Doris dried her hands, took off her apron, hung it up tidily, and went into the front room to watch television. Ten minutes later, when they were having coffee and Alec suggested taking her a cup, Frank said no, she'd have gone to bed. He said nothing more. Illness happened: it didn't have to be talked about.

Frank stirred his coffee. 'So how's that little sod Bladon? Settling in, is he?'

It was the nearest he'd get to asking Alec why the hell he'd gone to see him. That too, if Alec chose, didn't have to be talked about.

It wasn't.

Alec said, 'Proper little barrack room lawyer. Lectured me on the causes of drug addiction.'

'Don't tell me. Used to be potty training. Now it's bloody unemployment.'

Alec realized that, in his wish to be nice to Frank, to be on Frank's side, to share Frank's simplified view of things, he'd presented Trevor unfairly. In fact the little turd had made no excuses. The lecture had been on the need for proper drug education. *Ah, fuck it* ... Trevor was fireproof these days: Frank wasn't.

He let the unfairness stay. 'And now his mother's dead. Same part of town as Dancer, near enough same time.'

'If you're saying there's a connection, Chief, Merseyside'll never find it. Dancer's with A Division now, Mrs B will stay with F, out on Rose Lane. And never the twain shall meet.'

Alec laughed. 'Bring back the bike.' It was a standing joke within the Force that internal communications were far worse with computers than they'd ever been in the days of messenger boys on bicycles.

Frank finished his coffee. 'So what now?'

'Now?' Alec was cagey. 'We do the washing up.'

'The case, Chief. I know the signs. You're not going to leave it.'

'That was then, Frank. This is now. I've got better things to do.'

'What's that, then?'

'Can't a man move on?'

'Of course he can. Of course he can.'

Frank didn't believe it. He stood up, took his cup to the sink and turned on the tap. When the hot water arrived he put in the plug. 'Did she know him?' He paused, looked over his shoulder at Alec, then squirted detergent. 'Mrs Bladon, I mean. Know Dancer.'

Alec had no opinion. Frank reached for his wife's apron and put it on, pulling in his stomach so that the strings would tie. 'Her son and him were close. They must of met.'

Alec shrugged. Frank said, 'Who'd want the both of them dead? Why?' He paused again, stirring the water in the bowl until suds rose. 'Wasn't there a niece? Maybe she's got ideas. Maybe someone should ask her.'

Alec gave in. Moving on was too hard.

'I'll dry,' he said, getting up to fetch a dishtowel. 'The niece is Evie Fairbairn. Cut off from her cousin years ago. Works in the ice cream factory. I don't reckon I ever saw her address.'

Frank dunked a plate, rinsed it under the tap and passed it across. 'Shouldn't be hard to find. The factory'll tell you.'

'If she's still there.'

'Come on, Chief. They keep records, don't they?'

'Not for me. I'm not police any more.'

'You'll think of something.'

6

Evie Fairbairn still worked in the ice cream factory, and she'd gone in that morning in spite of the news about her aunt. Alec turned up around noon, asked for her, and the gate let him in without comment, directing him to the Finishing Shop where her supervisor pointed her out. She was one of a line of young women in white coats and caps, sitting in front of the ends of oblong stainless steel tubes suspended from the ceiling, out of which flowed endless columns of semi-solid pink ice cream. They guided the columns into cardboard cartons, slid the cartons sideways across the mouths of the tubes when they were full, closed the cartons' lids, put them in metal trays, and picked up fresh cartons. By which time the dangling columns of ice cream were six inches long and ready to be guided in again.

Alec negotiated open vats of yellowish something, went and stood close behind her. Raucous music played, and terrible metallic clashes came from the far end of the workshop. He pitched his voice just loudly enough to reach her.

'I was sorry to hear about your aunt, Miss Fairbairn.'

'*Christ* . . .' She tossed her head. 'All her life, and now this . . . I mean, sometimes God just don't give up. I mean, not once he's got it in for you. Didn't for Auntie Joan, any road.' Her fingers moved automatically, lift, slide, fold, close, as she peered at him sideways. 'Do I know you?'

'We've never met. The name's Alec. I was visiting the prison . . . Justice City. I was visiting your cousin.' It was a form of words – *visit* and *prison* – suggesting, he hoped, that he had some sort of official capacity. Perhaps he was a Prison Visitor. A deception, but preferable to going into the actual reasons for his interest.

She accepted it. 'Him? Our Trev? A grown man like you should have something better to do with his time.'

Alec agreed with her. 'He's very upset.'

'Boo-sodding-hoo.' Lift, slide, fold, close. 'So what'm I supposed to do about it?'

'Could we have a wee word, Miss Fairbairn? Mebbe lunch?'

'It's sodding piecework here. I only take half an hour. Twelve-thirty to one.'

'Twelve-thirty to one, then. In the canteen. My treat.'

'All I ask is, don't expect me to be sorry for our Trev.'

He left her to her lift, slide, fold, close. He himself, was he sorry for their Trev? Sorry? *Sorry?* What sort of word was that? He was dodging the question, knowing more about their Trev, about his situation, in the broadest sense of the word, than she did. Sorry? What bloody stupid sort of word was that?

He went out to his car in the factory car park, dumped his coat and slowly made his way to the canteen. Twelve-thirty was forty minutes off. Sorry? He felt sorrier for her, for her lift, slide, fold, close. Furthermore, she was crippled. A pretty face, wonderful wide brown eyes, but she had a hump on her back, not much of one but a decided hump, and her head was a mite too large on her crooked shoulders.

He found an empty table and sat down at it to wait. Sorry for Evie but sorrier still for Frank and Doris. In that order – Frank first? Yes. The love and inarticulacy between them would work against him. Doris had an important new job now, dying, and the habit of doing things well. She'd always coped with herself, and with him, and she would continue to do so. This left Frank only with service, with present loneliness and worse loneliness to come, and with the need to remake himself. Frank's new job was surviving and he didn't want it. Wouldn't accept it. Wouldn't even admit it.

Last night, over the two remaining cans of beer, after the washing up and the police talk, the Dancer/Bladon murders, Alec had offered him the chance. 'She's lost a bit of weight, your Doris.'

'She's not been well.'

'I can see that.'

'We've a holiday planned. North Wales. That'll set her up.'

'Her sisters live there, don't they?'

'That's right. And her brother.' Looking at the clock. 'A real family get-together.' Looking at his watch too. 'That's right.'

Alec had taken the hint. Thank-yous at the door. 'Wonderful evening, Frank. Convey my compliments to the cook.'

'Come again soon, Chief. She likes to see you.'

On his way home, driving very carefully with unlawful beer in him, Alec had got to wondering if he'd made a mistake. Jumped to wrong conclusions. He wasn't a doctor – whatever she'd had, mebbe Doris was over the worst of it. He hoped to hell she was. But now, thinking back as he waited for Evie Fairbairn, he didn't believe it.

That morning, in his coffee break, he'd called the ice cream factory from the porters' room at the hospital. The very mention of her name, a woman's, over the telephone in the porters' room at the hospital, had brought him ribald whistles and eye-rolling from the other men. Mostly black, they found him odd – he was one of them and yet he wasn't – so they welcomed any evidence of shared interests. It was entirely his fault. The pathetic thing was, he didn't know how to talk to blacks. In his Edinburgh school, the son of a middle-class white mother who'd forgotten herself, for just two Festival weeks, with a handsome black jazz player from Philadelphia, and then in the Edinburgh force, he hadn't had much call to, and he feared not matching up to their expectations. But the fact was he didn't, and apparently, even after the months he'd been at the hospital, they were still amused enough not to mind.

He'd quit the hospital early, to more joshing, so as to be sure of catching Evie before she disappeared on her lunch break. Now, waiting in the canteen's clatter, he thought about what he wanted her to tell him. What he wanted was a link – other than Trevor – between her aunt and Dancer Drew. Two of life's losers, on opposite sides of the law, yet something had brought them within hours of each other to their very similar deaths. Coincidence? A random mugging and a drug deal that went sour? Alec didn't believe a word of it.

The tissue on the beach pointed to a woman at the scene of Dancer's murder. If the woman was Joan, and she'd witnessed the crime, and the killer had gone after her . . . Witnessed the crime? Joan Bladon, down in Otterspool Park, just walking by, at one in the morning? It was possible.

Evie – did your aunt suffer from insomnia? Did she go for walks in the middle of the night? Did she favour the lonely riverside?

It was possible . . . But was it also possible that she could have run fast enough to get back to her kitchen before Dancer's murderer caught up with her?

On the other hand, mebbe she and Dancer had known something they shouldn't have, and had been killed for it. Or had shared the responsibility for some act that had required brutal vengeance. Or had—

'It's the first sign of madness.'

'I'm sorry?'

'Talking to yourself. It's the first sign of madness.'

Released from the white cotton cap, Evie Fairbairn's hair was dramatic: lustrous reddish-brown, long and seductively wavy. Alec's first thought was that its vividness transformed her prettiness into beauty. His second thought was that her body was more crippled than it had seemed in the workshop. Her legs were so short that, standing by the table at which he was seated, she looked him in the eye. Their heads were level. She'd seemed small before, but not small like this. Not crippled small. He supposed it went with the hump, and was angry that such things happened.

He said, 'I was miles away. I hadn't seen the time.'

They went and queued at the counter. His six foot two embarrassed him, but it didn't bother her. She was used to shouting up at people.

'I were close to Trevor once,' she told him. 'We aren't a big family, and Auntie Joan and my mum got on. In and out of each other's houses. Especially after Uncle Bert took off.'

'When was that?'

'Years back. Took off with a tart from the Social Security. Trev was only a kid. Started getting into trouble from that day on. Always the way, isn't it? Then Jack Fisher came on the scene.'

'Made things better, did he?'

'You wouldn't cocoa. Christ knows what Auntie Joan saw in him, but that's women.'

Alec nodded. That was indeed women. He slid his tray behind hers along the counter. Their turn came: minced beef pie, sausages or cod in batter, with peas and reconstituted mash. Products of the conglomerate that made the ice cream – different textures, same mono- and di-glycerides – and all of them less than delicious. Evie had the cod, on account of it was almost Friday, and an individual peach and apricot pie. No ice cream.

'They let you eat all you want on the job,' she said. 'After the first couple of days nobody touches the stuff.'

Alec chose the firm's sausages. He'd been known to eat them at home. Evie had a cup of tea and he joined her.

'Ta,' she said. 'It mayn't be the Ritz, but at least you know where it's been.'

By the time he'd paid she'd found an empty table. They unloaded their trays and stacked them and she immediately started eating. Alec was reminded that he had only half an hour.

Seated, she looked taller. Almost normal. 'Tell me about Jack Fisher,' he said.

'Drove a minicab. You know the sort.' She ate as she talked. 'Auntie Joan met him at the Garter . . . How come you're so interested?'

'Her son was worried about her. It was because of him that I went along, couldn't get in, called the police.'

It was hardly an answer but she didn't seem to notice. Perhaps he had an official aura. 'They think Jack did it? He didn't never. He was a sod, but never vahlint.' She squeezed red sauce from a large plastic tomato. 'Anyway, he's been gone years. Trev saw to that.'

'Trev?'

'Who else? He made it this choice, didn't he? There he was, knocking things off, playing truant, drugging it up, all sorts, and nothing Jack said made a sodding bit of difference. I can hear him now – "You're not my father . . ." How many men'd put up with that?'

Alec started on his food. 'So your aunt had to choose between them.'

'Little bastard. Broke her heart.'

Alec could imagine it. She'd have seen Jack Fisher as her last chance at a proper life. 'How old would she have been?'

'Back then? Younger than my mum. Couple of years back, I dunno, maybe fiftyish . . .' She looked up, stopped chewing. 'You never met her, then?'

He shook his head. 'I told you – I went along because Trevor was worried.'

'Bit late for that. Bit sodding late for that . . . Like to see a piccy?' She put down her knife and fork, rummaged in her bag, found a wallet, passed him a buckled photograph. 'August bank holiday. Took last year, before all this business. Anglesey.'

Alec saw a sturdy middle-aged woman in a round-necked dirndl summer dress, standing awkwardly on a sunless beach. The dress looked odd and old-fashioned and didn't suit her. Her face was plain, worn down, almost slatternly, not helped by frizzed, blown about, dyed blond hair. She was carrying several folded beach chairs. Alec stared at her, trying to think of something to say.

Evie saved him. 'Some people just don't photograph. Auntie Joan never did. She was a good sort, though. Broke my heart, seeing where it got her . . .'

Alec smoothed out the photograph. 'Can I keep this?'

'Whatever for?' But she was pleased, touched that he should want to. 'Go on. Why not? I got others back home, or my mum has . . .'

She put away her bag and returned to her lunch. 'I tried to talk to Trev, mind. Over and over. Piss off, he'd say. Stoned out of his mind. *Nasty* . . . Piss off he'd say, so one day I pissed. Shouldn't of, for Auntie's sake, but what can you do? Never saw him from that day to this. What happens to kids these days makes me sick.'

She was hardly more than a kid herself. No mention of a father, so mebbe a broken home like Trev's, yet she'd kept herself together. Alec struggled with his mash and reached for the tomato sauce to mask it. 'How did he get started? On the drugs, I mean.'

'How does anyone get started? We're talking Toxteth, mister. The kids were queueing up.'

He couldn't resist it. 'You weren't.'

'Yes. Well.' She hunched her shoulders. 'I were different, weren't I?'

He felt himself blush. At least she wouldn't see it. She was referring to her humpy back. It had kept her apart. Narrowed her options.

'I wanted to, mister.' She laughed, remembering. 'More than anything in the sodding world. But there were gangs and you had to be in one ... And in case you're asking aren't I glad now, the answer's no. I'd rather be human-sized and straight and given the choice, any day.' She laughed again and shovelled in peas. 'Anyone would.'

He wanted to tell her, human-sized or not, that she was one of the straightest people he knew, but it wouldn't have done. She didn't need it. He returned to why he was there. 'So you never got to know the dealers?'

'I got to know Dancer.' Alec choked on his food. 'We all knew Dancer. Everybody's chum. He wouldn't sell me shit, though. He said—' She broke off. 'Look, are you with the police or what?'

He put down his knife and fork. 'I'm no with the police. I promise. I'm no *with* anybody ... It's just that your mentioning Dancer surprised me. He was killed the same night as your aunt.'

'Dancer? Dancer Drew? Killed? I'd of said he was eternal. Whatever the word is. Immortal.'

'Not any more. Someone shot him. The way they shot your aunt.' He paused. 'Did she know him?'

'Auntie Joan?' Evie hesitated, thinking back as she swapped her empty dinner plate for the pie. 'She must of. Time was when him and Trev were real pals. Them being bum boys and that.'

She looked up from her plate, testing him. Oddly, Alec had never considered that Trevor might be gay. He'd assumed the HIV came from dirty gear. Now, with Evie watching him, he made no comment.

Satisfied, she went on: 'Real pals ... But that was before Trev took to the needle heavy. Dancer moved off then, the sod. Didn't want to know. Kept him supplied, mind, but moved off. Found a new bloke.'

'So he'd visited your cousin's home?'

'Plenty of times. Never actually saw him with Auntie Joan but they must of met. She had enough to say about him, any road. Chewed my ear off. I always told her, folks like our Trev go to hell in their own sodding way, don't need no help from outsiders, but she didn't listen. I reckon she needed someone to blame. Poor soul . . .' She tailed off sadly, spooned up pie filling, stared at it. Then she brightened. 'Maybe it was her done in the little sod.'

'Your aunt? With a gun?'

Evie laughed. 'Wouldn't put it sodding past her. I tell you who you are.'

Alec jumped. 'Me?' The remark had run on directly, no change of tone.

'Yeah. You're the bloke with the girlfriend our Trev done for.'

He tilted his head, admitting it. 'How did you know?'

'Two and two together. Blacks like you, nice suit, real quality, don't grow on trees. And I've been thinking back. Didn't see you at the trial, but the word was you was black. From up north. A black copper.'

'I'm no a copper any more. And I didn't go to the trial.'

'Auntie Joan did. Every sodding minute of every sodding day.'

She was eyeing him sharply. The suggestion seemed to be that he'd been wrong not to go to the trial, that he hadn't cared enough. He'd cared too much, of course, but it would have been ingenuous to correct her. He let the accusation go. 'I'm sorry I didn't tell you who I was, Evie. It wasn't honest. The thing is, I was afraid you'd—'

'Obvious, isn't it? I'd of told you to sod off.'

He pushed back his chair. 'Shall I sod off now?'

She wiped one corner of her mouth with a paper napkin.

Her eyes were on him still, but less judgementally. 'Not on my account. I'm the last of the family up here. Could be I owe you.'

'No,' he said. 'No, you don't owe me.'

Astonishingly, she leaned forward and put a hand on his, where it rested on the table. 'Trev was a cross country runner once. Toxteth Grammar. And he won the high jump. Did he tell you that?'

Alec shook his head. A mitigating circumstance? The boy *had* told him – but at a time, nine months ago, the day before he'd killed May, that Alec didn't want to discuss, even in his head. 'I'm glad you were there,' he said, 'when your aunt . . . During the trial, I mean, when she needed someone.'

She gave his hand a pat and returned to her peach and apricot pie. 'Mum came up too. From London. Took time off – she works for a vet in Balham, on reception. She loves animals . . . Not that we could do much. I mean, what's there to say? And then the folks on the estate started in.'

Alec sighed. 'It happens.'

'Neighbours. Folks you'd of said was your friends. Sodding bastards. If I told you the half of it you wouldn't believe me.'

He would. He'd seen the communal outrage, the viciousness, the hatred . . . housewives in their slippers, grannies, young dads, kids, united for once in their miserable lives. 'A paper helped, didn't it?'

'Helped? You could say that. Ten days in a Manchester hotel while some woman reporter got down her story – Trev growing up, Trev playing truant,Trev's dad leaving, Trev going on drugs, all that . . . Don't know why she sodding bothered, the lies she made up what they went and printed. Ten days in some hotel, a lump sum, nine thousand pounds, and she was dumped back where she started. Then the papers come out, making her some sort of angel, knocking the estate – Drug Hell they called it – and she was worse off than ever. We'd warned her but she didn't listen. The reporter wound her round her little finger. They're good at that. She was a woman, too.'

Alec pushed his plate away, he hadn't been hungry, and drank his tea. It was nearly cold. 'The council moved her?'

'Middle of the night. Just the basics, in a little council van. That was my mum – camped on their doorstep till they give in. Generous I don't think. You've been out to Riverview, you've seen what she got.'

'It's not much.'

'Sodding insult. Nobody wants them ground floor places. That's why she's dead, if you ask me. Empty for months on end – nobody wants them. They put up grilles once, but I ask you. They'd of done better with sodding Lego. It's an invitation to the sodding robbers.'

He saw a chance to lead her on, and took it guiltily. 'Your aunt didn't have much worth robbing, did she?'

'You've been there. What you see is what you get. A rented TV and a few bob in her purse. That's Riverview all over. Black kids – I'm sorry but it's true – sodding black kids'll turn you over for a couple of postage stamps.'

Most of the kids he'd seen had been white, but he didn't argue. She'd reminded him of what one of them had said about a Mrs Brown. 'Used a different name, did she?'

'My mum again. Auntie Joan wasn't hardly thinking. No point in advertising yourself, Mum said. Chose one with the same initial. Brown. That's B for Brown and B for Bladon.'

She looked up at the canteen clock and gulped her tea. 'Not that the Riverview lot would give a monkey's. Most of them's men is away on their hols. At her Majesty's pleasure, if you take my meaning. How come you're not a copper any more?'

'I reckon me and Her Majesty didn't see eye to eye.'

'You what? Once a copper, always a copper.'

'No.'

She sized him up and didn't press it. 'Not that I've anything against coppers. Not the straight ones . . . So what's you and me here for then?'

'I . . .' He had to be honest. 'I don't know. Your cousin really did ask me to check up on his mother. I feel . . . mebbe I feel responsible.'

'Nah. You hate him. You must do. I do. Look what he did.'

Truth or dare. How fierce she was. Uncompromising. And he'd bought her lunch. 'Hate, Evie? It's a big word.' He didn't like its rawness. He feared it. 'The point is, Evie, I know how the police tend to work these days. It being Riverview Heights, and him in LTI, they mebbe won't try too hard.'

She waited for him to go on, started to say something, then changed her mind. 'So what about Dancer? Feel responsible for him too, do you?'

'He's a puzzle. I don't like coincidences. If your aunt knew him, then there could be a connection.'

She patted his hand again. 'Once a copper, always a copper.' So young, and tiny, and humped, and she was mothering him. 'Time I went. Ta for the lunch.' She stood up. 'I shouldn't sodding say this, but Auntie Joan didn't have much. I reckon she's well out of it. Short and sharp. She'd been very down, too, the last few weeks. Not so much *down* – gone away, more like. I reckon she's well out of it.'

She went away between the ugly plastic-topped tables. At the door she turned and waved, her hand just visible above all the seated customers. She astonished him. Truth or dare, and he knew he'd cheated.

Alec's next call that afternoon was off Wango Lane, up by the racecourse. He wasn't sure what he'd expected of Dancer Drew's pad, but the street turned out to prove how successfully a man could compartmentalize his life. Its gentrified Edwardian terraced houses were socially, as well as geographically, a long way from the Funrama Videodrome and the estates where Dancer did most of his business. Skips outside several of the houses were loaded with last year's kitchen cabinets, junked now for new, and the neat ground floor bay windows were yuppie enough to scorn net curtains. These people felt no shame at being seen in their spotlit white and leather rooms, listening to their CDs.

Alec drove down the street looking for a parking space, and found none. Dancer's car was still in the police pound but dead men's shoes were worth their weight in parking tickets. Eventually Alec found a space two streets away and walked back, checking the scribbled address Frank had given him. The sun was shining. A light aeroplane buzzed overhead, making for the Aintree landing strip. Pop music and laughter and electric drill sounds came out at him from the houses with skips in front of them. He didn't hurry. This visit was on spec – he'd thought it more likely that he'd find Dancer's friend at home if he didn't phone ahead for an appointment.

Dancer's place turned out to be a ground floor flat, dustbins behind a neat privet hedge in the tiny front garden. Dancer's front window, being Dancer's and snobbish with it, was uniquely modest, net curtained top to bottom. Alec rang the bell, waited, then rang again. Stepping back quickly out on to the path, he caught a movement behind the curtain at the side of the bay and waved cheerfully. Curiosity had to be denied, if one seriously wanted to be not at home

Another wait. The glass in the door had fine wire mesh embedded in it. A red burglar alarm box gleamed on the wall beside the window. The door opened four inches, on a thick chain, showing one wary eye, probably male, and a flash of some sort of red garment. 'Yes?'

Alec stood very still and smiled. 'Jackie Patterson?'

'Yes?'

'I've been talking to Stan, Jackie.'

The eye narrowed. 'Yes?'

'Stan Falco, Jackie.' His ace. Right up front, the only ace he had.

'I didn't think it was Stan Laurel.'

'I'd like a word.'

'He's already had one.'

'That was someone else, Jackie.' Alec still smiled, still didn't move. He wasn't surprised that Falco had already sent someone. It was what he'd have expected. 'That was someone else – this is me.'

'It's not convenient. This is a house of bereavement.'

'Stan knows that, Jackie. He hoped you'd stretch a point.'

'What for?'

'Because.'

The eye looked past him, at the silent houses opposite, then shortened focus again. 'Don't have much choice.'

'That's very good of you.'

The door closed, reopened without the chain, revealing a haggard young man in sandals and a red cotton kimono printed with dragons. 'You'd better come in.'

'Thank you, Jackie. That's very good of you.'

Incense, matching the kimono, hung heavily in the small entrance hall. Jackie led him through into the front room, went to the filled-in fireplace. A long narrow picture of blue-white horses hung above it. They were galloping, their manes and tails flying, along crimson sands. Jackie turned. He didn't suggest that Alec sat down.

'This is a house of bereavement,' he said again.

'I know, Jackie. It's a terrible thing.'

'So what does Stan want?'

Alec regretted the deception. Not much though, given present company. And Stan's name had got him in, which was probably more than could have been said, back in his old life, for the Chief Constable's. As for what he wanted, Alec wasn't sure. He'd just have to poke around and see – in Frank Grove's favourite phrase – what eventuated.

He sat down on the curved brocade sofa facing the outsize

TV. 'A drop of whisky would be very nice, Jackie. If it's no too much trouble.'

Jackie hesitated, then went to the door. He paused there. 'Men like you make me sick.'

They made Alec sick also, but he had Stan to live up to. He smiled up at Jackie. 'No ice. Water in a jug. If it's not too much trouble.'

Jackie went away. Alec took the small voice-activated recorder out of his breast pocket and put it on the coffee table that stood in the exact centre of the sofa's curve. The room was precisely ordered and immaculate. Huge black loudspeakers were mounted high in the corners of the wall behind the TV set, a stacked sound system positioned beneath one of them, a rubber plant with polished leaves beneath the other. Centrally above the TV set CDs and videos were arranged in tidy rows on glass and chrome shelves. Two remote control units and a mobile telephone rested side by side on the coffee table, between a copy of the *TV Times* at one end and the *Reader's Digest Book of English Houses* at the other. Alec's recorder spoiled the symmetry. Behind him he was surprised to see the window bay filled with an electronic keyboard, its teak veneer stand supporting a white plaster bust of Schubert, and in front of it a stool with a cushion that looked used. Dancer, he felt sure, had not been the musician – any more than Dancer had done all the arranging and sweeping and dusting. The incense fumes were weaker in here, overlaid with lavender aerosol furniture polish.

Jackie returned with a red papier mâché tray, bearing whisky, a tumbler with yellow parasols painted on it, and a matching jug of water. He put it down on the *TV Times* and immediately saw Alec's recorder.

'I suppose you must?'

'I suppose I must.'

'You really work at it, don't you?'

'At least I'm being aboveboard, laddie. I bet Stan's last guy kept his recorder hidden.'

'He was another sod, though.'

'It comes with the job, laddie.' Alec leaned forward, poured himself whisky, added water, tasted it, raised the glass in an ironic toast. With his provenance, he thought, it would be difficult, if not impossible, to overdo things. 'So what've you got to tell me?'

'Nothing I haven't already said.'

'So say it again.'

Jackie sat down in the corner of the sofa furthest from Alec, wrapping his kimono carefully across his knees. 'I've no sodding idea who killed my Frederick. Could've been anyone . . .' He broke off, as if overcome by emotion.

Frederick? Alec was intrigued. Dancer'd never looked like a Frederick. He'd no idea what Fredericks looked like, but Dancer'd looked like who he was – Dancer. Most people did, of course: it was a result of the human need to see order when there was really only random happenstance.

Jackie cleared his throat. 'There was this black guy, mind, hanging around – no offence meant, that's what he was, black – but you need a motive, don't you?'

'A black guy, Jackie? What sort of black guy?'

'Flash. Bags of street cred. Strictly business, I thought . . . which is why I said he didn't have a motive.'

'Why mention him, then? There must have been other guys . . . hanging around.'

'Not really. Not in the same way. He was always trying to be helpful. I think he thought he was getting somewhere.'

'You mean friend Dancer might have been willing to deal him in?'

'How should I know? I'm saying what he thought, that's all. Frederick never talked shop to me. He always said, what I didn't know—' Jackie struggled again '—couldn't hurt me.'

At least, Alec thought, from Stan Falco's point of view this story of the black guy would have slotted in well with the bouncer's call from the Videodrome, explaining why Stan had been in such a hurry to pick him up.

'But you *did* know that the man dealt in drugs, didn't you?'

'Don't insult me, please.' Jackie lifted his head. 'He wasn't a slave to conventional morality. I respected him for it.'

Alec sat back, momentarily silenced, wondering if such bird-brained loyalty might be genuine. He checked himself, the hetero window through which he saw things – in a young woman it wouldn't be surprising, just part of being in love. Equally bird-brained, though.

'Did our young friend's unconventional morality let him carry a gun?'

'A gun? Never.'

'*Never?*'

'That's what I said. It wasn't morality, though, just common sense. We often talked about it – you see, frankly he worried me. There are nasty people out there and I wanted him defended. He said having a gun in your pocket was the best way to get shot. Not that he couldn't handle one – he was a crack shot once. But a man knows you've got a gun in your pocket and it ups the ante. He really believed it. And he said he *was* defended. Worked for Mr Falco, didn't he? Whatever people may say about Mr Falco, they know he looks after his own. I mean, that's why you're here, isn't it?'

Alec couldn't argue with that. He wouldn't argue with the theory either. It mightn't have worked for Dancer on Monday night but it had kept him alive longer than many in his business. Which in itself was interesting – whoever shot him had been either too new to Merseyside to know how things worked or too angry to care.

Of course, Stan Falco too had strong views about handguns. Not because he objected to their use but because there was a time and a place for everything. His time. His place. He agreed with Dancer: war on the streets, he said, did nobody any good. The two insurance salesmen he'd sent for Alec were typical Falco professionals, experienced and disciplined. They'd have police licences for their weapons – they were employed by Mr Stanley Falco who, as a legitimate Merseyside club owner, needed protection.

Dancer, on the other hand, was neither experienced nor disciplined. That didn't mean, knowing him, that he mightn't have had a go, but any gun he'd carried would have been strictly a private enterprise. 'You're telling me friend Dancer didn't even *own* a gun?'

'Why should he? He'd grown up, he said. Didn't have anything to prove . . .'

Jackie looked away suddenly, biting his lower lip. Alec could imagine the memory his words had raised, the sexual allusion, the moment between the two men that had been so light and was now so heavy.

Jackie cleared his throat. 'I never saw him with a gun, that's all. He didn't hold with them. He was a good shot, like I said, a crack shot, but he'd put it behind him. He didn't have the need.'

A crack shot . . . Alec could imagine that too. He could just hear him. Everything Dancer did he was best at, the man who had never actually been best at a single bloody thing. One of life's losers. But not to be pitied, he spread it around too much. He took too many others with him.

Alec sighed, and changed the subject. 'This black guy, lad. Does he have a name?'

'Carter. That's all he ever gave. Could be his first or his last, I've no idea. You know the way these blacks . . .' he checked himself but saw he was committed '. . . these blacks have names that could be either.'

Alec shrugged. It was a fair comment. 'But Dancer and this Carter got on . . . they were friends?'

'No. Not at all.' It was too fierce a denial. 'I mean, I've no idea. All I ever heard was business talk, and not much of that.

I mean, he never came visiting. He was just another punter with ambitions. Frederick laughed at him.'

'Laughed at him?' In some circles a more than passable motive.

'About him. To me. Privately. He laughed about him. About how hard he was trying.'

The kimono had fallen open, revealing nakedness save for white briefs. Jackie was better-built than his slightly wafting manner had led Alec to expect. His belly and thighs were well-muscled, surprisingly free from flab.

Alec looked away. 'And Carter was here on the day of the murder?'

'Did I say that?'

'Did you?'

Jackie flapped his hands, temporizing as he tried to remember what he'd told Alec's predecessor. 'The thing is, he hung around . . . I mean, I can't be certain.'

Alec emptied his glass. 'Did the police have any views on this Mr Carter?'

'Sod all. Fat lot they care.' He leapt angrily to his feet, furling his kimono together round his waist, and strode away to the window. 'Haven't been near me. Not a peep. Not even to tell me what happened. Saved that for Frederick's brother in Leeds, and they haven't been talking for years . . . Not a peep, I tell you. I thought of complaining but it's no sodding use.'

He stood quietly for a moment, his back turned to Alec. The day had clouded over and a fine drizzle was falling on the privet hedge outside the window. Alec was shocked that Inspector Pritchard hadn't sent anybody round. Keeping things simple was all very well, but this was neglect beyond the call of duty.

Jackie reached down and moved the bust of Schubert an inch or so to the left. 'The authorities look after their own, of course. Frederick was always an outsider. Why should they bother? Why should they bother to find his murderer?' He swung round. 'And you can tell Mr Falco from me, he won't either. He's all mouth. He may say he will, but he's all mouth . . . Ten years my Frederick gave him, and—'

His eyes were wild, his hands moving randomly. 'And d'you know what? They won't let me have the body. I know the things they have to do to it, dreadful things, but, Christ, it's days now. Haven't they done enough? Why won't they let me? I've begged them. Begged them . . . It's not a lot to ask. They won't even tell me when. How can I arrange a decent funeral if the sodding police won't let me have the body?'

His voice had thinned to a whisper. His question expected no answer, was addressed to a cruel universe, and he stood now, stiffly erect, biting on a clenched fist as his tears flowed nakedly. Alec found such unmistakable distress shaming. This wasn't performance, this was misery. He had misjudged Jackie Patterson from the start, seeing the signs but not imagining for an instant that a drug dealer's gay partner, with wafts of incense, and a crimson kimono, and his prissy *This is a house of bereavement*, could possibly be genuinely bereaved.

Alec turned and knelt awkwardly on the sofa, resting his arms on its back. 'You shouldn't be staying on here like this. Not alone. Have you nowhere you could go? Your parents?'

Jackie stared at him blankly, then focused and gave a bitter, ugly little laugh, removing his fist from his mouth and thrusting it deep into his pocket. 'My father's a Neanderthal. Gays are shit to him. It's the word he uses. Gays are shit . . .'

He tried to go on, failed, and hurried out of the room, his sandals soundless on the fitted oyster-coloured carpet. A moment later a door closed somewhere. Alec frowned. *Stupid, stupid* . . . He shook his head, looked at his watch, wondered what to do next. He'd harried witnesses before, and felt bad about it, but that had been in the line of duty. Now he had no excuse. According to Evie, once a copper, always a copper . . . a familiar enough saying, but now with pejorative overtones.

Once a copper, always a nosy, insensitive, foot-in-the-door bastard.

He got up. He was about to pocket the recorder and let himself out into the drizzle when Jackie reappeared.

'Sorry about that.' Bright as a button. 'I needed a hanky. You were saying?'

Alec decided an apology would only reopen doors Jackie had closed. Besides, he was a Stan Falco man, and Stan Falco men never apologized. They never sat on sofas offering well-meant advice about not living alone either, but luckily Jackie seemed not to have noticed.

'Tell us your end of what happened on Monday night.'

'Christ. You never give up, do you?'

Alec waited politely, steeling himself.

Jackie flashed a sudden bright smile and sauntered away, one finger trying the top of the TV set for dust. 'I . . . shouldn't have said that about Stan, you know. Of course I shouldn't. Stan's been good to Frederick and me. Very good. I shouldn't be ungrateful.'

Alec saw it was fear of Stan Falco that had brought Jackie back into the room. Perversely, it lessened his sympathy. There were emotions he approved, and others he didn't. Grief was worthy, fear was less so. He offered Jackie no reassurance, therefore, that the insulting things he'd said about Stan would go no further.

'You were telling me about Monday night.'

Jackie perched on an arm of the sofa. He paused, screwing himself up. 'Well, the car wouldn't start, of course. Sodding thing's been past it for months, but Frederick always said—'

'Go back to the beginning.' Alec sat down too, but squarely. 'When was this? Where were you going?'

'I wasn't going anywhere. Middle of the bloody night – I was ready for bed but Frederick had this business engagement. Plenty of battery but not so much as a fart, so he got me out in the street, giving him a push.'

'When was this? What time?'

'Twelve-thirty when we started. God knows when, by the end. Charming neighbours we have. There we were, double hernias all round, and up the windows went. How dare you this and how dare you that . . . Po-faced sods.'

'You were quarrelling and it disturbed them.'

'Quarrelling? Why should we be quarrelling?'

'Did wee Dancer often go out alone after midnight and not tell you where?'

'Who says he didn't tell me where?'

'I do.'

Jackie smoothed a crimson lapel. 'Haven't I already said? He didn't want me worried. He was very thoughtful.'

'And what you didn't know couldn't hurt you.'

'That's right. That's exactly right . . . And yes, of course his work often took him out at odd hours.'

'And where was Carter in all this?'

'Nowhere. That would've been earlier. Six or seven. If at all.'

'And as far as you know they didn't make an arrangement to meet later.'

'I know what you're saying. The trouble with your fucking sort is you think all us gays are like you. Always playing around. Promiscuous. Frederick wasn't like that. He wasn't fucking like that.'

Bingo. 'So you tell me. Business of some kind? After midnight?'

'Why not? Do you work nine to five, mister?'

'Fair enough. So you pushed the car for a bit, and finally it started, and off he went, and you weren't quarrelling.'

'That's right. That's what I said. That's exactly right.'

'So what did you do then?'

'Went to bed. What do you sodding think?'

'And you weren't worried.'

'Why should I be? I leaned in at the passenger's window.

The car's started, see, and it's going nicely, settled down nicely, so I lean in at the passenger's window. He says he won't be long and I tell him to be careful and he says he will. Then the door comes sort of open, it's been dicky for months, and I have to heave it shut, and he leans across and locks it and winds up the window, and then he drives away.'

Alec could see it all. Jackie fussing, Dancer already late and getting later, impatiently revving the engine to keep it going, struggling with the door catch, no, I won't be long and yes, I will be careful, finally winding up the window and getting away to the relief of all the neighbours. Very vivid. Jackie left standing in the road, and all this at one in the morning.

'So when were you worried?'

'Not till next morning. I took one of my tablets and slept like a log.'

Alec could see that too. The quarrel that hadn't happened, and the sleeping pill to calm nerves that didn't need calming.

'What did you do then? When you discovered that Dancer hadn't come home. What did you do then?'

'What could I do? Nothing. I rang around. And all this time the police were finding brother Malcolm in Leeds. He called me finally, but that was the middle of the afternoon. What was I supposed to do? All that time, what was I supposed to do?'

'You rang around. Who did you ring?'

'People. Business colleagues. Friends . . . What the hell does it matter who I rang?'

Alec honestly didn't know. It was the sort of question he'd have asked when he had the clout to demand names, and the back-up to check them. It was the sort of question that helped to establish a witness's general reliability. It was the sort of question that sometimes, like now, was a waste of everybody's time. General reliability was something Jackie Patterson didn't have. Heart, lots of that, but general reliability, nothing you could shake a stick at.

Alec allowed a pause. 'So who do you think is the murderer?'

'I don't. Frederick went to meet someone. It's as simple as that. I don't know who, and you don't know who, and Mr Falco doesn't know who, and the police neither know nor fucking care.'

'And what about why?'

'That's your area. It certainly wasn't sex. I've already told you. I told Mr Falco's other man, too – we were long-term, Frederick and me. It was his life that did it. His business. He knew he'd had a good run. He was going to quit. He promised . . . I know about jewellery, you see, objets d'art. I've worked in the trade. We were going to open a little shop. A boutique. Move away from this rotten city. Some place with a bit of style. Harrogate, I thought . . .'

Poor Jackie. *Some place with a bit of style* . . . His Frederick must have had plenty salted away. He didn't have a habit to service, which was what usually kept men like him poor. He'd been trading for ten or eleven years now, with mebbe a couple of token fines for possession. And not only drugs – the word was he fenced a bit on the side, sold a bit of this and that. All sorts. And he never spent out. This place wasn't much, nor was his car by the sound of it. He'd have had a nice litle nest egg by now, plenty for a little boutique in Harrogate. But there'd always been just that one more deal, that big final coup, the master stroke that would put them both on easy street. And now he was dead. Poor Jackie.

Alec just hoped that Dancer'd left a proper will and that the money was where it could be acknowledged and got at. Or else was in tenners under the bed.

He took out his wallet and offered Evie's photograph of her Auntie Joan. It was what, if anything, he'd come here for, which was why he'd left it till last. 'Ever seen that woman?'

'Never.'

'Look at it properly.' Jackie was still distant, grieving for

Frederick, grieving for Harrogate. 'It's an ordinary face. Think about it.'

Jackie leaned sideways and peered. 'It's a bloody awful face . . . Doesn't mean a thing.'

'You're positive?'

'Who is it?'

'I asked if you were positive.'

'I'm positive.'

Alec took the photo back. Witnesses weren't often willing to be positive – but why should he lie? So much for this end of the Joan Bladon connection. Where now? He had waited to see what eventuated and nothing much had. He got to his feet.

Remembering who he was, he stood very close and smiled. 'That's it, then. For the moment . . . If you think of anything, laddie, give Stan a bell, will you? If it's no too much trouble.'

He leaned past Jackie, pocketed his recorder, and walked out into the hall. Jackie joined him by the front door, put a hand on his arm.

'Tell Stan . . . if he needs someone over at the Videodrome, just temporary, tell Stan I don't mind, will you?'

Alec frowned. Poor Jackie? For Christ's sake, now the little shit was looking for a bright future in the drugs trade. 'I thought you didn't know about Dancer's business.'

'I can learn, can't I?'

So dumb. So fucking dumb . . . Alec couldn't help it – Jackie was so fucking dumb he actually felt sorrow for him. 'You had a partner, laddie. He's dead now. Learn from that.'

And thus, portentously, turning up his jacket collar, he went out into the drizzle.

7

When Alec reached his car the telephone was ringing. Unusually, he got the door open in time. He crouched, half in and half out of the car, his arse getting drizzled on while the Allerton nick made an appointment for Mr Alexander Duncan to present himself at nine the following morning, Friday, with the purpose of making a statement concerning his involvement in the events leading up to the discovery of the Bladon killing. Alec admired the desk clerk's copious flow. He asked if he could move the appointment on to the afternoon – Friday being another of his mornings at the hospital – and after a moment's muttered consultation Allerton said yes, that would be quite convenient. Would two o'clock suit?

Alec told the man two o'clock was fine. He rang off, eased himself sideways into the car, sat down damply, and closed the door. Something about all the courtesy didn't ring true. Back at Riverview he'd given Constable Baynes his home number yet here Allerton was, calling him in the car. Not beyond their research facilities, of course, when the number given by the witness failed to answer, but a job that in his experience got shoved to the back of the desk. He wasn't exactly material . . . So why the extra effort? And then the flexibility, when they could quite well have insisted? For old time's sake, because they'd worked out who he was? It didn't seem likely.

No. Well, time would tell. Tomorrow afternoon, to be exact. Sufficient unto the day was the evil thereof . . . He had a sudden vivid picture of his mother, thin hands clasped at her thin waist. She had words of ancient wisdom to decorate every occasion. They made her life manageable, gave her the company of others who had trodden very similar paths before her. There wasn't much of a family left, a cousin or three or four but all of them away down south or gone to Canada, and otherwise only himself. Not that she moped. She'd suggested he return to Edinburgh a couple of months back but she hadn't pressed it. It wasn't healthy for a man, going home to mother. He had his own way to make in the world. He had to work out his own salvation. He had indeed . . . He stared out at the drizzle and wondered if she worried. He should go and see her. At least give her a call. Go and see her – Edinburgh wasn't the end of the world.

His trousers were damp and itchy against the backs of his thighs. Brought back to the present, Alec shifted uncomfortably on the Rover's leather seat. Trevor. Trevor's mum. Evie. Jackie Patterson. Events were gathering momentum and he needed to consolidate. Consolidate what, for heaven's sake? The afternoon's two interviews were hardly mines of useful information. Nuances, yes, particularly from Jackie; hard facts, no. According to Evie, Joan Bladon had been well-acquainted with Dancer, and according to Jackie, she'd never been to his home. That was it. Oh, and Dancer's business engagement on Monday night must have been important: if Jackie was to be believed, Dancer'd insisted on going to it in the face of quite a major domestic.

If Jackie was to be believed . . . Alec sighed. An evening house-to-house when the neighbours had got in from work would settle it one way or another, and establish a time frame too, but these days he didn't have a team of eager constables. He didn't have a free evening either. At least Jackie's version of Dancer's departure fitted in with the nuances. His insecurity. His possessiveness. They presented a coherent picture. And the final vivid moment could hardly have been invented.

Alec glanced at his watch. He was missing Frank badly. He needed a sounding board, but at this time in the afternoon Frank would still be at work, waiting on two hundred-odd resentful remand men, trying to keep them happy (*happy?*) while the mills of justice (*justice?*) ground. Phone calls to the main Bridewell were out. Alec stared at his carphone. He realized he was itchy to be pressing buttons, itchy for the comforting feel of plastic pressed against his ear, the reassurance it brought that he was in touch, that he existed, so he got out his dog-eared old notebook, looked up Stan Falco's number, and rang him instead.

Falco's switchboard swung into action. Surprisingly, he could be found and, for Mr Duncan, was available. Alec had no compunction about calling him. This case was Falco territory.

Falco came on the line. From the background racket he was on a building site somewhere. 'Alexander? Great to hear from you. Have you reconsidered my offer?'

'The job? Thanks but no thanks. I'm no that desperate.'

'You may be. You may be. It's a hard old world . . . So how can I oblige?'

'You can tell me about a man named Carter. He's black, I gather, and he—'

'I'm impressed, Alexander. You don't waste time. You've been talking to that little shit Jackie. But that leaves me with a question. Do you know what I say, Alexander? I say, what's in it for you? You'd retired, I thought. Looking for fresh pastures ... So what is it about Dancer Drew's abrupt departure that's stirred up the Old Bill in you?'

'It's the fields that are fresh, Falco. The pastures are new. It's mebbe a tautology – fresh fields and pastures new – but it's what the man wrote.'

'I stand corrected. So you aren't going to enlighten me.'

Alec hesitated. To explain about the Joan Bladon connection risked exposing Evie to Stan Falco's heavies. Which was a garbage excuse – the only real risk was of exposing the Trevor Bladon connection. The only real risk was of exposing himself. 'If you don't want to tell me about Carter,' he said, 'then fucking don't. I reckon I'll survive.'

'I do love it, Alexander, when people beg. It makes me feel so *needed—*' His voice changed. He'd turned away from the telephone. 'For fuck's sake, Blakey, the spec says sixty-thirty. The concrete mix these oafs are using'll wash away if the borough surveyor so much as fucking spits at it. Yeah . . . Yeah, Blakey. Do that thing . . .' Falco returned. 'Alexander? Look, I got to go. And take my advice, friend – stay out of property development. It's brought me more grue than all my other interests put together . . . Oh, and by the way, Alexander – don't worry yourself about Carter. He left town.'

'Left town?'

'That's what I said. Left town. Ciao.'

He rang off. Alec stared at his receiver, wondering what Falco was telling him. He remembered the man's parting words the last time they met: *Them as killed young Dancer, they're already dead.* Alec had taken this as a promise, boastful, typical Falco, but – linked in now with Carter's having 'left town' – it might well have been a simple statement of fact. There were many ways of leaving town, not all of them survivable.

Alec replaced the receiver on its rest. If Carter was at the bottom of the Mersey, tied to a couple of hundredweight of scrap iron courtesy of Stan Falco, where did that leave his inquiry? Mebbe if he'd been more open with Falco, told him about Joan Bladon, then Falco could have set his mind at rest. If Carter had 'left town' after shooting Dancer and then Trev's mum, for whatever reason, then Falco would know all about it. Alec reached for the receiver, intending to call Falco back.

On the other hand . . . Alec changed his mind. On the other hand, if all Carter had done wrong was to make a play for a tiny slice of Stan Falco's business, then 'left town' might mean exactly what it said. Falco was a pro: he kept murder for the guys that mattered. A sly little operator like Carter would simply get his marching orders, delivered in such a manner that he would obey them.

Alec decided to wait until he could ring Frank Grove. Frank would have been in touch with his friends in both A Division and the Allerton nick. He might well have new information.

He did. Alec drove back to Sefton Park, stopped off at the supermarket on the Aigburth Road, bought lamb chops and frozen tagliatelle and boil-in-the-bag kippers and other lonely bachelor fare, peeled potatoes back at the flat, and put them on to boil. By then it was after six, so he rang Frank on the kitchen phone.

Doris answered. Frank had his feet up in the front room, reading the paper, waiting for his tea. She'd fetch him. Alec thought how proud her Betws-y-coed mam would have been of her.

'Chief? I thought you'd call. Any luck at your end?'

'Not much. The two victims knew each other. Oh, and our Trev's an even greater sod than I thought he was . . . How about you?'

'Phil's had a look at A Division's inventory of Drew's effects. He says they found a hundred and fifty pounds in his duffel coat pocket. Two bundles – the hundred still in a blue bank wrapper.'

'Traceable?'

'Not a chance. Old notes, standard wrapper . . . The coat has an extra inside pocket, what you might call unofficial. Preliminary examination shows traces of white powder, almost certainly cocaine.'

'Recent?'

'Impossible to tell. Probably within the last couple of weeks. Outside right-hand pocket has traces too, this time of gun-oil.'

'There's an odd one. Quite wrong.' The potatoes boiled over. He reached out and turned the gas down. 'Dancer with a gun? Friend Jackie swore he didn't have one.'

'Could've come from an oily rag, Chief.'

'Be your age, Frank. Rags with gun-oil on them mean guns. That's how they get gun-oily . . . So Dancer'd taken to carrying a shooter his partner didn't know about. I wonder why.'

'It's tough out there, Chief.'

'It always was.' Alec wondered if Stan Falco hadn't known about Dancer's shooter either. 'Pity he didn't have it with him Monday night,' he said.

'Means he wasn't expecting trouble. Just a business transaction – hand over the goods, take the money.'

'Interesting that whoever shot him didn't take the money back . . . I'm out of touch, Frank – how much would a hundred and fifty buy these days?'

'I asked Phil that. Not much. Straight heroin, a couple of days'. Designers, less than that. More coke or pot, of course, but nothing to get excited about. And no profit margin worth trekking all the way down to Otterspool in the middle of the night for.'

'So if there *was* a drugs deal then they *did* take their money back. In which case the one fifty's something else, Dancer's cash float, and they just didn't find it. Mebbe they were interrupted.'

'By the woman who left the tissue on the beach?'

'So it *was* a woman?'

'Woman's make-up, at any rate. Look, Chief, what if we've got this wrong? If the money's got nothing to do with it, what if it wasn't drugs at all? What if it's a crime of passion? Love, jealousy, sex . . . whatever. Drew'd never take his gun if all he was doing was going off to meet a woman.'

'He was gay, Frank.'

'I know. But he might've been bi. Or perhaps it was a man he was meeting, a man who wore blue eye-shadow.'

Alec appreciated the neutral tone. It did Frank credit. He had a problem with gays. It was his one serious blind spot.

'So they quarrelled, you think, and the lover shot him?'

'Could be, Chief. That many shots look like an amateur job. Emotional.'

'Aye . . .' It fitted in with Falco's *Unnecessary quantities of lead.* And with the suspicions Jackie denied so strenuously. An amateur killer was more likely also than a pro, who would've known he was messing with one of Stan Falco's. Apropos of which: 'Any word round A Division, Frank, of a black, name of Carter?'

'Carter? That's a new one. *Carter?* Look, Chief, you know the way I'm out of things. Phil's an old mate, but there are limits . . . You can't just throw out new names and expect—'

'Sorry, Frank. You're absolutely right. I was thinking aloud, that's all.' Frank was touchy these days. Alec told himself he'd be touchy too, in Frank's position. 'Sorry . . . Make a note though, will you, *black called Carter*, for the next time you ring Phil?'

Frank muttered something. It sounded suspiciously like, 'If there *is* a bloody next time . . .' Then he cleared his throat. 'Carter, you said? No first name?'

'Carter's all I've got, Frank.' He'd apologized enough. 'And start with the morgues.' But if Carter was in one of them, that would prove there hadn't just been a lover's tiff. Falco needed more than that to put the man there. Falco only killed when hard cash or power was involved. Had Carter represented either? 'By the way, what does Chief Inspector Pritchard say about all this?'

'He's sticking to the official line. Underworld killing. Territorial . . . Drew was a dealer, so what more d'you need? The gun's a problem – it *was* a police calibre weapon and you and I know the crims don't like 'em – but he's not letting a thing like that worry him.'

'He'll go far . . . He's a wise man, Frank. He hasn't even been to see the official boyfriend. And he never sent someone round to tell Jackie his partner was dead. He's keeping things simple. What the A Division eye doth not see, the Public Prosecutor doth not grieve over . . .' Alec sighed. 'So that's it, then. A dry night, so no footprints, I presume. No sign of a struggle. And nothing yet from forensics, of course.' Since privatization, forensics were a farce. Endless delays, lost evidence, rushed jobs, shoddy so-called experts, everything on the cheap. 'So that's it, then. Thanks, Frank. I'm very grateful.'

'Don't you want to hear about Mrs Bladon, Chief?'

'You've already done so much, Frank. I didn't dare ask.'

'A couple of phone calls, that's all. And it makes a change from the Bridewell.'

Of course it did. Alec was forgiven. Frank hadn't stopped being CID, just because they'd packed him off to Cheapside. 'So tell me about Joan Bladon.'

'Not much to tell. Shot at close quarters. Seems the sod held the gun to her head. Came up behind her and grabbed her. She struggled, so he let her have it. That's from the doctor who signed the certificate – there's not going to be a forensic examination.'

'There's *what*?'

'Like you said, Chief, a straight robbery with. Healthy woman, clear cause of death, no unusual circs, so let's save the poor bloody tax-payer a bob or two.'

'That's crazy.'

'That's Allerton.'

'Meaning?'

'F Division's overspent. According to Harry the housing riots back in July cost a bomb in brought-in special gear and vehicles – and overtime, of course. One Riverview resident the fewer isn't going to get the *Gazette* up in arms, so they're burying her cheaply.'

'I don't believe it. Pritchard's sitting on one, and now Allerton's sitting on the other. Who's the investigating officer?'

'David Clarke.'

'He's all right. Bit of a bastard, actually . . . but he can't fight Finance. I tell you, Frank, I'm glad I'm out of it.' Alec prodded the potatoes. He needed them soft – mash was his staple. 'So what's Clarke doing?'

'The usual. Prints. House-to-house. Two constables for half a day, Harry says.'

'Christ.'

'Nobody's admitting to seeing anything. Could be intimidation, could be the truth. A couple upstairs heard the shot. It woke them. No idea of the time, though. They listened for another but there wasn't one so they went back to sleep. After midnight but they won't say more than that.'

'Mebbe I could try.'

'I was going to ask for names, Chief, but Harry says they're pretty old, scared stiff, bolts and bars and chains from floor to ceiling. Wouldn't let the constables in, didn't trust their ID, shouted through the crack. I don't think you'd get much.'

Alec agreed with him. Particularly if the old folks were white. 'Did the half-day include the wider question of what Mrs Bladon did with herself? Was she seen around? Did she go for walks? Did she go for a walk on Monday night?'

Frank paused before answering. Finally, 'Harry'd have mentioned it, I think, if she'd been seen the night she was killed.'

Which was his polite way of reminding Alec not to expect too much. This was a friendly contact, for God's sake, not a Home Office case report.

'She was calling herself Brown, by the way.'

Alec nodded. So Evie'd told him. So had someone else . . .

one of the kids on the estate. He should have paid more attention – nobody intimidated them, their bright little eyes were everywhere, and they wouldn't have come within the remit of a half-day's house-to-house. He'd have to go back.

Frank sighed gustily down the phone. 'No news of the stolen telly, Chief.'

'That's no surprise. They don't hang around.' Alec held the telephone under his chin while he rummaged for spinach in the freezer. Time was passing and he hadn't yet put his mind to what he'd give the punters at Tony's. 'Frank? We're missing something. I don't believe matey really held a gun to Joan Bladon's head for the sake of a bloody TV. There's something else.'

'The niece didn't help?'

'She doesn't think the common law husband did it.'

'Me neither. Any reason?'

Alec cut open the plastic spinach bag with scissors. 'He drove a minicab.'

'That's nice.'

'I'm sorry, Frank. I'm not paying attention. I've lamb chops to do, and then I've got to be at Tony's . . . Look, if Joan's death had anything to do with Dancer's, then we've got to connect them. Evie says they knew each other, but that was back in Trevor's time. This is now. Evie's given me a photo of her aunt – mebbe we should show it round a bit in Dancer's stamping grounds.'

'We, Chief?'

'The Funrama Videodrome, Frank. Over in Wavertree. I'm sure you know it.'

'Can't keep away, Chief. Me and Doris, every Saturday night.'

'The thing is, there's a wee bruiser there, fancies himself as a yakuza, and he's marked my card. But if you went in, all official, with the photo, he wouldn't be able to refuse.'

'Wavertree, you said.'

'It can wait till Saturday. I'll get a copy of the photo to you.'

'Saturday, you said.'

'Keep you in practice, Frank. Do you good.'

'I remember it now. Used to be Dancer's base.'

'That's what I mean. If Joan and him met anywhere, it's the best chance.'

'What's wrong with them talking on the phone?'

'Want to bet Dancer's ex-directory?'

'Why wasn't it *him* calling *her*?'

'The Funrama Videodrome, Frank. Saturday. I'll drop the photo off with Doris tomorrow, on my way to the hospital.'

Alec rang off, unwrapped the chops, started heating the grill. The potatoes were done and the spinach would take three minutes in the microwave. Frank and the Videodrome bruiser would get on – he wished he could be there to see it.

One of the good things for Alec about piano playing was that while he was doing it everything else went away. He hadn't done enough gigs for the job to be automatic. Even when his fingers remembered the notes for him, all that did was leave his mind free for the music. He had to listen very hard. Once in a while he'd coast along on a Scott Joplin straight from the printed sheet, but mostly his arrangements were original and needed all his attention. No room was left for questions of Trevor Bladon, of Joan, of Dancer. No room was left for May.

He was winding up for the end of his first set, 'Cocktails for Two', which only aficionados would remember, leading into Porter's failsafe 'Begin the Beguine', resplendent with Art Tatum twiddles. Tony's was filling up this Thursday evening, and the level of conversation was rising. If he wanted their attention he'd have to crank up the volume. Leave blood on the keys.

Later on, with Tony's as busy as this, it wouldn't be worth

the effort. Later on, unless the punters were dancing, he could retire, be strictly background, and play to please himself. But there was always a balance to be struck. Bar pianists could be too strident. They could also be too self-effacing.

After a couple of bars someone out there recognized the beguine intro, and it got applause. People stopped talking to listen – not all of them, and not for long, but enough of them to give Alec that performer's unique sense of being, of the moment, of here-ness and now-ness. It worked out well. A hammy tune – and Alec Duncan, the King of Swing, black at his white piano, was hammy too – but he got away with it.

He got a good hand. Standing to acknowledge the applause, smiling and bobbing his head and looking round, he saw familiar faces in a booth. Some time during the last couple of numbers, Morag and Iain had arrived. He was surprised and delighted. Sitters for Jamie were hard to organize, and when the McKinleys did get out they usually went to the theatre. The Everyman was very left wing, and Iain liked his faith in humanity restored.

They had a woman with them Alec didn't recognize, collar-length dark hair and a red jacket with ugly padded shoulders.

As the applause died he got down off the stand and walked over.

'Iain, Morag – why did you no tell me you were coming? Charlie could've saved you a ringside seat.'

'Tell you?' Morag laughed. 'When were you last there to answer your phone?'

Iain stood up as much as the narrow booth would let him. 'Alec – this is Rachel Hewson. She plays in the Liverpool Philharmonic. She's a jazz fan, too.'

She held out her hand. 'I was here last week, Mr Duncan.'

They shook hands awkwardly in the crush around the booth. Her voice was pleasant, non-regional, standard English middle-class. Alec caught the flattery implicit in the fact that she'd heard him last week and was here again tonight. Morag made room and he slid in beside her. One of Charlie's lads fought his way over, and Iain ordered drinks.

'I've been out a lot,' Alec told his sister. 'And I sent the answerphone back to Multirent. You should have tried the one in the car.'

'I didn't think you still had it.'

'I may be hard up, Mor, but I can still—'

'In any case, Alec, it really doesn't matter.' She was uninterested in the current priorities of the New Poor. 'This was an impulse anyway. Jamie's staying the night with a kid from school, so we thought why not? and I rang Rachel.'

Iain sat back in his observing way. 'I'd forgotten how well you played, Alec.'

'Good of you to say so. With me it all depends. I've no the experience yet – some nights are great and everything works. Other nights—'

'Rachel and I met at the clinic, Alec.' Morag was driving on, impatient of family courtesies also. 'I can't remember how we got round to it, but suddenly we were talking about jazz, and you, and I thought, you've really got to meet.'

It seemed an odd sequence. He suspected that Morag, not wanting to be too obvious, had left something out.

'You're a member of the Philharmonic, Miss Hewson?'

'That's a grand way of putting it. I'm reserve team – fifth desk in the double basses. They send for me when they're boosting numbers for the big Romantics. Ten of us for the Berlioz. That sort of thing.'

Alec smiled to himself. He'd known all would come clear. 'But you play jazz too?' Piano and double bass, the perfect team. Morag was match-making. 'Off duty, I mean.'

'Not really.' Not really? He knew about that *Not really*. 'I've a living to earn. There isn't any off duty – I teach every hour God gives. Flute and composition.'

'And the big fiddle to anyone who wants it.'

She laughed ruefully. 'I haven't yet found one. If it was bass guitar, of course, there'd be a queue halfway down the road.'

'Rachel has a little girl,' Morag explained. 'She works from home.'

'It can't be easy.' Perhaps she really didn't play jazz. Alec looked at his watch. If Charlie's lad didn't get back from the bar soon he'd have to return to the piano sans drink.

Iain cleared his throat. '"Out a lot," you said. So what've you been up to?'

It was a question he'd been dreading since he first saw them. Its answer seemed to him for some reason shameful. 'Mrs Bladon,' he said minimally. 'The mother of the young man who killed May. She was killed herself a couple of days ago. I've been . . . looking into it.'

'Murdered?' Iain frowned. 'That seems a bit hard. Considering what she's already been through.'

'I agree. That's why I—' He was spared further elaborations by the arrival of Charlie's lad. The drinks were claimed and distributed, and the conversation wandered off to the problem of play schools in Liverpool for the under-fives. Miss Hewson's daughter was four.

Alec noted that no explanation of May's killing had been necessary. Clearly Morag was delivering him to Miss Rachel Hewson with a full case history.

'I've been thinking,' he said suddenly, emptying his glass. Another thirty seconds and he'd have to go. The punters needed him. 'I've been thinking about Mrs Bladon and her son. What he did to her. He ruined a second marriage for her with his bloody-mindedness. He turned out gay, you see, which she probably didn't like much, and a drug addict. The new bloke couldn't take it and buggered off. Then he became a murderer too, after which all hell broke loose. She lost her home. Actually had to go into hiding. Changed her name. Had damn-all left, some dump in a no-hope estate . . .' He looked round the booth. 'So mebbe you women with kids can tell me. Did she forgive him? If she'd lived, could she ever have forgiven him?'

There was an awkward silence at the table. The tone he'd struck was wrong for an evening out on the town, but he didn't care. He'd been burdened with Joan Bladon, and her miseries, on his own, for far too long.

'Whatever their kids may do,' he said, 'do mothers forgive them?'

Miss Hewson moved first, shaking her head. 'People talk a lot about a mother's love. It's not indestructible. No love's indestructible. For myself, given all that you said, I don't see mine surviving.' She gestured apologetically. Her hands were big and square – bassist's hands. 'That's only me, though.'

Alec nodded, then turned to Morag. His thirty seconds were long gone, but he needed to know. 'Can you imagine forgiving Jamie?' he asked her.

She was still thinking. 'I'm not sure what you mean by "forgive". Once bad things have happened you can't make them un-happen. You certainly can't forget them. You probably shouldn't excuse them . . . So what does "forgive" mean? Stop wanting to punish?' She looked down at the table. 'That's awfully mechanical. Besides, it assumes you wanted to punish in the first place, and that's something else . . .'

Alec stared at her. Oh, Morag, dear Morag, he thought, what a different, beautiful world it would be if all its Mrs Bladons worked like you. He stood up.

'I'm sorry,' he said. 'This was supposed to be you people's evening out.' He turned to Miss Hewson of the big broad hands. 'I'm not usually this earnest.' An appalling thought – perhaps he was. 'In any case, it's time I did my duty. See you after the next set, mebbe.'

Morag reached for his hand. 'We can't stay, Alec. This was very much an in and out. Rachel's got an itchy sitter.'

'Ah . . . Well, another time, then.' He disengaged his hand, nodded, and went away. He knew he'd behaved badly, but he didn't choose to work out why. Back at the piano he sat for a while, not thinking. People close by eyed him curiously. He straightened his back and flexed his fingers. A chord arrived, followed by others.

One of the good things about piano playing was that while he was doing it everything else went away.

8

Alec liked to think he wasn't a superstitious man. He used the word rigorously. It seemed to him that for most people a superstition was any irrational belief or practice that they didn't agree with: for him, a sensible person who resisted irrational beliefs and practices of whatever kind, they were all superstitions – everything from not walking on the lines in the pavement to the Pope's infallibility, from rain-making dances to the healing power of crystals or the existence of an interested creator. In particular, given his previous line of work, he had little sympathy with the irrational beliefs and practices that surrounded dead human bodies.

Corpses, to him as a sensible person, were the rubbish left behind after the animating consciousness, which was the person, had for whatever reason departed. Not that he was unmoved by the mutilations he had seen in the course of his police career. They had been perpetrated upon the living, they added to humanity's pain and wretchedness, and they outraged him deeply. But the notions that the body itself, once dead, should be revered, and its disposal ritualized, were to him distasteful – one might as well revere a worn-out torch battery or ritualize its dumping. One might more reasonably do so, in fact, since at least torch batteries did not need boxes to keep in the stink of rotting meat and innards.

Certainly the disposal of corpses, as of any other rubbish,

should be hygienic and ecologically sound, which suggested cremation, but if people preferred burial he'd no great objection. Funerals were out, though – as well as usually involving vapid wish-fulfilment stuff about some sort of afterlife, funerals also emphasized bodies, as did graves – and for survivors to show respect for a dead person, let alone love, via their decaying remains seemed to him (having seen the bloated, maggot-eaten reality of all too many) to be perverted. He was all for some sort of get-together, to celebrate the departed life, if that were in all honesty possible, and to sanction the survivors' grief, but the corpse didn't belong at it. Neither, save perhaps for some civic/tribal importance, did any memorial. As a sensible person he found it slightly insulting to the dead that their survivors should need expensive arrangements of stones as *aides-mémoire*.

May, for example. She'd known where he stood and, in the absence of any strong feelings to the contrary, she'd stood there too. In principle, since no moment had ever seemed quite right for a more specific, written declaration, they'd agreed that funerals were out, and graves and memorials. As to an afterlife, she'd been if anything more vehement than he. The notion insulted her intelligence. The universe was whole, and finite – it couldn't keep on being added to. If one survived at all, it was in other people, in their lives and minds and hearts.

But May had had parents, and a brother and a sister. Not close, not what you'd call close, but around. And not noticeably religious either. But when she'd died, when she'd been murdered, when she'd been slashed and stabbed until she'd died, and Alec away at work, doing his job, his ill-considered, unconsidered job, when her animating consciousness had departed in pain and terror, then the parents and the brother and the sister had suddenly and unexpectedly come into what they considered their own. Into what the law, too, unexpectedly considered their own. Alec was the deceased's cohabitant. He was nothing.

He'd tried. He'd reasoned with them. He'd told them how he felt. How May had felt. She hated shiny hearses and portentous lines of limos, the coffins gentled into place as if the bodies in them cared a damn, the ministers threatening them with resurrection. And now she was dead, and he'd loved her more than anything in the world, and didn't his wishes count for anything?

No.

A plot in Allerton's overspill cemetery, out by the ring road, was currently available, and dear May had left nothing in writing, and he was only dear May's cohabitant, and the words 'decent Christian burial', once spoken, acquired mythic power. It would all have been quite different, of course, if he and dear May had been married.

He fought them all he knew. He reasoned with them quietly, together and separately, on their own, in terrible official rooms, the parents, the brother and the sister. He should have known he was wasting his time; wasting the tears it cost him. They smiled, with tight lips, and shook their heads. He begged and ranted. They asked him whose fault it was that May was dead, anyway. He appealed to their better natures. They reminded him, revealingly, that May had left him her flat and most of her money. He sought legal advice. It told him he was only the deceased's cohabitant. He threatened, most dire of all to May's parents and brother and sister, to make a scene at the ceremony. But they, although never completely comfortable with him, with his blackness, knew that he wouldn't really. And besides, there were ushers at funerals, men who kept order, weren't there? – certainly at the proper decent funeral their dear darling May deserved and would get. And would get. And would get.

Ushers could deal with anything poor distressed Mr

Duncan – they were nothing if not charitable – anything poor distressed Mr Duncan might feel obliged to come up with.

He'd realized, in the middle of one desperate night, his folly. He'd been building the whole thing up quite foolishly. May's funeral was unimportant. So was her grave. He had to laugh – he'd been falling into the same superstitious error as her parents and her brother and sister. It simply didn't matter. Why should he care if there was one ritual more or less, one shrine more or less, in this ritual-ridden, shrine-ridden world? He was being mean-spirited. Undignified. Superstitious. Rituals, shrines, they gave comfort to many, and they were no skin off *his* nose.

Just so long as May's parents and her brother and sister didn't expect him to take part in the one or visit the other.

Which they didn't.

They sent him a notification of the date and the time of the funeral (no flowers, please – donations to the Law Society's Benevolent Association), and the location of the grave, as was only right, but no mention of the repast, the cold collation, organized in conjunction with May's legal partners, that followed the interment. He'd read about that next day, in the *Liverpool Gazette*.

Faced with getting through what he'd imagined was the hour or so of the funeral, he'd spent it in what was then still, pending probate, May's Sefton Park flat, sitting at what was then still May's grand piano. Not playing. Mostly he'd wept. He was there on sufferance, at May's lawyers' discretion.

His donation to the Law Society's Benevolent Association had been generous. It pleased him that someone, somewhere should benefit from the whole wretched affair, and he'd nothing against lawyers. He'd been the cohabitant of one, for heaven's sake.

As it turned out, Allerton's overspill cemetery wasn't too bad. Not late at night, when the traffic on the ring road was sparse. He visited it occasionally after playing at Tony's – the gates would be locked but in one corner the railings had been bent apart by local children in need of a quiet place for sniffing glue, or fucking, or whatever it was they did these days. He'd visited it on the Thursday night after Morag and Iain had come to the pub with Rachel Hewson.

He never went so far as to find May's grave, it was enough simply to walk along the paths. The children had all gone home by then, and he didn't need to fear being seen, a black man in a dark suit on the unlighted paths. It wasn't as if the cars on the ring road ever stopped.

Chief Inspector Clarke leaned forward across the interview room table.

'I'll ask you again, Mr Duncan. Why the hell did you drive all the way out to Justice City? You say you wanted to see Ms May Calcott's murderer. What for? Why the hell did you want to see Ms May Calcott's murderer? And on the day after his mother, too, had been murdered? Why on that day of all days?'

Clarke spoke loudly, with unnecessary emphasis, being as offensive as he could. *Ms May Calcott's murderer* . . . the words were so raw. Alec had done the same sort of thing in his time. It unsettled the suspect, made him want to punch the interviewing officer's teeth in.

Alec said nothing. He wanted to punch Inspector Clarke's teeth in.

'I'll phrase it differently. What did you and Trevor Bladon talk about? On that day of all days?'

'I don't remember.' Which, oddly, was true. They hadn't talked about anything, really. 'Why don't you ask him?'

'He says you went there to look him over. He says you went there to gloat.'

Oh, Trevor. Shame on you, Trevor . . . Unless Clarke was lying, of course. This was outrageous. 'Do you no have a tape, Chief Inspector? A video? In glorious technicolour? A record of our blood pressures and our pulse rates? The acidity of our saliva? A report on our marital status? The size of our bank balances and the combined volume of our farts?'

Clarke's sergeant smirked, covering it too obviously with his hand.

Clarke lowered his voice. 'I wouldn't try to be too clever, *Mr* Duncan. What goodwill you ever had, *Mr* Duncan, you used up last January. Rotten apples hurt us all. We're very hard on them. I think you know that, *Mr* Duncan.'

A rotten apple? Was that what he was? He'd honestly never thought of himself in that way. 'I always understood that the City ran recorded surveillance of the men in LTI.'

'Not . . . invariably.'

So that was it. Something had gone wrong with the gadgetry and the prison electronics men had egg on their faces. Alec thought back. What *had* he and Trevor talked about? Drug addiction? Mostly drug addiction. And guilt.

'My trip out to Justice City has nothing to do with this case, Inspector. If you had those tapes you'd know that.'

'Not fucking so, Mr Duncan. All I'd know was that you'd known you were being recorded . . . So why did you go out there? On that day of all days, why *did* you go?' Clarke no longer expected an answer so he didn't wait for one. 'You see, Mr Duncan, there's this remarkable coincidence. Early on Tuesday morning – a time for which you have no alibi – a woman was murdered. Then, only the very next day, you conned the VSA into letting you visit her son, the man who stabbed Ms May Calcott to death, who stabbed your partner to death nine months ago and has been in jail, safe from you, ever since. Nine months ago, that is, and not a peep out of you to the VSA in all that time. Not until Wednesday. Not until the day after someone did in his mother. So what am I to think?'

Alec was on his feet. 'You can think what you bloody—'

He checked himself. This was formula stuff. Disgusting.

He'd done it himself, so why was he falling for it? . . . He'd gone because of Morag. He'd gone because of Hardcastle. He'd gone because of the way he'd shouted at the vigilantes. He'd gone because he'd gone. How could he tell Clarke that?

He shook the sergeant's hand from his shoulder and sat down again. 'So what *do* you think? Do you really think I went to gloat? Vengeance at last? At one remove? He kills May so I kill his mother? Like in some TV serial?'

'It's this record you have, Mr Duncan.' Clarke spread his hands, as if regretfully. 'This record of violence . . . And they tell me you and Ms Calcott were very . . . close.'

Alec's anger flared again. This time he checked it sooner. His pulse raced and his mind lurched briefly, but he didn't move. 'I've worked with you, Clarke. Don't forget that. I know how you work. You're not going to get to me.'

Chief Inspector Clarke smiled, seeing that he had. 'And then of course the crime *was* committed by a police calibre weapon, which you would be in an excellent position to possess.'

More garbage. Didn't fucking Clarke know the lengths the authorities went to, making sure you didn't leave the Force with so much as a shirt button that wasn't yours? The idea of getting out into civvie street with a police issue handgun was as outrageous as the idea that he hated Trevor enough to . . . enough to . . . But mebbe Clarke didn't know that. He hadn't left. He was still in.

Alec took a deep breath. Ordered his thoughts. Motive, opportunity, reputation, weapon . . . no case as yet, no hard evidence, but in the inspector's place he might have considered it worth pursuing. Technically speaking, the gloat trip out to Justice City was a risky elaboration – devious enough to fascinate a jury, but any halfway decent defence counsel would make hay of it – but in the inspector's place he might have considered it worth pursuing.

This, then, had been the reason for yesterday's relaxed

approach. In the absence of evidence you needed time. You needed to wear the suspect down, to confuse him, to demoralize him, so you got him to come in just to make a formal statement – morning, afternoon, anything to oblige. That way he'd hardly think it suitable to arrive equipped with his solicitor. Why should he? It would make him look guilty, and only real pros weren't bothered by that.

The first rule of any police investigation: you keep suspects from their solicitors for as long as is humanly (inhumanly) possible. First you jolly them along – Alec had been as jollied as anything, making his statement to nice Sergeant Baker and signing it, not a rubber hosepipe in sight – and then you move them quietly on to the next stage, nothing sudden, nothing rough, nothing they could take exception to, until all at once they find themselves 'fessing up, it's a fair cop, guv'nor, and they don't know what came over them . . . Not that they fucking 'fess up to anything very much these days, not since all the fucking media exposés, but you can always hope.

In any case, Clarke could hardly have expected it to work with Alec. The minute the chief inspector had ambled into the room, on a social visit that nevertheless required the presence of his sergeant and the tape recorder, Alec had rumbled him. So he hadn't been worried, and he still wasn't. His innocence didn't greatly reassure him, but the lack of evidence did. He didn't need a solicitor.

Famous last words? No. There was no way that Clarke was going to connect him with the flat in Riverview Heights, with the gun that had killed Joan Bladon, with the stolen TV.

Also, he didn't have a solicitor. There was the man who had handled the sale of his place down by the river when he'd moved in to May's, but he couldn't imagine that ancient twit standing up to the likes of Inspector Clarke.

Alec was glad to see he was keeping his sense of humour.

'If you're not going to charge me,' he said, 'which you're not, then you've got thirty-six hours.'

'I don't need them.' Clarke glanced at his watch. 'Another ten minutes, at the most. This is by way of a softening up. Presumably you threw the gun in the Mersey? It's just down the road from Riverview and you knew, with the tides, that we'd never find it.'

'Tell me something, Chief Inspector.' Alec had thought of a little game of his own to play. 'Did the dead woman wear blue eye shadow?'

Clarke was brought up short. 'You what?'

'Blue eye shadow. Did Mrs Bladon wear it. I didn't get far enough into the kitchen to see.'

'I'm not here to answer stupid fucking questions.'

'No?' Alec let it ride. The question wasn't stupid. He wasn't going to explain, but on its answer, and on the reason for it, might hang the resolution of the Dancer Drew as well as the Joan Bladon murder cases.

Clarke gathered his thoughts. 'You'll have driven to Riverview from that manky club you play in. They're a restless lot down on that estate. Someone's bound to have seen you. Seen your Rover. It *is* still a Rover, isn't it?'

'I went straight home. Mebbe I woke up someone in one of the other flats. Slamming the car door and that.'

'We've asked, and you didn't.'

Alec was surprised. He remembered what Frank had said about Allerton's resources – two constables for half a day didn't sound like a trip out to Sefton Park. But mebbe that was before Clarke had heard of his Justice City visit, and had made two and two come to more than five. A vengeful ex-copper on the loose would get a bit more out of Finance than some random robbery with.

Clarke looked again at his watch. Clearly it was he who was fitting Alec in between more important matters, not the other way round. 'I'm interested to know why you waited so long, Mr Duncan. Nine months. At first I expect it was because of the publicity. Then she went into hiding. She was calling herself Brown. You knew that, of course.'

He was putting together a case. It was what a policeman did. It was his job. First he found a suspect, then he looked for evidence. He put together a case. It was how he worked, how he had to. He looked for evidence that fitted.

This time round he'd find there wasn't any.

Alec humoured him. 'People need to make plans, mate. You don't just go out and shoot someone. It takes time.'

'You wore gloves, and you dumped the TV. It might be anywhere. Even if we found it, it wouldn't prove anything. You know all this and so do we. But we'll still get you.'

'Can I go now?'

'You murdered that poor harmless woman.'

'Ten minutes, you said.'

'You were getting at her son. It was the only way you had.'

'I don't have to sit here and—'

'You put a gun to the side of her head and shot her.'

Alec nearly lost it then. More than any other weapon, he feared guns. He feared their ease. Knives, ropes, razors, coshes, broken bottles, they required involvement. Squeezing a trigger was small, remote. And it shifted responsibility. The result was so gross, so disproportionate, the noise and then the blood and destruction, that some other agent must have intervened. God? It didn't matter. Any intermediary, so long as there was one, would do. He feared guns, yes, but his unease went far deeper than that.

He covered his face with his hands. He felt, otherwise, that he might make a fool, or a monster, of himself.

Chief Inspector Clarke stood up. 'Don't leave town,' he said. 'We're going to want to talk to you again.'

He left the room. Alec heard his shoes squeak on the floor, then the latch of the door. Sergeant Baker signed off for the tape: 'Chief Inspector Clarke has left the room. The time is three-thirty-seven.' He gathered up the things on the table, the forms and pens and pencils.

'You can go now, sir. And thank you for the statement. We'll be in touch.' Then, as Alec reached the door, 'Not everybody thinks you got a square deal, sir, back in January.'

Alec lifted his gaze up from the floor. 'I know, sergeant. Thank you.'

'And for interest's sake, sir, she *did* wear blue eye-shadow.'

When he got back to the flat the door scuffed noisily over the pile of mail on the mat. He picked it up, flipped through the envelopes. Half the British insurance world was trying to sell him cover. There were charity appeals, Unit Trust prospectuses, Victoriana catalogues and a chauffeured car hire brochure. His affluent chief inspector days had got him on to all the best mailing lists. It was comforting, in the silent flat, to know that somebody still loved him.

Alec looked up Rachel Hewson in the book and called her. The phone rang for quite a while before she answered.

'Miss Hewson? This is Alec Duncan. Morag's brother.'

'Yes?' A wary lady.

'Are you busy?'

'Busy?'

'Is this a bad time – I mean, are you teaching?'

She laughed. 'Not at all. I was taking down the rubbish. It's an upstairs flat.'

'That must be a bother. For your work I mean.'

'Not really. Having people overhead would be worse. Doesn't sound rise?'

'I'm sure you're right.' Silence fell. 'I called to apologize for last night. I'm not always so heavy.'

'You said what was on your mind.'

'There's a time and a place, Miss Hewson. I'm sorry.'

'There's really no need. We certainly didn't leave because of it. Your sister was right – I had an itchy sitter.'

Alec leaned on the kitchen wall by the phone. That morning, before going to the hospital, he'd had to leave early to drop Joan Bladon's photo off at Frank's place, and he now realized that he'd forgotten to get anything out of the freezer for the evening.

'You said you taught flute. Isn't that an odd one for a bass player?'

'The flute came first. And piano. But at college there were dozens of us swaying young ladies. What the college orchestra wanted was double basses. They loaned me an instrument. I found I liked it. And I was good at it.'

A purposeful lady. He wondered how she'd come to purpose a four year-old daughter. 'But you don't play jazz?'

'It's all plucked – not enough bow work. And a classical training makes you afraid to improvise.'

It hadn't him. Only school level, of course, but his mother'd moved heaven and earth to keep him on the classical straight and narrow. It wasn't that she'd been ashamed of his father, but look where it'd got him. An Edinburgh Festival gig, then back to Chicago and what next? Not a thing. She'd looked for his name but she'd never seen it. If his son wanted to play then he'd do scales, and sight-reading, and classy partitas.

He'd done them. He did them still. But they weren't what he did best, and he didn't think they'd made him noticeably afraid to improvise.

He laughed. 'I once heard Menuhin. With Grapelli.'

'It wasn't very good.' Not a question. She knew the recording.

'No. No, it wasn't . . . I must go now.' He'd done a glance up at the clock, *gosh, is that really the time?* but it was wasted on her. 'I just wanted to say I was sorry.'

'You needn't have.'

'Aye. Well . . .'

'And I like your music. Really.'

'It passes the time. Still, I'm glad . . . I must go now. Good luck with your students.'

He rang off. He was going to have to do an omelette. He opened the refrigerator door to see if he had enough eggs. There were plenty. He'd have an omelette with frozen oven-ready chips. It was a matter of principle with him, at times like this, that he didn't turn on the radio.

He picked up his mail and took it through into the sitting room. It was a fine big room, shadowy now as evening approached. He sat down on the sofa, slipped off his shoes and put his feet up. The trouble with telephones was that they stopped people writing letters. His mother, for example – in an earlier age the mail now in his lap might have included a letter from his mother. They'd been out of touch since March: he wondered how she was doing.

One of the catalogues was in a transparent envelope. The come-on of its green-and-gold cover worked and he poked at the plastic, but it wouldn't tear. Another trouble with telephones was that, unlike letters which could be simply chat, people – certainly people like his mother – expected phone calls to be weighty. If he telephoned her (she liked the three syllables, *tel-e-phoned*, they went with her formal nature) if he telephoned her with nothing in particular to say she'd suspect him of hiding something. Something bad.

He got up and dumped his letters in the box in the hall, ready to go for recycling. He decided suddenly, in the empty flat, to take Sunday off, drive up to Edinburgh, pay his mother a visit. Inspector Clarke wouldn't like him leaving town, but sod him. They'd been out of touch since March. It was a long time. There were reasons, but even so it was a long time.

He'd need to telephone her after six, cheap rate, avoiding accusations of extravagance, to be sure that she was free. Jeanie Grant wasn't a woman who wilted meekly, waiting for her children to appear. She had her bridge and her golf, a job in the Oxfam shop on Princes Street, and a gentleman friend,

Hamish Fraser, a neighbour with whom she went on city walks. They charted the rise and fall of restaurants, hastening from menu to menu. They never, ever ate out, but Mr Fraser had a shrewd eye for over-extended kitchens hoping to get away with shared sauces.

Alec filled in till six, sweeping the kitchen floor and emptying the dishwasher. May's dishwasher. Reminded by Miss Hewson, he took his rubbish out to the bins round at the back of the house. He had no patience with solitary men who lived in squalor as if it proved their manhood. He always put the ironing board and iron away in their cupboard once he'd done with them.

Coming back from the bins he lost impetus on the gravel drive.The last time he'd gone up to see his mother had been soon after May had died. He'd stayed three days, no more, and not gone back. His needs had been too much for her. He didn't blame her, now, but he'd learned from it. His needs, he saw, had always been too much for her. She'd done what she could for him, she was a good mother, but white daughter Morag was the most she was really up to. A son, and so black, was more than she could manage. Her college bursar father, the only other man she'd known, had been so pared away, so different. Morag's father, perhaps, had been more abundant, but significantly he hadn't stayed. And Alec's father a long-ago aberration of youth and innocence, a single, crazy, abandoned, unregretted but never ever again, Festival-long fuck. . .

'Penny for 'em.'

'Wasting your money.' Alec came round. The voice was Chas's. Chas and his wife Janet, both retired from the Civil Service, lived in the flat at the back of the house. 'I was . . . just thinking.'

'I saw you. Fact is, old man, I was lurking. *Horr, horr.* Waiting to pounce . . . I've had this thing too bloody long.' He held out Alec's electric drill, borrowed back in June. Chas was lean, prematurely white-haired, with a clipped military moustache and manner. According to his wife he'd been the terror of his department. 'I said to Jannie this morning, I really must make an effort. What will the feller think of me?'

'You needn't have worried, Chas. I'd completely forgotten.' There'd been a shelf or two to put up when he'd first moved in and was making the effort. Since then, nothing. 'Why not hang on to it? You're the DIY man.'

'So I ought to buy me own – nothing worse than a neighbour always on the bloody scrounge. Eh? Eh? Still, if you *really* don't . . .' He withdrew the drill, held it warily against his chest. 'At least you'll know where it is . . . Reminds me of a film I saw once. Bloody stupid. Woman threw her engagement ring into the sea. When her chap asked her why, that's what she said: "At least I'll always know where it is." Bloody stupid. Made Jannie cry. That's women for you. Bloody stupid.'

'Aye. Well . . .' Alec shifted his feet uncomfortably. He wanted to be off. Where was all this leading? 'I doubt I'll be needing it for a wee while yet.'

'Maud and Harry. That's what the film was. Harry and Maud. Something of the sort. And the bloody woman was old enough to be his grandmother . . . In a spot of bother, are you?'

'I'm sorry?'

'Don't mind me asking. Don't mind me mentioning it. Only want to help, old man. Know what I mean?'

'I'm afraid I'm not with you.' Alec was with him completely. He just wanted him to say the words. Chas had indeed been lurking, *horr*, *horr*. All day, probably, behind his net curtains. Ever since Dave Clarke's men had called. The drill was no more than a pretext.

'Your old mob, old man. The boys in blue. Didn't you know? They've been round on the knocker. I mean, you could've bloody warned us.'

'Warned you?'

'Didn't know what to say. Felt bloody stupid – Jannie wasn't even dressed yet, for God's sake.'

Alec thought of his 'record of violence'. Just then he felt like adding to it. 'They have a job to do, Chas. You can always complain if you think they called too early.'

'It's not that. I mean, two coppers, crack of dawn, it'll be more than just a bloody parking ticket. We're broad-minded, Jannie and me, but it's just not what you expect, old man. Not on Sefton Park.'

Alec was sorely tried. 'I'd have warned you if I'd known, Chas. I—'

'It's not as if it's the first time.'

And suddenly, between them, there was total silence. Not a bird, not a radio, not a barking dog, not a sound from the city. When angry enough, Alec had that ability. He was, as some men are, most powerful in his stillness. It was a quality that not even Chas was proof against.

He stepped back a pace and raised a hand to protect himself. 'Sorry I spoke. Not your fault, that. Quite uncalled-for, old man . . .' He gathered courage as the moment passed. 'Doesn't look good, though, you must admit – the coincidence, I mean. That, and now this . . .' He paused to check the buttons on his lovat-green cardie. 'I mean, what on earth, old man, have you been bloody up to?'

Alec didn't feel capable of answering. He turned and walked away, then paused by his door. Other people dealt with this sort of situation every day. Had he ever thought enough about what his men were leaving in their wake?

'The police think I may have murdered someone, Chas. If you or Jannie had heard me come in on Monday night it might have provided an alibi.'

'Not a sound, old man. We had to tell 'em. Sorry about that, but we had to tell 'em. Always quiet as a mouse. Marvellous neighbour. Marvellous bloody neighbour – we told 'em that too but I don't suppose it helped much ... Murdered, you say? That's a bit steep, isn't it?'

'Very steep, Chas. Very steep. Thanks for the offer of the drill. As you said, I'll know where it is when I need it.' He went into the house and closed the door. He'd made Chas and Jannie's evening.

At five past six he telephoned his mam. Jeanie said she'd have been charmed to see him the coming Sunday. The only trouble was, Mr Fraser was going to visit his married daughter in Portobello that day and she'd promised to go with him. The daughter was a witch, a real witch, but with the dearest wee bairns, and the poor man was relying on her ... The better the day, the better the deed. And it *was* rather short notice.

Alec agreed that it was indeed rather short notice. It was just that he'd been—

Jeanie wondered how he was faring. Was he well, and hadn't they had a rare summer, and she didn't want to interfere, but had he thought about a job yet?

He told her he was well, and agreed that they'd had a rare summer.

Jeanie must have noticed the omitted answer for she retaliated by showing concern for how much the call was costing him. Money didn't grow on trees. And as for his visit, what about the Sunday following? That was as free as the birds of the air. And a wee bite for lunch? Nothing grand, mind.

He told her, fine. Fine ... He'd have expected nothing else. Always something clean and suitable, never something grand. Grandness was for the ungodly. He'd no idea what he'd be doing the Sunday after next but he could always cancel. See you Sunday, then. Around noon. Aye. He rang off.

The talk of food reminded him that he'd eaten lunch early, at the hospital canteen before he left, so as not to be late for his appointment at the Allerton nick. He dug the chips out of the freezer, knocked off weeks of frost, arranged the chips in neat lines on a baking sheet, and put them in the oven. While he waited for them to thaw and sharpen up he sat down at the table and looked at his notes on the case. His case. The game he was playing.

Things were working out. Nothing he could put his finger on, no suspect, no evidence, just some blue eye-shadow on a scrap of tissue, in a world where eight women out of ten wore it, and men too, and some gun oil in the pocket of a man who never used a gun, together with a hundred and fifty pounds, which wasn't enough to make sense, and two people killed with similar calibre bullets, but he still felt that things were working out.

Joan Bladon had known Dancer Drew, and according to his partner, and believably, he'd gone down to Otterspool on business, always a dangerous matter, even for a Falco man, in such an isolated place, especially after midnight. Business with Joan Bladon? It was unlikely yet the best hope, for it explained why he'd dared. And it might not have been for business – he might have been meeting her for some personal reason, some personal reason he didn't want Jackie Patterson to know. Personal reasons, between him and Joan Bladon, were hard to imagine but they weren't impossible.

In any case, someone else must have known about the meeting and lain in wait for them. No, that didn't work. If the plan had been to kill them both, then why leave her alive till she'd got back to her kitchen? No, the killer must have been after Dancer and reckoned to do the job and get away before she arrived. Or mebbe after she'd gone ... Unless of course the meeting had been with the killer all the time, and she'd just happened along. But why leave her alive anyway? Once she'd seen Dancer's murder, which seemed the best reason for hers, then the sooner she was dealt with the better.

So mebbe there'd been a need to keep the bodies separate. God knows what, but nothing else made sense. In which case, why bother with stealing the telly? The actual effect had been to make her death look like a random mugging, nothing to do with Dancer's, so mebbe that had been the intention. But why should the killer mind? And anyway, nobody could have counted on her going back to her flat – most women in her position would have made for the nearest phone box, or knocked up a neighbour.

Why *had* she gone home? Could it be that she'd known the killer and they'd gone back to her flat together? She mightn't have realized the danger she was in as a material witness. *Ah, fuck it* . . . Known the killer? Just happened along? For God's sake, how convoluted could you get?

Through the glass oven door the neat lines of chips mocked him. Not much else in his life was so orderly. He left the table and beat up eggs in a jug. His dietetic conscience told him he needed a second vegetable so he sliced and peppered some tomatoes. Then he waited until the chips' time was up, and made the omelette. And though he said so himself, it was a triumph.

Later, in the empty flat, he watched the television in the living room and wished he hadn't telephoned his mother.

9

Alec was woken early next morning, after a restless night. A telephone call again, but for once incoming: Evie Fairbairn.

'D'you know what? The sods've just been on the blower. They've released Auntie Joan's flat and maybe I'd like to see to her kitchen. The sodding cops, I mean. It's been nearly a week and they say the place is stinking. Well, it would be, wouldn't it?'

Alec tried to swallow the sour taste of not enough sleep. 'I'll pick you up.'

'Would you? I was going to ask. I looked you up in the book. I don't have a car myself and there'll likely be stuff to bring back. You don't mind? I could scrounge a lift here on the estate but I'd rather not give folk here the thrill. You don't mind?'

'Of course I don't.' He was oddly flattered. These days Evie Fairbairn was his favourite woman. He took down her address and arranged to be there in an hour. This trip to Riverview was, on second thoughts, a golden opportunity, always assuming that he was arrogant enough to believe he could pick up something the Allerton team had missed. Even if he couldn't there were still the kids who might have seen Mrs Bladon. Mrs Brown.

After midnight? There was always the chance.

Evie was waiting for him on the pavement near her home,

empty shopping bags on her arm. It was a sunny morning and the Toxteth estate looked personable. Drug Hell? Not here. Evie's place was at its 'good' end, low rise maisonettes with some grass left between them, where the tenants didn't break each other's doors down and mostly paid the rent. There was little visible despair. The cats were calm. A policeman, even in uniform, could visit here alone.

He leaned across to open the door and she got in. 'Phoo.' She settled her seatbelt, which lay too high. 'Nice wheels.'

Alec nodded. The phrase jarred, until he realized that the snob in him had been falsifying her. She was Toxteth and if he didn't like it he could do the other thing. He drove off. From here to Riverview wasn't far, just through the city centre and then out a couple of miles along the Aigburth Road. He asked her, 'Are you going to find this hard?'

'Auntie's place an' all? I expect so. But it's got to be done. 'Sides, if I disgrace meself, sodding blub an' that, I reckon it won't be the first time you seen it.'

True. He cleared his throat but she got in first. 'How's the coincidence going?'

'The coincidence?'

'The connection. Auntie Joan and that Dancer. What we talked about in the canteen.'

He smiled. 'No very well.'

'You've been out a long time.' She patted his leg. 'Maybe you've lost your touch.'

'Mebbe I have.' The car in front braked abruptly. Ahead the traffic was solid. He should have known that even as early as this on a Saturday morning the new prison had a costive effect. He remembered the boarded-up shops and burnt-out tenements that had been here before. Now, according to the mayor and city council, Liverpool would have a new pride. The prison would be convenient, too, for family visits, once that privilege had been properly earned – not like the old-style jails that went up a few years back, miles from anywhere.

The mayor and the city council were humane people.

Alec sighed. He asked Evie, 'Have you thought about a funeral?'

'Trev was on the phone to me last night. Wants me to fix it. He's a mess – feeling sodding guilty, I reckon.'

'A mess?'

'Crying. Blaming people. You know what I mean.'

Alec glanced sideways. 'Blaming people?'

'No one in particular. The blacks out at Riverview. The housing committee for not protecting her. I let him have his say.'

The traffic edged forward. Alec drummed his fingers on the steering wheel. 'Did you mention Dancer?'

'He already knew. Seen it in the paper. Worked up about that too. Upset. Boo-sodding-hoo. They've been split up for ever. Little creep like that – made me sick.'

A tough woman. And she really didn't like her cousin. 'Did you tell him that his mother's death might be connected?'

'Nah. He was nutty enough without that.'

Alec was relieved. He'd have warned her if he'd thought – even from LTI Trevor could stir things up. He wondered briefly why it was so important to him that the Merseyside Force wasn't alerted. Revenge for the way they'd treated him? He hoped not – they'd treated him fine. It wasn't their fault if justice, as understood in this country, made him sick. If prisons, Justice City in particular, made him sick. It was there that the woman he'd assaulted worked, it was what she stood for, it was why, mostly, he'd assaulted her. No wonder he'd resigned. But they'd treated him fine.

'So what about the funeral?'

'He wants the lot. He says Auntie paid into a club.'

Alec nodded sadly. She probably had. Out of a lifetime's weekly pittances, so that at least she could hold her head up once she was dead. So that her son could hold up his.

'It'll get him compassionate leave, of course,' Evie said. 'I wouldn't be surprised if that's why he's so sodding keen.'

Not only tough. Merciless. The telephone conversation with her cousin hadn't warmed her to him.

'An afternoon off,' Alec told her. 'It's no big deal.' But he knew just how much it would mean to a man in LTI.

'Anyway, she'll have left a bit of money. Some of the paper's nine thousand. She was always careful. . .' Her voice broke and she fussed with her shopping bags. Alec was disconcerted. He'd judged her harshly, not recognizing the pressures of grief. 'It'll go to Trev now, I reckon. Sodding crazy . . .'

He turned off the main road, down to Wood End and Riverview. 'Won't she have left a will?'

'If she has, it'll all be for him.' She wiped her eyes unobtrusively, spreading the damp across her cheeks with her fingers. 'It's not me I'm thinking of, mind – don't think that. I'm doing fine. It's just the sodding waste, him in there now for how many years is it? It should go to folk who need it, maybe the homeless. Maybe the old. Folk where a couple of thou would really make a difference.'

'You can't be sure she's left it to Trevor. Not after the hard time he gave her.'

Evie snorted. 'Want to bet? The sun shone from his arsehole. Everything was other people's fault, never sodding his. . .' She checked herself, maybe hearing her shrillness. 'I know what it was, of course. Don't have to be no head-shrinker to see she blamed herself for Uncle Bert's going. All that how he'd never of took off if she'd treated him proper. And then the boy'd've had a father around to keep him on the straight an' narrer.'

'Aye. Well, it might have made a difference.'

'Of course it sodding would. But she'd never of kept that man, not if she'd danced around all night starkers in fishnets and a black satin suspender belt. He'd got bored, see. Ten years' marriage and he'd got bored. The tart he went off with wasn't all that much, but he'd got bored. And when a man gets bored—'

She made a cutting sound, a sharp breathy hiss, *phttt*, and laughed bitterly. Alec wasn't surprised that she had no opinion of men – she'd have been very lucky indeed, with her crippled body, to have known anything other than rejection or the crudest exploitation. He was reminded of the condoms in Joan Bladon's purse and wondered how hopeful they'd been. The woman on the beach in Evie's photo would have turned few men's heads, and the way her life had panned out left little chance of a more commercial basis for sex. Most probably, he decided sadly, they were a leftover from Jack Fisher. Throwing them out would have been too final, too much of an admission. But it wasn't a thing, today, that he could ask her niece.

They arrived in Riverview Heights. The place hadn't changed much since his last visit. It hadn't changed at all. Even at nine on a sunny Saturday morning it looked worn out. The kids were there too, the smaller ones rolling about on a stained rubber mattress while the bigger ones stood talking in a furtive group. Alec parked the Rover and wound down the window. He called out, asked who was boss and did a deal with the lad who answered. He was visiting a friend – five pounds if the car wasn't beat up when he got back to it. Two fifty now, in advance. Expensive, but he had no choice.

He lingered for a moment, eyeing the group. Last time he was here one little kid had remembered Mrs Brown – fat old tart in a Red Indian jacket, he'd called her. That would be the Aztec thing Alec had seen on her dead body in the kitchen. The carroty kid in a T-shirt printed with fake bullet holes looked familiar, but Alec couldn't be sure. He'd try later, once he'd got Evie settled in the flat.

He and Evie went along the path to the tower entrance. She'd been here before and knew the way. She walked quickly, not looking round, absorbed in getting the key out of her bag.

Not seeing, in order that she should not be seen. She led him into the foyer, down the short corridor, and opened the door. Its frame had been repaired but the marks of Constable Baynes's jemmy still showed. The air in the flat's tiny hallway smelled of the acetate used by the SOC team to lift fingerprints. Presumably, since Frank hadn't mentioned them, they hadn't found any. The dumbest opportunist lad wore gloves these days.

Evie hesitated in the open doorway. 'Where'd it happen? You were here. You saw. Where'd it happen?'

Alec shook his head. 'It doesn't matter, love. Things happen, then they're over. Done with. Your aunt's gone . . . she was here once and now she isn't any more. It doesn't matter, exactly where it happened.'

Evie stared at him, then accepted what he'd said. She went on into the flat, making straight for the closed kitchen door. Alec followed her.

The kitchen stank. Alec leaned across the sink, raised the venetian blind and opened the window. Sunlight flooded in. Behind him Evie was down on her knees in front of the refrigerator, muttering disgustedly. It wasn't working and the police had left its door open. Alec tried the cooker switch – nothing was working. Of course not. Allerton would have notified the electricity company, who would have been worried about their bill. Dead people, in Riverview Heights, got themselves immediately disconnected. It was a tough old world.

Evie looked up and pointed. 'There's plastic bags in that drawer. At least, there used to be.'

There still were. Alec handed her a couple and she started scooping mouldy tomatoes into one. She sniffed some bacon and that went too. She handed him a carton half full of lumpy sour milk which he emptied with some difficulty down the sink. He flattened the carton and stuffed it into her plastic bag. Over her shoulder he saw a bowl of mashed potato, just the sort of thing he might have kept to fry up the following day with some onions. It brought home to him the bleakness of Joan Bladon's death, a woman he'd never even spoken to, the bleakness of anyone's death, the inexpressible bleakness. It had been the same with May. It would be the same with him. One day his mashed potatoes would have to be scraped into someone's plastic bag. That, however, would be their problem – this was Evie's. He rested his hand on her shoulder but she twitched it off so he went away.

He'd no idea what he should look for, but if the Allerton lot had made any sort of effort at all it would have been in the kitchen, where the body was found, so he tried elsewhere. First, the bedroom. He didn't ask for Evie's permission because he knew what she'd say. She'd said it before – *Once a copper, always a copper*. He opened her auntie's wardrobe, saw slacks hanging, blouses, a dress or two, a winter coat and a heap of shoes on the floor. He stirred the shoes with his foot: there was nothing hidden under them. The chest of drawers was equally unrevealing – the untidiness might have been Allerton's but it might equally well have been Joan Bladon's. He was putting together a picture of her now, and it wasn't orderly.

The bed, unmade when he'd seen it last, had been stripped, the bedding folded and piled on its foot with the pillows. He glanced under it, lifted the edge of the mattress. He was wasting his time. The youngest trainee constable could have scraped this room clean. There was nothing in it. The woman had been camping out, waiting till the fuss died down and she could go home.

The bathroom offered a mirror-fronted cupboard with medicines in it. Not many. He read their labels – headaches, constipation, piles, indigestion, flu, nothing you couldn't buy over the counter at Boots. No sleeping pills. If Joan Bladon had been down by the river in the early hours of last Tuesday morning it didn't seem to be because she had a pattern of insomnia. Also, she hadn't been a drug addict. All the addicts he'd known were patent medicine freaks. Not that there was any question of that – still, it would have been useful if she'd had such an obvious reason for meeting Dancer.

Her cosmetics were stacked on a shelf below the cupboard. Again not many, among them several well-used plastic pans of blue eye shadow. A box of tissues, too. What progress he could have made, given the Force's facilities for analysis. He could have proved that Joan Bladon and the person down by the river where Dancer was killed – and ten million others – used the same popular brands.

He looked for loose tiles, an unobtrusive panel in the side of the bath. There was still the possibility that the two murders were unconnected and she'd had something worth stealing. If she did, then she probably revealed where it was before the thief killed her. The floors of the flat were concrete, the walls unadorned plaster. That left this room, after the kitchen, as the best hope.

Alec found nothing, looked quietly back in at Evie. She'd finished at the refrigerator and was filling one of her shopping bags with dry goods, flour and sugar and tea and coffee. Faint noises suggested that she might be crying. He went away, past the coat cupboard in the hall for which he'd have needed a torch, and into the living room.

So bare. Sofa, drop-fronted desk, chair, carpet square, curtains, lamp, TV stand. The curtains were drawn back, revealing at one side the door out on to the wired-in balcony. Unlike the front door, it had been not so much mended as crudely boarded over. How long the boards would last was anybody's guess. For form's sake Alec felt down the sides of the sofa cushions, then tipped it up to examine the sagging canvas underneath. The curtains too, their hems. The lamp was a lamp. The TV stand was a TV stand. Looking under the carpet square was a chore which would involve moving everything off it. He turned instead to the open desk, the most obvious place.

Pad, envelopes, several ball-point pens, rent book. He looked in it: Joan Bladon had been paid up, a good tenant. It didn't seem fair. With so little time left she could have kept the council waiting, spent her money on something else. He was willing to bet that every other sod on Riverview Heights did ... The desk's top drawer had an opened box of Dairy Milk chocolates in it, a circular sewing basket with little Chinese heads on the lid, a bundle of papers, mostly bills and receipts by the look of them, in an elastic band, an instruction manual from Multirent TV, and a building society savings book. Prompted by his discussion with Evie on the way there, Alec checked among the papers for a will and found none. He wasn't surprised – if she'd made one it would be with her other important papers, birth certificate, marriage lines, whatever, back in her Toxteth flat. He turned to the building society book. The balance on the last page with entries was £5374.57. He stared at the figure thoughtfully. Out of nine thousand, over six months or so, most of them unemployed, it was a decent amount. Evie's Auntie Joan was no reckless spender.

More interesting, though, above the final amount, was a withdrawal, last Monday, of a hundred and eighty pounds. He gaped at it, not believing. A withdrawal, last Monday, of a hundred and eighty pounds. Twenty pounds found by Constable Baynes in her purse with her Social Security card and the condoms, ten pounds gone on this and that, and the rest, a hundred and fifty, exactly a hundred and fifty, some with the bank strip still round them, turning up in Dancer Drew's pocket. It was almost too neat.

He looked round the room. Where else could all that money have gone? In this whole flat, what on earth had cost a hundred and fifty pounds? Where else could all that money have gone?

He stared at the book again. He could hear Frank Grove's sceptical wheeze. Anywhere. It could have gone anywhere. A dentist. Months in advance to Multirent. A package trip to Disneyland. It could have gone anywhere.

Not so. Any legitimate destination for a hundred and fifty pounds would supply a receipt, which careful Joan Bladon would keep. He turned to the bundle of papers and scrabbled through it. Electricity, telephone, TV licence, nothing else . . . and nothing in her purse, or Baynes would have shown it to him. That left him with the non-legit, and Dancer Drew at the head of the list. She might have paid a hundred and fifty pounds in cash to a bookie or a toyboy but he hardly thought so.

The connection. The definite connection he'd been looking for. A transaction between the two of them some time between her visit to the building society and her death. What the transaction might have been he'd no idea. If Dancer had sold her something then that would be what the thief had stolen, for it certainly wasn't here now. The thief and murderer, killing her for it.

He closed the book. She might have had the hundred and fifty in the flat, in which case that was what the thief had stolen, and Dancer's hundred and fifty was something else altogether. The flip answer to that was that two hundred and fifties were too much of a coincidence, and he didn't believe in coincidences, but he did. They happened all the time.

Not last Monday, though. He didn't believe in that particular coincidence, happening on that particular Monday.

In the kitchen Evie had cleaned out the refrigerator and was standing on a chair, looking in cupboards.

'Anything you fancy?' she said brightly. 'Teacups? Veggie dishes? The council'll want the whole sodding lot cleared and there's only me. Mum won't want to hump stuff back down to London. She's coming up this afternoon – I said she wasn't to but she's family so it's right really. It's the soonest she could get away.'

'If I were you,' Alec told her, 'I'd get in touch with one of the hostels. Mebbe a halfway house. They can always do with things.'

'Great. They'll have a truck too. They can come round and take the lot.' She sat down wearily on the work surface, her feet still on the chair. 'There'll be Auntie's Toxteth place too. Piled high – she was always a squirrel. Christ knows when I'll get round to it. Trust our Trev to be somewhere else when he's sodding needed.'

Alec held up the building society book. 'I found this. There's over five thousand pounds. If your aunt left a will things'll be simpler, but in any case a solicitor will fix it so you don't have to do a thing. It's no your problem.'

'Easy for you to say.' Evie rested her head on her knees. 'Whose is it then? Don't want sodding strangers picking over Auntie Joan's things. Mum says she's stopping over till the funeral, whenever that is. Soon as may be, I can tell you.'

Alec noticed that the matter of Joan Bladon's body was being skirted. Presumably Allerton hadn't released it yet. If Inspector Clarke was going to keep it on ice until he had him, Alec, in the bag, then Evie and her mum would have to wait a while for their funeral. But it wasn't for him, Alec, to say so.

'According to this wee savings book, Evie, your aunt drew out a hundred and eighty pounds on the day she was murdered. Is that something you'd know about?'

'A hundred and eighty? No sign of it here, and the cops never said nothing. That's what she was sodding killed for, then. That and the telly. A hundred and eighty lousy quid. . .'

'Then you don't know what she'd have taken it out for.'

'Me? Wasn't one for confidences, Auntie Joan. More so ever since Trev was taken away. Kept herself to herself. Know what I mean?'

Alec could well imagine it. People like Joan Bladon didn't

flash their shame around. 'She probably needed the money to live on,' he said. 'The state isn't generous.'

'You wouldn't cocoa. Starvation rations, that's what.' She stood up and got down off the chair. 'I've said it before and I'll say it again, Auntie's well out of it.'

Looking round the kitchen she'd died in, the flat she'd died in, the estate she'd died in, Alec didn't argue. She was well out of it. Dancer, on the other hand, had been on the verge of great things: a boutique, jewellery and objets d'art, with Jackie in Harrogate. It was Joan Bladon's life, then, that Alec mourned, not her death. He closed the kitchen window and lowered the blind again. Then he helped Evie gather up her plastic bags and carry them out to the car. It looked in good shape so he handed over the second two pounds fifty.

The carroty lad with the bullet holes didn't seem to be around. It didn't matter – he was as sure now as he'd ever be that Joan Bladon had met Dancer down in Otterspool late Monday night. She'd given him a hundred and fifty pounds. Why, and what had happened next, were other questions.

He gave Evie her aunt's savings book. 'I wish I could help more but you need to go to a solicitor. The police will surely give you the death certificate if you ask. Take it with you. Tell the solicitor how things are. It's Trevor's job really, but you can explain about that.'

Evie took the book, not speaking, and put it away in her handbag. They got into the car and he drove her back to Toxteth. It was still a fine morning: the good end of the estate still looked personable. Even so, the sour smells and sad aching emptiness of the Riverview flat hung over him. He stopped the car, cut Evie's thanks short, told her he'd be in touch, watched her cross the pavement, waved to her, and she was gone.

By way of late breakfast he had coffee and a doughnut in the city centre, a filthy American habit, then drove over to Frank's place. He could have rung him to find out what luck he'd had out at the Funrama Videodrome, but he wanted the reassurance of Frank's all too ample flesh. And if Frank wasn't back yet he could pass the time of day with Doris. He needed to make up for his unawareness, that he hoped she didn't know about.

His unawareness stretched to his not considering the possibility that, with Frank gone off early to Wavertree, Doris might have decided to have a lie in. It was something Doris never did.

Luckily Frank drove up as he was opening the gate. He didn't call out, just wound down the window and signalled, a finger to his lips, the other pointing up at his and Doris's bedroom, above the glassed-in entrance porch. Alec waited for him, and together they went round the side of the house and in at the kitchen door.

'Park your bum, Chief,' Frank said, moving a chair out from under the table with his foot. 'I'll be down in a minute.'

'No rush.' He sat down. No rush? The tension was killing him.

At the door Frank turned. Had mercy. 'Matey didn't exactly fall over himself,' he said, 'but he did go so far as to admit as how he might have seen the woman in the picture I showed him. . .'

'Might have seen her?'

'Might have seen her talking to friend Dancer.'

'Ha.' Alec rubbed his hands together. 'That means he did. Any idea when? No – don't bother. It doesn't matter. Go along now.'

'Ten days ago, actually. Middle of last week. Wednesday. He remembers because it was his first day back. He'd been on his hols.'

'Hols? Matey goes on hols?'

'Tenerife. So he says, and I believe him. With the wife and the kids. Can't rely on anything these days, Chief.'

Alec tried to imagine that many tattoos being allowed on a charter flight. 'He didn't happen to hear what the two of them were talking about?'

'In that place? Not a word. Which is half the point. . .' He patted the doorframe by way of punctuation. 'Shan't be a tick, Chief. Put the kettle on for some coffee if you like.'

He went out. Alec heard him thumping up the stairs. He went to the sink and filled the kettle – he had no interest at all in more coffee just then, and in any case Doris's instant was the foullest own-brand he'd ever come across (she was a tea person, herself), but her rules of hospitality, and therefore Frank's, demanded it. He put the kettle on the gas and leaned on its handle, staring out at the tiny patch of garden that wasn't given over to conservatory. . .

The connection. Dancer and Joan Bladon had definitely been up to something. First the money, and now they'd been seen together over at the Videodrome. It was a pity, then, that he'd drawn a blank with Jackie – in a perfect world the boyfriend would have been able to fill in all the missing pieces . . . He'd had no reason to lie, had he? Alec straightened his back. The reasons people had to lie were legion. He had the tape of their interview out in the Rover. Mebbe he could pick Frank's brains.

By the time he got back from the car Frank had come downstairs, the kettle had boiled, and two mugs of brown were being stirred. He held up his pocket recorder. 'I've something I'd like you to hear, Frank.'

Frank sat down heavily. 'I wondered where you'd gone . . . Falco's got in a replacement, by the way. In the Videodrome. For Dancer, I mean. Busy with the morning trade – till matey sussed me out and sounded the alarm.'

'Don't tell me, Frank. A sharp young black by the name of Carter?'

'You can forget Carter, Chief.' Frank topped up his mug with milk and added sugar. 'I should've called you. You never said what your interest was, but Carter's Drug Squad. He was under cover, till one of Stan Falco's men rumbled him. Now he's pushed off back to London . . . No, Dancer's replacement is a right shifty little git. Won't last a week, if you ask me.'

Under cover Drug Squad . . . and not very good at it. According to Jackie he'd tried too hard. No doubt that was how Falco'd rumbled him. And if he was back in London now and wasn't tied to scrap-iron at the bottom of the Mersey, presumably that was because Falco'd felt sorry for him. Alec remembered Falco's words on the phone: Carter had 'left town'. It was as if he'd personally put Carter on the train. Oh, the shame of it.

'Carter was never more than a vague possibility, Frank. Now he's one possibility less. Which is all to the good.' Alec reached for the milk. He saw that no breakfast was being made, no pot of tea even. 'You and Doris got any plans, Frank? How is she?'

'I heard that Clarke had you in, Chief.'

'He's doing his job. Pursuing his inquiries . . . How is she?'

'Not sleeping well.'

Alec waited. 'I'm sorry to hear that.'

'It's nothing much. I told her to have a lie in. What's Clarke's idea, then?'

Reluctantly Alec took the hint. 'That I killed Mrs Bladon, Frank, because her son killed May.'

'That's daft.'

'It won't go anywhere. It made a change though, to be on the receiving end. Every officer should be suspected of a major crime. It's an educational experience.'

'Clarke always was a hard young sod. I remember him when he was a detective constable. A sod then and he won't have changed.'

Alec tackled his coffee. 'There's room for all sorts.' He moved them on. 'I've just been over to Riverview with Evie Fairbairn, Frank, helping her clear out her auntie's flat.'

Frank widened his eyes and slapped both his palms down on the table. 'Surprise me, Chief. Allerton missed something.'

'Not really. I mean, they couldn't know.' He told Frank about the savings book and the hundred and eighty pound withdrawal. 'A bit of a coincidence, wouldn't you say? Remembering Dancer's one fifty?'

'A bit of business, Chief. Has to be. The old girl would've known where to find him from Trev's days. She wasn't a natural for the Funrama, though – she'd only of gone there if she'd really wanted something.'

'Something illegal.'

'What else? From friend Dancer, what else?'

'Something she asked him for when she was out there on the Wednesday. Something he said he'd need time to get. Something he said he'd have for her the following Monday night.'

'Something sizeable, Chief. And very illegal. Something he wouldn't want to hand over just anywhere.'

'Something that didn't come with its own wee book of instructions.'

'Something he'd need to show her how to work.'

Alec laughed. They'd played this game many times before, in the old days. In the good old days. 'Frank, Frank . . . what the hell did Joan Bladon want with a handgun?'

'Protection?' Frank rubbed his chin. He hadn't shaved well that morning. 'Riverview's a rough place. It's not right for her, I know, but maybe she'd been seeing too much "NYPD Blue".'

Alec sat back from the table. 'It's the reason she'll have given Dancer. . .' There was another reason, though, and he'd heard it first from Evie Fairbairn. He remembered her giving it, in the factory canteen, and he remembered laughing. 'Maybe it was her done in the little sod,' she'd said. 'Wouldn't put it past her. . .'

He looked across at Frank. 'Maybe it was her done in the little sod.'

'Ah . . .' There was sugar spilled on the table by Frank's coffee mug. He wetted a forefinger with spit, blotted up the sugar, and sucked it off his finger. 'Got him to get her the gun, ta very much, then shot him with it . . . Now that, Chief, is what I'd call not very nice.'

'Possible, though. If she'd hated him enough.'

'And she would. She'd blame him for every bad thing that ever happened . . . Her son on drugs. Her second bloke who pushed off. The murder. Trev banged up and the key thrown away. The rough time she'd had after. Her whole bloody awful life. It was all, the way she looked at it, down to him.'

'So she killed him . . .' Evie Fairbairn again: *She'd been very down, too, the last few weeks. Not so much* down – *gone away, more like.* That would be after she'd made up her mind. Not easy, deciding to kill someone. Or mebbe, when the someone was Dancer, very easy. A relief. *Gone away* . . . 'Is that no a bit on the melodramatic side, Frank?'

Frank shrugged. This was another game they played – I agree with you so persuade me – but this morning he couldn't be bothered. 'Either she did or she didn't. And, without the bloody gun, we'll never prove it either way.'

'Me, Frank, I'd have tossed it. Thrown it in the Mersey.'

'Hundred and fifty quid's worth, Chief. She'd need to break the habits of a lifetime.'

'She'd already done that. I tell you one thing, though, all this gives us an excellent motive for her murder.'

'Squaring things? Marking his territory? Leaving a sign?' Frank shook his head. 'An old tart like that – even if he'd known that quick, Falco'd never bother . . .'

'Not Falco.'

'. . . And if he did, he'd want people to know the whys and wherefores. He'd make sure the bodies was left close together. And the gun too. His man would have his orders.'

'You're not listening, Frank. I'm not suggesting Falco.' Alec reached for the recorder. 'I'd like you to listen to a couple of minutes of Jackie Patterson. He's very good.'

He fitted the earphone, ran the tape back to where he thought was the right place, over-shot it, ran forward, listened. 'Right, Frank – this is where Jackie's saying his goodbyes on Monday night.'

He removed the earphone and Jackie's voice came, tinny and hollow, out of the speaker: . . . *leaned in at the passenger's window. The car's started, see, and it's going nicely, settled down nicely, so I lean in at the passenger's window. He says he won't be long and I tell him to be careful and he says he will. Then the door comes sort of open, it's been dicky for months, and I have to heave it shut, and he leans across and locks it and winds up the window, and then he drives away.*

Alec's voice: *So when were you worried?*

Not till next morning. I took one of my tablets and slept like a log.

Alec switched off the recorder. 'So what d'you think?'

'I can just see it.'

'Aye. Too well?'

'Is there any more?'

'The next one's different.' Alec searched again. He'd been showing the photograph, just about to leave.

Ever seen that woman?

Never.

Look at it properly. It's an ordinary face. Think about it.

It's a bloody awful face. Doesn't mean a thing.

You're positive?

Who is it?

I asked if you were positive.

I'm positive.

Alec stopped the tape. 'Lets him off the hook, doesn't it? I mean, if he's never even seen Joan Bladon he couldn't possibly have killed her.'

'There *are* some faces, Chief, that you can look at and know at once that you've never seen them.'

'Of course there are. And your average Mr Joe Public, given the chance, would always rather know nothing. It keeps things simple. So why aren't I convinced?'

'I could say that's because it doesn't fit with your theory.'

'Aye, you could.'

Frank stood up. He went out into the hall and Alec saw him listening at the foot of the stairs. In the silence Alec heard a neighbour's lawnmower, the distant siren of an ambulance, probably on its way to the Park Hospital on Orphan Drive. Frank came back into the kitchen.

'I'd be happier doubting the first one, Chief. The car and that. I'd say he's worked on it. It's just too good, like something in a bloody book.'

'The last time he saw his partner alive, Frank. It's the sort of thing you do remember.'

'Were they close?'

'Very.'

Frank took his empty coffee mug to the sink and washed it out. 'Who did you tell him you were, Chief? That's private stuff. Personal – why did he bother?'

'I told him I was from Stan Falco.'

'See what I mean? He'd no need to say all that – not to one of Falco's men.'

Alec peered into his mug. 'I've let mine get cold.' If he was completely honest he'd have to admit that he hadn't come on one hundred per cent as a Falco man. He'd allowed himself a smidgen of sympathy . . . but hardly enough to invite, as Frank put it, such private stuff. 'No, I agree with you, Frank. It's all too smooth. Too detailed. I don't believe a word of it.'

Frank accepted the mug without comment, and emptied it down the sink. 'So what happened?'

'I tell you one thing – Jackie was jealous as hell. He had a lot riding on the relationship.' A boutique in Harrogate, for heaven's sake. Not to mention love. 'And he had his suspicions of Carter's romantic intentions.'

'Carter?' Frank laughed briefly, his mouth shut, blowing out his cheeks. 'So you think he followed Dancer down to Otterspool?'

'His name was Frederick, by the way.'

'Well I never.' He rinsed Alec's mug and began drying it. 'Do we know if this Jackie has a car?'

'He must have. Living out on Wango Lane he must have. And I'd expect some smart little number.'

'So he nipped into his smart little number and followed friend Dancer down to—' He caught Alec's eye '—and followed sodding Frederick down to Otterspool. What then?'

'You know the park there, Frank. A dark night. Plenty of trees and bushes.'

'So he peeks out and sees young Dancer on the receiving end of—' This time he caught the correction Alec hadn't made. He flung down the dishtowel. 'Look, Chief, I'm an old dog, and I've called the little sod that since before he jerked off his first social worker, and he's dead now, so do you mind?'

'Mind? Of course not.' It was the first time, ever, that Frank had turned on him. 'I'm sorry.' The man had other things on his mind, the silence upstairs, and this Bladon thing was simply foreground. Useful foreground? He hoped so. 'If Joan Bladon did the murder, and Jackie saw her, then he'd have been pretty desperate. She was armed, though, and she'd just shot someone, so there wasn't much he could do.'

'Gone for the police?' Frank returned to the table. 'Not him. I expect he's a user.'

'Actually, I doubt he is. Dancer never was. But I agree with you – he'd want to sort things out himself.'

'So he followed her back to Riverview. Neat on his feet, is he?'

'Very.' The TV made following people look easy. It wasn't. 'It was a dark night, Frank. And she'd have been shook up.

Pulling the trigger's easy. . .' He understood the number of shots now, the convulsive hatred behind them. 'It's afterwards that catches up with you.'

'He'd found out where she lived. But she was still armed.'

'Unless she'd tossed it in the river.'

Frank frowned. 'He'd need to have a gun himself, then. Same calibre.'

'He says he doesn't have a gun at all, but I wouldn't bet on it. Still, he needn't have had it with him – I doubt he was planning to shoot poor Carter. No, he has to have gone home to get it. Once he knew where she lived he went back to where he left his car. He wasn't in a hurry. In his place I'd leave things an hour or two, wait for her to go to bed.'

'Only trouble was, Chief, she didn't. So she surprised him and there was a struggle and he got lucky. Either with his gun or hers, it doesn't matter. He pushed off with the telly to make it look good, and Bob's your flipping uncle.'

Alec laughed. 'We always did make a wonderful team, Frank. If telling a good story put villains in jail we'd have been head of the league.'

Frank glanced up at the clock with its painted waterfall. 'So it all comes down to the telly.'

'He'll have dumped it.'

'Wouldn't be so sure. Some blokes get greedy . . . makes no never mind, though. All the men in the Force, just one more telly, we'll never be able to trace it.'

'No, Frank. What it comes down to is the gun. I reckon he saw hers go into the river. Else he'd never have taken her on. I doubt he's a coward, but he'd just seen her shoot Dancer so she'd nothing to lose.'

Frank grunted. 'So he had a gun all along, and it's the same calibre?'

'Stranger things have happened.'

'Then what we need is a search warrant.'

'That, or a bit of private enterprise. For which I'm not volunteering.'

Alec thought about it. An exciting tiptoe at dead of night. Luring Jackie away to Huddersfield with a fake phone call like in the books, and turning his nice little place upside down. And what then? Finding the gun and taking it to Inspector Clarke and hoping to be believed? And all so that Jackie could be brought to justice? *Brought to justice* . . . Ah, those terrible words. Suddenly his evidence game had got heavy. Society had to be protected. A lifetime in LTI for a man who avenged the murder of his lover. The deterrent that had never been known to deter. He wondered what Evie would think. But you couldn't let things like that influence you. Justice was justice. Evie had said she thought her Auntie Joan was well out of it.

Something had been niggling at him. All at once, like waking in the morning after his subconscious had been beavering away all night, he remembered. 'I'll tell you something else, Frank. If he didn't dump that telly, if he tried to fence it locally, then we may be in luck. She was renting it from Multirent. I saw the book.'

Upstairs a toilet flushed. Frank stood up, nearly tipping over his chair, then slowed himself with an effort and went to fill the kettle. 'Nice spot of tea,' he murmured. 'What was that you said about Multirent?'

'It doesn't matter.' Alec stood up too. He walked to the back door. 'I've picked your brains enough, Frank.'

Frank didn't argue. He'd put the kettle on the gas and was spooning tea into the teapot.

Alec opened the door. 'I really must go. And I'm really grateful for your help. This thing's important to me . . . Tell Doris I'm sorry I missed her.'

Frank looked up, focused on him. 'Don't Multirent make all their own stuff?'

'That's what I need to confirm.' He would have liked to

look them up in Frank's phone book and he was tempted to stay. But tempted only for the briefest moment. 'I'll keep you posted, Frank. And thanks again.'

As he closed the door Frank was already fumbling bread from the bin on the counter, one hand stretched out to the refrigerator. Alec hurried down the side of the house and out to his car. He was being tactful, he told himself. But he also knew he was running away. Behind Frank, out through the door into the hall, he'd seen Doris's hand on the banister rail.

He drove off quickly. Out of sight of the Groves' house he stopped again and called up Directory Enquiries on the carphone. A computer voice gave him the number of Multirent's main showroom, in the centre of town. He noted it, thanked the computer, and sat for a while, imagining Frank and Doris in their cluttered, homely kitchen. Perhaps he was being melodramatic. Perhaps Doris had simply lost some weight and was showing her age. Perhaps, that morning, she'd been enjoying a perfectly ordinary Saturday lie in. But Frank's evasions, and obvious anxiety, told him otherwise.

He dialled Multirent.

'Multirent International.' A young woman, smiles in her voice. 'How may I help you?'

'I'm interested in renting a television set.'

'We have the biggest range in the country, sir. May I suggest that you—'

'I've seen a set of yours that's just right. I'm calling to find out if one just like it is available.'

'What model would that be, sir? Do you have a model number?'

'I'm afraid not. I was hoping you could look it up. The one I saw is rented by a Mrs Bladon. That's Mrs Joan Bladon.' He gave the address. 'I was hoping you could look it up.'

'We do not give out confidential details of—'

'I only want you to find the model number of her set. Then you could tell me if you have one like it.'

'We have a very wide range of models available, sir.' The smiles were wearing thin. 'If you cared to come in to our showroom, perhaps—'

'Of course I'll come in to your showroom. But I know exactly what I want and I just want to be sure I'm not wasting my time. Would you look it up for me, please? I'm sure it's somewhere there on your computer.'

'And your name is?'

'Duncan.' Why not? 'Alexander Duncan.'

'Hold the line please, Mr Duncan.'

Electronic notes arrived, playing 'The Arrival of the Queen of Sheba' over a solid rock percussion base. Alec held the receiver away from his ear, then put it back. Mebbe there was something he could learn from it. He couldn't stay for ever, just being the King of Swing.

'Mr Duncan?' The young woman was back, and her smiles too. 'I am delighted to be able to tell you that we have Mrs Bladon's model ready in our local warehouse for immediate delivery. It comes with its own built-in VCR , high definition twenty-seven-inch screen and digital stereo.'

'I know.' Evie's auntie had done herself proud. 'That's why I liked it.'

'There's simply the matter of the rental agreement, Mr Duncan. If you could call in at our—'

'I'll do that. And thank you very much, miss. You've been very helpful.'

'That's what we are here for, Mr Duncan.'

'One last thing – do you happen to know who makes this set? What firm? Philips? Sony?'

'We are the biggest rental firm in the business, Mr Duncan, and we make our own sets. That is, we have contracts with all the world's best manufacturers. But they are Multirent sets and we stand by them. We do all our own servicing. We offer a two-hour call-out and you can rely completely on our—'

'I'm sure I can. And thank you again for your help.'

He rang off, slapping the handset triumphantly back into its holder. He'd known it – his answerphone had been from Multirent, and advertised the fact. All Multirent goods did. It was a sales feature – no thief who knew what he was doing bothered with them. They were available only for rent and there was no way they could be sold on as legit. They shouted *Stolen goods!* and never made it on to the market.

Jackie Patterson, on the other hand, probably hadn't known that. He'd have tried to unload the set and he'd have failed. And whoever'd turned him away would remember. Fences would be cagey, not likely to say a word, but if they were sure Alec wasn't police they might be persuaded. His only concern, at the moment, was to tie the set to Jackie and therefore Jackie to Joan Bladon's death. Once he'd managed that he'd decide what to do next. That was when the game got heavy.

He drummed his fingers on the steering wheel. What next? He knew the most obvious fences, a fair range of them, but the problem was, did Jackie Patterson? He didn't believe, he dared not believe, that the laddie's life with Dancer had been as innocent as he'd claimed. Dancer'd never gone in for thieving, he'd never had the need, but there hadn't been a petty fiddle within a twenty-mile radius that he hadn't known about, even if he hadn't had a hand in it. That was the way Dancer's business went, and Alec couldn't believe that his lover hadn't been a part of it. What else had Jackie done with himself all day, for God's sake? Dusted his bust of Schubert?

Where would Jackie have gone, then, to unload Joan Bladon's telly?

Alec's next few hours were straight out of a tourist guide to Liverpool's seedier dens of naff iniquity. Men in backstreet lock-up garages, always on the brink of the deal that was going to see them on the Costa Brava. Men in cluttered rooms with sagging, dry-rotted floorboards, behind junk shops fronted with 1930s bric-a-brac that had gone out of fashion for the second and final time a good ten years ago.

Men sitting smoking at bars in pubs, with a nice little van parked just round the corner, leaving for Holland in the morning. Women too, in this equal opportunity age, tending to be better presented, with antique jewellery boutiques and such – in one case a perfectly legitimate dry-cleaner's.

Alec had a passable story, a woman friend with a son he was trying to save from a life of crime, and only one man didn't swallow it: otherwise his marks were helpful. It cost them nothing. They'd nothing to lose, no deal had gone through so they'd no need to lie. This young lad, trying to sell you a rental TV, as if you were so stupid you wouldn't know it was stolen. Or as if he thought you wouldn't care. And you someone with a reputation in the neighbourhood to think on . . .

It wasn't until well into the afternoon that he struck lucky. He remembered the place from his time as a lowly detective inspector. Stan Falco had been putting his frighteners on the man, a specialist in stolen car radios called Doug Finch with a shed and a soggy inspection pit and a sign MOT INSPECTIONS WHILE YOU WAIT, and a ministry licence too (who the hell inspects the inspectors?), who'd been trying to diversify into designer uppers from Sweden, a direction Falco didn't like. He'd had the brass neck to complain to the police about Falco's threats, and Alec had ended up going round with a message from his Super. First a sharp reminder that times were hard and the police couldn't always be everywhere, and then the advice, in most general terms, that people were better off if they avoided the clever stuff and stuck to what they did best – in Doug Finch's case this was obviously MOT inspections, which both of them understood to mean car radios. He mightn't get to the Costa Brava on them, but he wouldn't incite a certain irresponsible criminal element to GBH (at the very least) either.

All this had been some years back, and frankly Alec was surprised, when he drove past on the off-chance, to see that

Doug was still in business. Still, if he'd taken Alec's advice Falco wouldn't have bothered him, and the car radio trade had boomed ever since the manufacturers introduced removable fascias as an anti-thief device – they gave owners a nice sense of security and you could buy assorted replacement fascias for five pounds a dozen, quite legal, across the river at a stall just down the road from Birkenhead Central.

Alec double-parked beside a rusty camper van lacking both rear wheels, it was that sort of street, terraced black-brick houses with cracked windows and four doorbells each, bed-sitters, no children, and walked back.

'Anyone at home?' He didn't think he'd be recognized. It was several years now since his last visit, and anyway blacks all looked the same. 'Anyone at home, please?'

'You what, squire?' Doug Finch, in grease-blackened T-shirt and jeans, a lengthy dog-end behind one ear, appeared from behind an untidy stack of second-hand tyres. He looked Alec over. 'So what can I do for you, mister?'

The demotion was small, but significant. Alec chalked it up.

But he took his cue from it also and looked down at his feet, showing suitable humility. 'Folk round here tell me I should talk to a Mr Douglas Finch.'

'I'm Doug Finch. Talk what about? I said, talk what about?'

'Pleased to meet you, sir. I'm Mr Jones.' He held out his hand for it to be ignored.

'Talk what about?'

'It's . . . it's, like, a delicate matter, sir.'

'I fix cars, mister. I said, I fix cars. Nothing delicate about that.'

'It's the son of a woman friend of mine, sir. I'm afraid he is getting into bad ways, into bad company.'

'It happens.' Doug found a rag in his back pocket and wiped his hands on it. 'So what's all this to do with me?'

Alec lifted his head. 'I come to talk to you, sir, because folk in these parts tell me you are a good man to turn to. Square and aboveboard, sir. And you have been around here in this neighbourhood a while. You hear things.'

'Can't say as I'd argue with that.' He eased the crotch of his jeans. 'What sort of things?'

'Well, sir, my friend's son isn't, like, what you would call real bad, just young and stupid.' Reluctantly, as if much shamed, Alec met the other man's gaze. 'I'm afraid, sir, he has turned to thieving.'

'Tell me something new, mister. It's a wicked old world. I said, it's a wicked old world.'

'And I'm a friend of his mother's so I would like to help. She tells me he has stolen this old pensioner's TV, sir. He says he hasn't, swears it, but I'm afraid she is right. He has been seen with it, sir, trying to sell it, sir, just up the street there.' Alec pointed solemnly. He was basing his Mr Jones on one of the most believable witnesses he'd ever interviewed, a clerk with British Rail. 'Tuesday. Tuesday morning. He was seen with it on Tuesday morning, sir, just up the street there.'

Doug stared at him thoughtfully, not answering, whistling through his teeth.

'And the situation is like this, sir. Up to now I have persuaded the old gentleman not to go to the police. I'd like the young man to stay out of trouble – it would break his mother's heart. But the old gentleman will not wait for ever, he wants his TV back, and the time is running out. So perhaps, sir, if you have heard of anyone round here who's bought a TV cheap, a good TV, sir, VCR included, then maybe I could make him an offer for it. Then the old gentleman would get his TV back and the police would not have to be involved, and my friend's son would—'

'What sort of TV?'

Doug had been making up his mind. It was Alec's first positive response of the afternoon. He kept his head. 'I mean, if I was to talk to the young man, sir, then maybe he would straighten out his life, and . . . What sort of TV, sir? I do not know what sort. It was rented. I do not know what sort.'

'Rented, you say?' Doug sniffed derisively. 'Young and stupid, mister. You said it yourself. Young and stupid. . .' He fished a lighter from his jeans pocket, took the dog-end from behind his ear, straightened it carefully, lit it. 'Thing is, Mr Jones, I'd say you came to the right man. I'm no gabber, mind, but I do hear things. And you saying rented like that, it rang a bell. Could be I'm wrong, mind, but I don't think so. I said, I don't think so.' He moved closer, honouring Alec with his confidence. 'Fact is, Mr Jones, blackberry like you, no offence meant, trying to help his own, I like to see that. If *you* don't, I mean, fair's fair, who will? And there's too many of these young fucking blackberries, don't know they're born, trying to make an easy bob or two. Nip just one of them in the bud, Mr Jones, and I'm with you all the way.'

One of his own? A young fucking blackberry? Alec's hopes died. This was crazy. He nodded wisely. 'They don't know they're born, Mr Finch.'

'That's what I said. So you catch 'em young, before it gets to be a habit. I mean, here's this blackberry kid, knee-high to a duck, trying to flog this rented set all up and down the street. Not a hope, of course, 'cause it has to be nicked. Being rented and that . . . Dumb kid. Asking for trouble. Nip him in the bud, Mr Jones, and I'm with you all the way . . . Thing is, he'll still have it, betcher, if he hasn't dumped it. Stashed it with one of his friends. Dumb blackberry kid – can't of been more'n twelve. Fourteen, maybe.'

A dumb blackberry kid with Joan Bladon's Multirent TV. Alec was dismayed, his Jackie Patterson theory blown to shreds. He trod water. 'That's the way it is, sir. Young and very stupid . . . And you think he will not have sold the TV set? That is very good news, sir. Thank you, sir. I'm very grateful.' What now? Problems. He needed a name and, ideally, an address, yet he'd said this dumb blackberry kid was the son of his friend. 'Tell me, please, Mr Finch, this stupid young person, if the police come asking, will they be able to trace him? Was he telling people his name, sir?'

'His name? Not him. His mates called him something, though. Joe, I reckon.' The cigarette was scorching his lip. He pinched it out between first finger and thumb nail, checked it, then flicked it away. 'Not that I talked to him myself, mind, but that's what I heard. His mates called him Joe. That'll be his name, will it? Joe? Joseph? Calls himself Joseph, does he?'

Alec chose not to commit himself. 'Mates, sir? He had other persons with him?'

'Had to. I mean, he can't hardly hump that dirty great TV just on his jacksie, and he's too young to drive the car himself.'

'They came in a car, sir?'

'What else? They were flogging a fucking TV, weren't they?' Doug glanced at his watch. He was losing patience. 'And I'll tell you something for nothing, Mr Jones. Your young Joseph's got in with a ropy lot. You need to get him out. I know the car, patched it up a few months back. String and chewing gum. A proper heap. It's them chummies down on Riverview. You need to get him out. Nip him in the bud. Like I said, Mr Jones. Nip him in the bud.'

'I will, sir. Believe me, Mr Finch, I will. And thank you.' Alec's hand moved briefly in the direction of his wallet, then away again. The Mr Jones he remembered would never have thought of such a thing. 'Thank you very much, sir.'

'Nothing to it. You came to the right man, that's all. Look after your own, Mr Jones. No one else fucking will. I said, no one else fucking will.' Doug turned away, went back to whatever he'd been doing behind the stack of tyres.

Alec walked slowly out into the street, returned to the Rover. Joseph, a black teenager living on the Riverview estate . . . It wasn't a lot but it was probably enough. And he'd got it, ironically, because, like Joseph, he too was a fucking blackberry.

His contact group on the Riverview estate wasn't in its usual place. He parked the car, nonplussed. The mattress was there, its centre blackened by the remains of a small fire, but the children were nowhere to be seen. He checked the time – Christ, it was nearly seven. Where had the afternoon gone? He had to be at Tony's, washed and changed, with a programme in mind, by nine. So where, at nearly seven on a Saturday evening, would the children be? In their homes, if they were lucky, if they had any, watching TV, having supper.

He got out of the car. Whom else could he ask? A cat shot by, disappearing through an open doorway, panicked for no apparent reason. The place was deserted, canned television laughter or police sirens coming from windows. He wandered to the end of the turn-around, looked up between a couple of buildings, saw nothing. A teenage black called Joseph, two tower blocks, any number of surrounding four-storey units – it was ridiculous, in the time available, to try to find him, but Alec was fired up, so near now, mystified, his theory shot to hell, pursuing his investigations. . .

He returned to his car, stood beside it in the middle of the road, feet apart, hands on hips, and shouted. He could think of nothing else to do.

He shouted, 'Joseph?' And again, 'Jo – seph?'

He was a biggish man, his voice biggish too. He shouted again, more loudly. *'Joseph? Jo – seph?'*

This was going to take time. He filled his lungs and shouted again.

His mother would have been shocked at such behaviour. He was shocked himself. But the thing was, fucking blackberries could do these things.

'Joseph? Jo – seph?'

A young black woman appeared on a first floor balcony on

one of the side blocks. 'Hey – you down there, wack, making all that racket. Belt up. Is it Joseph Kakimbo you're wanting?'

'Black kid. So high.' He repeated Doug Finch's estimation. There might be two four foot ten Josephs, black, on the estate, and Kakimbo the wrong one, but it was a risk he'd have to take. 'Just about so high. . .'

'Didn't think it was his pa. Big Joe's been gone years now.' She leaned on the balcony rail, one hip jutting. 'Are you police?'

'Do I look like police?' Another risk, but not much of one.

She smiled slowly. 'So what's it you're wanting?'

'That's between me and Joseph, and Joseph's ma.'

'So it'll have to wait.' A baby started crying in the flat behind her. 'They've took off into town. Some movie.'

'Maybe I could leave a note.'

'Not with me, you couldn't.' She jerked her head upwards. 'Fourth floor, 'long at the end. Number twenty.'

'I'm much obliged to you.'

'Then you can spare me Janice knowing who it was pointed you in her direction.'

'I'll do that. No problem.' Whatever it was he wanted, she'd decided it wouldn't be welcome. She'd still passed him on, though. It looked as if Joseph and his ma weren't her favourites. 'Fourth floor up, you said?'

'You'll have to walk, lift died on us couple of days ago. Welcome to Riverview.' She went back into her flat and a moment later the baby stopped crying.

All the noise Alec had been making, and only one person had chosen, for whatever reason, to be seen taking an interest. Welcome to Riverview.

Alec walked up, found number twenty. He rang the doorbell, just to be sure, but no one answered. He didn't leave a note – he'd simply wanted to be certain he knew where to come in the morning. Sunday, fairly early, seemed a good time to catch the Kakimbos at home. What he'd do when he'd caught them was another matter. Even if Joseph had stolen Joan Bladon's TV, it didn't necessarily mean that he'd killed her. At least, Alec hoped it didn't. Knee-high to a duck, dumb enough to try to flog a stolen Multirent TV, no more than twelve years old, fourteen, maybe, and black, Alec would find it hard to turn him over to Inspector Clarke, but harder still not to.

He made it to Tony's with hardly five minutes to spare. The place was filling up, and busy, but not so much that a *shshshhh* didn't spread round the booths as he stepped up on to the low platform and started sorting sheet music. His pulse quickened, the familiar showbusiness thrill blotting out Joseph Kakimbo. One of the good things about piano playing was, when you were doing it everything else went away.

He liked Saturdays. They were boisterous, and hard work on account of the high level of groundswell that had to be drowned out, but they were more fun than the mausoleum conditions earlier in the week. At least the punters were alive on Saturdays, and it was his fault, at least until the bar goods took over, if they didn't pay attention.

He stood by the piano, putting his music into a reasonable sequence. Usually he saw to this at home but tonight there hadn't been time. He seldom did more than glance at the sheet music but he liked to have the pieces in order on the stand, saving him from the mental block – *what next?* – that might descend at the end of a number. The new title, and a key signature, were mostly all he needed. He enjoyed thinking up far-fetched ways round the modulation, and sometimes got a hand when a sharp-eared fan noticed.

He stood there fussing by the piano long enough for the noise level to rise again. He liked to insert the first chords unobtrusively, getting the music noticed gradually, no reverent opening hush. That way he was covered if his fingers were slow to remember what they were supposed to be doing. He sat down, looked round the room, spotted Tony himself, front-of-house, as was his Saturday custom. Alec hoped tonight's punters would behave themselves. His boss knew damn-all about jazz, but he could tell a good house from a bad house as well as the next man.

Continuing round the room, Alec's gaze settled on another familiar face. He looked away quickly. What the hell was Aiken Hardcastle doing here again? Couldn't he take no for an answer?

Playing these gigs, he'd said, *it's not enough*.

You're taking your time, he'd said, *but how much longer can you afford to?*

Alec's fingers were shaking. He stretched them, closing his eyes and breathing deeply, and drifted into an eight-bar intro. When he opened his eyes again the music on the stand was 'Jeepers, Creepers', upbeat, key of D major. Aiken Hardcastle joined Joseph among the unimportances.

At the end of the second set, though, in response to the by now traditional single malt that he could have refused, Alec went over. It was a measure of the man that, although by then Tony's was packed, Hardcastle still had a booth to himself. He didn't get up. 'I got last Monday's presentation wrong,' he said. 'Wrong approach, wrong follow-through, wrong clincher.'

Alec smiled. 'Good evening, Mr Hardcastle. Very well, thank you. And how are you?'

'A man like you needs something definite. A definite proposal. Something he can get his teeth into.'

'I can't stay, Mr Hardcastle. I just wanted to—'

'Please sit, Mr Duncan. What I have now is exactly that – a definite proposal. So please sit.'

Alec sat. The new, super-forceful Hardcastle was more amusing than the old, understated one. 'I just wanted to tell you that—'

'Job description. Terms of employment. Salary scale.'

Hardcastle produced papers from the briefcase on the seat beside him. 'You'll refuse to look at any of it, I know, not just at the moment, so I intend to provide a verbal summary.'

'I really can't stay, Mr Hardcastle. I just wanted to—'

'You wouldn't have come over if you weren't interested.'

It brought Alec up short. Three times Hardcastle had interrupted him, and a good thing too, because he'd have been hard put to it to finish. *I just wanted to tell you* ... what? *That I've found out where I'm going, and it's not with Guardians Plc* ... was that it? If so, then why come over? Especially since the new, super-forceful Hardcastle in fact wasn't amusing at all.

'Crime prevention, Mr Duncan. Your special interest.' Hardcastle rolled the papers into a vertical tube, rested his chin on it, and regarded Alec intently. 'Guardians Plc have been looking at all these vigilante groups. Like the police, we aren't happy. Blundering amateurs, and no good at all for public perceptions of the actual job professionals do. Besides which, they'll be demanding to carry guns soon, and none of us in the trade wants that, but this government won't like to say no ... Unlike the police, though, we don't see the answer in more restrictions. We see the answer in proper training. And that's where you come in.'

Alec detested vigilante groups. The public liked them and they were a cheap way of getting the government off the Laura Norder hook, but they were no substitute for a properly funded police force. Also they gave small men big authority.

'Guardians Plc is establishing training courses, Mr Duncan. Plans are well advanced. Courses in all aspects of proper policing. Fee-paying, naturally. Response from the groups themselves is excellent. What we need is a chief instructor. A very senior man. A director of studies ... someone who can turn the present shambles into an organization along the lines of the Territorial Army.' He unrolled the tube of papers. 'I'm authorized to offer you the job. Eighty thousand a year plus the usual extras. And the chance to make a difference.'

Alec sat back. Aiken Hardcastle had been quite right about his earlier presentation – approach, follow-up, clincher, compared to this it had been fucking useless. Especially the clincher. He reached out and took the papers, which had rolled up again of their own accord. He left them that way.

Hardcastle said, 'You have questions.'

'Of course I have questions. But now is no the time.'

'I understand that. But you don't have unlimited time. Guardians Plc needs an answer.'

'How much time?'

'Read the papers. There's a prospectus of the proposed courses. We need your input.'

'How much time?'

'A week. Two at the most.'

Alec stood up. 'I'll be away back to the piano. This isn't a conventional way of doing things.'

'This isn't a conventional job. You aren't a conventional man.'

'If that's understood, Mr Hardcastle, then we're halfway there.' Wasn't he conventional? He'd never thought of himself that way. But in any case, who cared? What he'd need was the leeway not being conventional gave. 'I'll be in touch, Mr Hardcastle. And one week should be plenty.'

He went back to the piano, sat down, stared at his music. This was ridiculous. He'd been offered jobs before, in security, and he'd turned them down, but this was ridiculous. He had Joseph Kakimbo to think about. A director of studies . . . and Joseph Kakimbo . . . and a chance to make a difference . . . and, fortunately, on the stand in front of him a tired stride arrangement of 'My Blue Heaven' that always needed a lot of perking up. He sighed, finished the single malt Aiken Hardcastle had bought him, and got stuck in.

10

Alec was back at Riverview by ten next morning. He'd decided this was the earliest he should disturb Mrs Kakimbo and her son, after a night out at the movies. Teenagers liked their beds. So did their mothers.

He could have been there a lot earlier – Aiken Hardcastle, combined with his Joseph worries, had given him a bad night and he'd been wide awake since five. Everything about Hardcastle put his back up, yet what did his present obsession with the Bladon case prove, except that the sooner he got back to some sort of policing, the happier he'd be? The money was preposterous, of course, but that didn't matter: he'd just have to be sure not to catch greed from it. There were plenty of good enough causes he could pass it on to. No, the eighty thousand wasn't a problem. But, policing or not, the job was.

He'd be teaching aspiring vigilantes, for one thing, and he was suspicious of their motives. Also, he didn't want to be responsible for putting more guns on the street. Most of all, though, he didn't want to work for Guardians Plc. He knew too much about them, about how they operated. In their PR they were endlessly pious about law and order: in their practice law was distinctly disposable – order was what counted.

Running in frantic counterpoint to this, as he battled with

his gritty, scrunched-up bed, was the problem of Joseph Kakimbo. It was just possible that the boy had been surprised by Joan Bladon in the act of stealing her TV, that she'd still had her gun, that there'd been a struggle, and that somehow a bullet from her own gun had killed her. But why not in her living room, where the TV was? Or in the hall, if he was going out that way instead of back through the window, which made sense, given the fact that he was knee-high to a duck and carrying a 27-inch TV. But the rest of the flat had been undisturbed – so how come the two of them had ended up in her kitchen?

Increasingly Alec was returning to Stan Falco as the moving force. 'Them as killed young Dancer,' he'd called down the stairs as Alec was leaving, 'they're already dead.' Mebbe he'd meant it literally after all. Joseph had stolen the TV, no doubt of that, but mebbe Stan Falco's man had done the killing. Frank didn't believe that Stan would interest himself in such small fry as Dancer, but a Falco man was a Falco man, at any level. Stan didn't offer his employees much else in the way of job security.

But if that was the case, then how the hell had he acted so promptly? The deaths of Dancer and Mrs Bladon seemed to have been two hours apart, at the most. Even supposing that Jackie Patterson, or someone, had watched from the bushes and seen Dancer's murder, and had reported it to Stan Falco, organizing a response still needed time. Hit men weren't sitting around, instantly available, and Stan would hardly go out at two in the morning and do the business himself. In any case, he surely wouldn't have known where Joan Bladon lived, and if Jackie had followed her home first, before reporting in, then that took at least another half-hour out of the time available.

On second thoughts, once Alec had accepted that one person, Joseph, had stolen the TV, and another person, X, had done the murder, then why couldn't X be Jackie after all?

The scenario as before, but without Jackie stealing the TV, which had never really made all that much sense ... No evidence, of course, but that wasn't Alec's problem. Alec's problem, as a law-abiding citizen, ho-ho, was to get Joseph honestly and genuinely off the hook. That was essential. If the boy wasn't a lost soul already, he would be by the time Inspector Clarke and the British justice system had finished with him.

So he needed Joseph to have left the flat in total ignorance of the body in the kitchen. Or possibly he'd looked round the door, and seen it, and fled.

Would he know if Joseph was telling him the truth? He'd cross that bridge when he came to it.

At ten to ten, red-eyed and sick with nervous tension, Alec turned right off the Aigburth Road and drove slowly down to Riverview. He continued through the estate, on to the fancier parts beyond, leaving his car out of immediate vandal range, where the road ended and the path to the river began. House owners there, so close to Riverview, would be fierce and watchful. He walked back up the road. If he and Frank were right, and Joan Bladon had shot Dancer, this was the route she'd have followed afterwards. It wasn't easy, on a sunny Sunday morning, to imagine such a woman, the woman on the beach in the holiday snap, the woman he'd built up in his mind, so passive yet now a murderer, making her way up this road with Dancer's death still pervading her. Had she wept? Had she danced in the darkness, Trevor avenged, and all her suffering? He didn't know about revenge. He found it hard to imagine.

He reached the Kakimbos' block and started up the stairs. Four flights were enough. Chief inspectors rode in cars or sat at desks. Add to that pianos, and so did ex-chief inspectors. By the time he arrived at the fourth floor his heart was pounding. He paused to let it settle. Three doors opened on to the landing, number twenty, the Kakimbos', at the far end.

The previous evening the landing had been peopled with murmuring sitcom voices and TV laughter: this morning shrill American cartoon characters competed with whoops and splats and extravagant explosions.

When he was ready, as ready as he'd ever be, he rang number twenty's bell. A pause, a movement behind the spy lens, then the door opened three inches, letting out muffled reggae, before being snubbed convincingly by a thick chain. Brown and gold flowered fabric showed in the gap, and a strip of very black face beneath lifeless, cheaply straightened black hair.

'Mrs Kakimbo? My name is—'

'You're the man making all that noise last night.'

'I'm sorry about that, Mrs Kakimbo. I didn't have an address and I needed to find you. I—'

'I hear all about it. You got no right.'

'I need to talk to you.' He lowered his voice. 'I need to talk to your son, Joseph.'

'We don't need to talk to you, mister. No fuss, now. Just go away.'

'I'm not police, Mrs Kakimbo.'

'I know that. This door would be down by now if you was.'

He leaned closer to the three-inch gap. 'I'm a friend, Mrs Kakimbo.' He hoped he was. 'I want to help. Let me come in. We don't want everyone out here hearing your business.'

'We don't need no help.' She glanced sideways, in the direction of the music inside her flat. 'Help with what?'

'I think you know that, Mrs Kakimbo.' She must do. She was worried. She hadn't slammed the door. She was telling him to go away and asking for his help at the same time. 'It's a family matter. I don't like to see a boy giving his family trouble.'

'They all do.' She stood back slightly from the door. 'They all do, Mr—?'

'My name is Alexander Duncan. And they all don't, Mrs

Kakimbo. Not if they get the right help. From the right person. At the right time.'

He waited while she examined him. He was smart and clean, wearing jeans and open-necked shirt under a short showerproof jacket. He was on her side too, but that wasn't so obvious. Finally she took a chance, gave in to her fears for her son, and unchained the door.

The flat was a larger, right-handed version of Joan Bladon's, with an extra bedroom, its door closed, through which the music, now changed to a computer-generated techno beat, was unpleasantly loud. She took him straight ahead, into the over-furnished living room. On every flat surface photographs in silver frames were arranged: family snaps, coloured studio portraits, a series of photographs of the same cheery little black boy, taken at yearly intervals. None seemed to be recent. At some point Joseph had gone off having his picture taken.

Mrs Kakimbo was a big-boned woman, and stout, with suffering legs, and feet in feathery slippers, and the brown and gold flowers were on a brocade, satin-lapelled dressing gown. She didn't ask him to sit down. She was taking her time with him.

He looked round, saw that her fourth floor window gave a view over the city's rooftops. The familiar landmarks of the Liver Building and the two cathedrals had been joined by a fourth: beneath its restless cranes the black outer wall of the new juvenile P & P Centre was already visible. He realized that when the prison was completed the city would have a new focal point.

Mrs Kakimbo's brocade rustled and he turned back to her. She said, 'Are we talking about the same thing, Mr Duncan?'

'A TV set?'

'He says some friends gave it him.'

Alec looked at her squarely and shook his head.

She stood behind an armchair, smoothing the lacy antimacassar on its back. 'Who told you where to come?'

'Your son was seen trying to sell the set, Mrs Kakimbo.'
'The police don't know this?'
'I haven't told them.'
'So why are you here?'
Alec hesitated. He didn't want to lie to her. 'I know the family that owns the set. I said I'd try to get it back.' He felt he was sounding abrupt and reached a hand out to her. 'And I also came because I thought, mebbe I could help. It's no good when a boy takes to thieving so early.'
She retreated. 'That's between me and Joseph.'
'If you say so.'
'I do say so. I know your sort of help, Mr Duncan. It's all pie in the sky. Selling folks Jesus. What's Jesus ever done for me?'
She thought he was from some church. It made sense, and would have kept things simple, but he couldn't allow it. 'I'm no that keen on religion myself, Mrs Kakimbo. I'd say life is here and now. Every moment. People need to pay attention. And to be given a better chance.'
His manifesto. Earnest stuff for ten in the morning, but he'd not apologize.
She stared at him for a moment, making up her mind, then turned away. She was distancing herself. 'You won't beat him?' Half of her hoped he would. She stood very still, painfully straight and stiff, and before Alec could answer she said, 'He's in his room.'
Alec moved towards the door. 'Do you call him Joe, or Joseph?'
'Joseph. He's Joe at school.' She moved a photograph on a crowded side table. 'He thinks you're police.'
Alec checked. 'Who told him that?'
'He didn't need telling. He's been expecting you all week. He's got a guilty conscience.'
She'd told him herself. Standard bogeyman stuff, the fulfilment of months, perhaps years of warnings. *Didn't I say? And*

now it's happened. Didn't I say? It was interesting, though, that Joseph hadn't run. He'd gone to ground instead.

'How old is he?'

'Fourteen in January.'

It meant nothing. Children littler than that ran away. Children littler than that stayed. They played tag, and mugged defenceless old women, and faithfully kept house for their younger brothers and sisters while their parents fought, and drank themselves unconscious. Being fourteen in January was no indicator of what might be expected.

Alec sighed. 'Do you want to come with me?' She shook her head. 'What about his father?' He had to ask it. She shook her head again, still not looking at him.

He went out of the living room, down the passage to the closed bedroom door. The music, electronic patterns over a techno beat, was very loud, and it seemed to Alec that a no-win situation was being created for him. If he knocked on the door, Joseph wouldn't be able to hear him. If he pounded, it would be typical fascist bully-boy tactics.

Alec tried the knob. Surprisingly, it turned and the door opened. He went straight in. The windows were obscured. A bare red electric light bulb hanging from the ceiling provided the only illumination.

'*Don't move!*'

A wild shriek, louder than the music. Joseph was waiting for him, had been here, like this presumably, ever since Mrs Kakimbo let him in. Dressed in standard black paramilitary gang gear, the boy was crouched in the farthest corner of his bed, pressed against the wall, a lightweight police issue .45 automatic pointed waveringly in Alec's direction, the safety catch off. He had a small boy's skinny little neck and wide eyes.

Alec was willing to bet that his mother didn't know about the gun. Hoping to keep things that way, he nudged the door shut behind him with his heel.

'I said, don't move! Fuck you, asshole, fuck you, I said don't move!'

Alec leaned against the closed door, all his hopes unravelled. Frank had been quite right, a hundred and fifty pounds was a hundred and fifty pounds. Joan Bladon hadn't thrown her gun away, and now Joseph had it. Probably he'd hoped it would make him brave, but it hadn't. He was very afraid. The pounding music wasn't anything clever, hadn't been meant to wrong-foot him. It was Joseph's security blanket.

'Asshole! Don't move, asshole! Don't move!'

Alec kept his hands away from his sides also. The boy would have seen enough cops and robbers TV to be edgy about pockets and imperfectly understood holsters. Joseph had the initiative, and now it was up to him to think what next he could make happen. Till then, all Alec had to do was wait. Joseph was frightened enough to be a little crazy, but Alec thought he'd need pushing before he'd kill.

In the meantime, Alec had a problem. He could imagine Joseph panicking if Joan Bladon had surprised him, firing at her, killing her. But he was so scrimpy, and on Monday night it had been she who had the gun. Would he have attacked her, struggled with her till she ended up dead? Wouldn't he just have run away? He couldn't have wanted the TV, or the gang status it represented, so badly. Had she cornered him?

Alec peered round the tiny room. On the floor by the bed, resting crookedly on several old shoes, with a cardboard take-away pizza box and several Coke cans on it, was the combined TV set and VCR from Multirent. Quite an unimpressive affair. Disappointing. The walls of the room, which seemed to be painted purple, had Megadeath and Kung Fu posters stuck on them, and a stuffed yellow Garfield hanging from its tail. The bed itself was covered by a cotton bedspread printed with vintage racing cars. A plastic model of a space monster, not finished, stood among comic books and a chest expander and dozens of audio cassettes on a flat-topped, home-assembled desk. Clothes, drooping from hangers, dangled against the outside of a matching wardrobe. On shelves above the desk Joseph's multi-amp sound system, flash matt black and probably nowhere near full volume, was bright with bands of rising and falling red and green lights. Apart from the stolen TV, and the gun in Joseph's hand, his bedroom was like ten thousand, a hundred thousand others.

'*All right, asshole. Where's your back-up?*' Joseph had thought of something else to fear. '*You fuckers come in twos, don't you? Where's your back-up?*'

'I'm not police, Joseph. I don't have any back-up.'

'*Louder, asshole. I don't hear you. Tell me louder.*'

'No.' Alec shook his head. Any communication between them, at that decibel level, would be hyper and confrontational. He gestured at the sound system, and mimed turning it off.

'*No way, asshole. No fucking way. If the music's too loud, man, you're too fucking old.*'

Alec had heard the joke before. He shook his head again, more firmly. Joseph was coming down a pitch or two, and Alec needed to make territory for himself, so he repeated his mime and took a step towards the sound system.

'*Don't move, I said! Don't you ever touch my system. I'm not kidding, asshole. You touch my system and—*'

Alec had already stopped moving, but the damage was done. He'd misjudged the situation. Joseph's hand was twitching uncontrollably: the gun went off.

Alec saw it as much as he heard it, saw the gun leap in Joseph's hand. Its sound, against the techno beat, was insignificant. Surprisingly, despite the very short range, he felt no impact. His relief, oddly, was more for Joseph's sake than his own. Being hit would have created, for them both, a whole new ballgame.

He didn't look to see where the bullet had gone – the gun held all his attention. The gun, and then the boy . . . Joseph was gaping at it, shocked, fumbling to get a firmer hold on it. The gun had jerked up in his face when fired, and he'd nearly dropped it. The gun terrified him.

Time had slowed. Become more capacious.

At the moment of the shot, Alec had been appalled. There was room for him to be angry at Joseph, disgusted with himself for letting it happen, and heartbroken at the clear implication that the boy who had shot at him could have shot at Joan Bladon. But now, an age later, he felt happiness blossom, lifting a great weight from his spirit.

Joseph had never fired a gun before, had never been close to a gun when someone else fired it. Watching him now, how scared he was – for himself: the possibility that he might have hit someone obviously hadn't occurred to him – watching him now, there could be no doubt that this was a first.

No, Joseph might be a less-than-ideal individual in any number of ways, but the poor dumb blackberry wasn't Joan Bladon's murderer.

Time speeded up again. Joseph flung the gun away, down on the foot of the bed, and retreated still further into his corner, curling up, arms round his knees, eyes squeezed tightly shut. He wasn't there. None of this was anything to do with him. He wasn't there.

Alec picked up the gun, then crossed to the shelves above the desk and turned off the music. Silence, high and thin, sang in his ears. He sat on the far end of Joseph's bed and rested his head in his hands. The stink of cordite was sharp. He felt exhausted, as if he had climbed a mountain.

'Joseph?' He spoke softly. His voice sounded strange to him. Unexpected. 'Joseph? It's all right, lad – no harm done. No harm done.'

The boy hunched in on himself, snivelling.

What about literal harm? Alec looked up at the wall behind where he'd been standing. There'd have to be damaged plaster somewhere, but he couldn't see it. The light was dim, of course. Joseph liked it that way – the window panes had been covered with thick black paint and the red electric light bulb was of low wattage. Alec thought about opening the window and decided this was not the moment to assault the boy with daylight.

'You're a bloody idiot, Joseph. You know that?'

Joseph muttered something.

'You what?'

His head was burrowed into the corner. 'I didn't kill her.'

'I know that. Nobody says you did.'

'She was dead when I went in. I didn't kill her. You don't believe me.'

'Try me.'

'She was in the kitchen. I was poking around. I didn't kill her. She was in the kitchen, sitting at that stupid little table. I didn't kill her.'

Alec remembered Joan Bladon's kitchen table. It was small, certainly, with ugly metal legs, but why stupid? And she hadn't been sitting at it, she'd been lying on the floor. 'She was at the kitchen table?'

Joseph looked back over his shoulder, suddenly uncurled and faced him. 'You can't fucking bang me up,' he said. 'I'm a fucking juvenile.'

Enough was enough. Alec leaned forward, grabbed what he could of Joseph's clothing, and heaved the boy up the wall in the corner above the bed. 'I can do what I like with you, laddie.' He shook him. So much for the more obvious forms of tender loving care. 'I'm not police and I don't have to play by their rules. So pay attention, and less of the lip.'

Joseph gaped at him. 'I didn't kill her, mister. I fucking *didn't. . .*'

'But she was sitting at the kitchen table.'

'That's what I said. How was I to know it'd give up on me?'

'Give up on you?'

The boy fought him. 'Put me down. You've no right. You—'

'Give up on you?'

'All right, so I wanted the shooter. I got my eye on it. But she was fat, and heavy, and sort of leaning on it. And when I went for it . . . well, she fell over sideways, didn't she, off the chair, and the stupid table went with her, and the chair too, all over the place . . .'

He tailed off, remembering the moment. Signs of a struggle, Alec thought. Constable Baynes's signs of a struggle. So simple.

The truth about Joan Bladon's death was simple too.

Alec sighed. He let Joseph slide slowly down on to the bed and released him. It was the absence of the gun that had fooled them. And the lack of a forensic examination that would have shown up lead residues on her hand, neutron transference. An elementary examination of the wound had revealed powder burns, but not who'd fired the bullet. The doctor'd said it was at close quarters.

'So she fell on the floor. But you still took the gun?'

Resentfully the boy straightened his black jacket. 'She didn't need it. What did she need it for? She'd done herself in with it, for fuck's sake.'

Yes. She'd done herself in with it. He believed Joseph. Of course she had. It made the only sense. First Dancer Drew, and then herself. What else was there? Where else could she go? It was so simple. She'd never had much, even before Trevor, and bugger-all after him, so she'd nothing to lose. And mebbe squaring things with Dancer Drew had let her die happy.

Happy? He wished he could believe that. Or even that she'd enjoyed the irony in killing Dancer with the gun he'd just sold her, but he thought not. She'd have been so tired, simply wanting to get home. A woman like her didn't kill herself untidily, out on the street.

He sighed again. 'You said she was leaning on the gun.' He needed things spelled out. Corroborative evidence. Once a copper, always a copper. 'Was she holding it?'

Joseph nodded. 'It sort of fell out of her hand when the table went. It landed by my feet.'

No rigor mortis. 'What time was this?'

'Late. Two or three. I didn't look.'

Why should he? It had been a stupid question. 'And you turned out the light?'

'It seemed, like, well, sort of . . . *right*. Her being dead and that.'

It was a fair point. He had another question. 'You wore gloves?'

'I'm not stupid.' Joseph fidgeted. He was getting edgy. 'See here, mister, I took the bullets from her bag, mister, but I never touched her purse. I never touched it.'

He looked at Alec anxiously, as if hoping that would make everything all right.

Bullets. That was a new one. Still, it made sense – Dancer Drew would have had to sell her bullets. The gun was useless without them.

Later, with Mrs Kakimbo keeping cave, Alec carried Joan Bladon's TV set down a couple of flights of stairs and along some corridors. He dumped it beside a rubbish chute and carefully wiped it off. With luck, someone at Riverview would find it and take it home with them. If not, and the police got hold of it, there was nothing to connect it with number twenty.

The .45 and the spare ammunition clip remained a secret between him and Joseph. He took them away with him and when he reached his car he went on the extra hundred yards or so down to the river, and the shore was deserted so he threw them in, far out beyond the low tide line. He'd talked to Joseph and he hoped they had an understanding. Joseph had helped him look for the mark made by the bullet on the wall, and when they'd found it, high up by the ceiling, he'd moved one of the posters to cover it. The bullet itself Alec had pocketed, along with the gun and clip. They'd had a serious talk. He'd suggested that Joseph's mates, the guys who'd driven him round hoping to do business with fences like Doug Finch, were losers. Noisy guys, but small-time. And the record among the next age-group up from them wasn't good – too many of them shot each other, and the police got a fair percentage of the rest. If Joseph wanted money there were better ways. Mebbe five pounds a week wasn't much, but if Alec brought his car round Saturday mornings that's what he'd get for washing it and cleaning it out.

The money was a feeble bribe – no sum would replace the other things gang membership gave Joseph – but it provided an excuse for Alec to keep in touch. He hadn't had a chance yet to explain this to Mrs Kakimbo, but she hadn't objected to the deal. No doubt she'd thought about him molesting Joseph and she'd decided she could keep an eye out. She knew where her son was heading and she didn't have many options.

She'd raised the question of punishing the boy. He'd stolen a TV and now he was getting away with it, and that wasn't right. Alec said it was up to her of course, but he didn't think the TV had given Joseph much joy. The gun had, probably, simply owning it and handling it, but Alec didn't mention that. The morning's nightmare, he judged, had cancelled things out. And it *had* been a nightmare: the music and the red light, the shrieks, the fucks and assholes, the gun . . . they pumped up Joseph's adrenalin but he was still young enough to remember different, and happier, ways. Family outings. His mother's broad knee.

Joseph's father wasn't around, admittedly, but that need not necessarily be regretted. Fathers weren't always an unmixed blessing. In any case, children survived their lack, and Mrs Kakimbo had impressed Alec. She was loving with her son, quiet when she might have been frantic, and sorrowful when she might have been enraged. Also she'd helped Alec without a lot of fuss when it came to disposing of the stolen TV.

After he'd thrown the gun and clip into the Mersey he stood for a while on the tussocky shore, staring out across the water. His double murder had reduced itself to a single murder, followed by the immediate suicide of the murderer. It was, in many ways, the ideal resolution. It left no loose ends. It was self-contained, made no demands on him as a responsible, law-abiding citizen. It required no further action. It was available if he ever needed it to get him off Inspector Clarke's hook, but he was off that anyway. Dave Clarke was just having fun: his sort of fun. Allerton would waste a few more days, a few more man-hours, but nothing significant. Dancer's death had already come and gone, and Joan Bladon's would soon follow it.

Reopening both cases and involving Joseph wouldn't help the cause of law enforcement, and would do a great deal of harm to Joseph. The Merseyside force would be made to look foolish. Also, the subsequent investigation would be highly labour-intensive – mebbe ten thousand of the tax payers' pounds spent proving something that nobody finally could do anything about. So, let sleeping dogs lie. The just-another-Riverview-mugging syndrome would quickly take over. He'd let her son know the truth – the poor wee sod had a right to that – but otherwise, *stumm* . . . The ideal resolution.

He shuddered. For Christ's sake – that was balance sheet stuff. This was flesh and blood. A person. It didn't need the sensibility of a Tolstoy to be able to envision Joan Bladon's life, her death, her wretchedness. The grinding banality. Even her hatred of Dancer Drew had been greyed down to a calculated, weary transaction, no fervour, no triumph, just loneliness and bitter determination. A matter of duty, really. Of obligation.

Her suicide, too, in a Riverview slum kitchen: weariness, duty, loneliness, determination. The ideal resolution?

He shuddered again. Such desolation should not be. Trevor's failures, and her community's, cast a long shadow . . . He turned and walked back up to where he'd left the Rover. He sat in it, staring bleakly out. He wasn't the only victim on the block. It wasn't a thought that gave him comfort.

He tried calling Morag but the McKinleys weren't at home and all he got was the answerphone. He didn't leave a message. If anyone had answered he'd no idea what he'd have said. It was all too long, and sad, a story. Morag didn't even know about his trip out to Justice City – she'd have wondered why and he wasn't up to explaining. He rang Frank Grove instead. Old Frank and he went back a long way – it was a male condition, with strengths as well as limitations.

11

Alec was left with a heavy sense of anticlimax. He felt weary, scarcely able to drag himself through the hours. His first thought, heaven help him, had been that he was missing the traditional station party, the booze-up with the lads that marked the successful close of a major investigation. The glass he'd raised with Frank and Doris late that Sunday afternoon had been no substitute.

But he'd never much liked those parties – not in recent years, at any rate. He'd never admitted it, of course, but he'd been a loner even then, edgy, secretly unconvinced that filling up more and more prison cells was a job he wanted to do. His interest had increasingly been in crime prevention, which was something else again.

No, his weariness came from the fact that the closing of the case should have meant he could move on, draw a line, start whatever came next, and of course he couldn't. Closing the case, like riding out to Justice City to see Trevor Bladon, had changed nothing. May was still dead. The flat was still empty.

Monday came, and he still pitied himself and despised self-pity. Nine months were still too long and nowhere near enough. He'd rushed about Liverpool asking questions and making sense of a couple of killings, and he was still unready. Still paralysed. Trevor Bladon, the poor wee sod, was still unfinished business.

He felt unclean, too. Rotting somewhere inside. It was a result, he thought, of too much sorrow.

At least he'd drawn a line under Aiken Hardcastle. He called him on Tuesday and told him, no. Thanks for the offer but no thanks. It so happened that the previous evening the artistic director of the Everyman Theatre had been at Tony's and had come up to him afterwards and offered him a job playing piano in a revival of a small-scale musical show, *Forever Plaid*. It had died the death in London but it was a good piano showpiece, rehearsals were beginning in October, four hundred a week, and he'd more or less taken it, but that wasn't the reason he'd turned down Hardcastle. He'd thought about it a lot and that wasn't the reason. No, among the few people he knew since he'd left the Force, if he had to tell them he worked for Guardians Plc, he'd find himself apologizing, and that was no way to run a life. So he'd called Hardcastle on Tuesday morning and told him he wasn't accepting Guardians Plc's offer. Hardcastle had taken it surprisingly well – mebbe he'd thought about it also and had decided that employing Alexander Duncan might let him in for apologies too. Guardians Plc could presumably be quite nasty if hiring decisions didn't work out.

Alec celebrated by collecting Jamie from school, and giving him the lunch box he'd talked about, with a real lock and key. It was spoiling the boy, but he didn't care. Jamie would survive. It was himself he was spoiling, really. Over tea in their jumble of a kitchen he told Morag his Hardcastle decision, nothing more, and she fed him Jaffa Cakes and didn't press him. It was her way, and he was grateful. He was keeping the Everyman job to himself until after he'd met the music director – there was a fair chance he'd back out if he could find some halfway decent excuse, the key signatures he'd be expected to play in. He didn't need it. Tony's was fine. Morag would say balls to that, Tony's was easy and he was just being chicken, and he didn't need that either. The King of Swing, for the moment, was just his speed.

He didn't mention the Bladon case, of course. She knew nothing about it. Telling her, at any stage, would have needed too many explanations. She didn't even know he'd been out to see Trevor . . . Explanations, explanations.

Allerton's interest, as he'd expected, was winding down. He'd been called in again on Monday afternoon, just as a salve to Dave Clarke's pride, and warned that the case would stay open. It was just a form of words. The inspector'd gone on to remind him that officers who let the Force down weren't worth shit. A form of words too, if less anodyne. Alec went away bruised – he would always have trouble with the way he'd left the Force – but unanxious. There was the small matter of evidence. An enterprising officer could make bricks with very little straw, but not with none at all.

Meanwhile, he still had a responsibility to Trevor. The poor wee sod had a right to the truth about his mother's death – a son did, surely, no matter how painful? – but getting it to him wasn't going to be easy. It needed to be kept strictly between the two of them, obviously, so a simple letter was out of the question: all mail going in to Justice City LTI men was opened. A cell visit was out too: such visits were routinely taped, and the fact that the machinery had failed once in Trevor's cell was neither here nor there. Telephones, similarly, were monitored, as were all forms of computer access. Notes hidden in boxes of chocolates or whatever were hard to take seriously – and besides, little goodwill gifts passing between Alec Duncan and his partner's murderer were unlikely to go unexamined.

No, although he was determined to do the right thing by the lad, for the moment he couldn't see how.

Then, on Wednesday afternoon, Evie Fairbairn called. She was organizing her Auntie Joan's funeral in the cemetery out by Springwood Avenue – Allerton had released the body –

and she wondered if he'd want to come. Saturday. Eleven in the morning. Not a man for funerals, Alec was racking his brains for a reasonable, unhurtful excuse when she went on to mention, in all fairness, well aware that it would probably put him off, that Trevor would be there. Governor Ransome was giving Joan Bladon's son compassionate leave to attend his mother's funeral, six whole hours away from Justice City.

Alec made hasty synapse reconnections. 'Saturday morning, Evie? I can manage that.' If he was ever going to have an opportunity to get Trevor Bladon on his own, it would surely be at his mother's funeral. 'Thank you for asking.'

He hadn't told her about her Auntie Joan's suicide. There'd been an earlier phone call between them, when she'd thanked him for driving her over to Riverview, and he hadn't mentioned it. That would be up to Trevor, once he knew. Alec himself could see no point. It wasn't as if she'd taken his investigations seriously. She liked the random mugger theory and anyway she wasn't all that interested. Her auntie, she said, was well out of it. She'd no great wish, clearly, to hound whoever'd helped Joan on her way.

Alec timed his arrival at the cemetery so that he'd miss the service in the chapel. He'd looked up the C of E burial service in the public library, so that he'd know what to expect, and it distressed him. Not on account of its emphasis on sin and misery and the compensations of everlasting life (whatever that might be): these obviously suited Joan Bladon's situation very well. No, what distressed him was the page's heading: *Not to be used for any that die unbaptized, or excommunicate, or have laid violent hands upon themselves.* In other words, not to be used for the most needy of all. So much, he thought, for the same page's holy and most merciful Saviour.

But it was all yet another reason, for her family's sake, to keep quiet about the terminally violent hand Joan Bladon had laid upon herself. Evie, and Trevor, and Evie's mum coming up from London . . . There was no need to add insult to their injury.

For the same reason he organized a black armband for himself and an expensive wreath for the coffin. He'd done the same for May's family, the charitable donation their announcement had asked for, but for a different reason. He'd wanted to make them feel small. He never told them, though, and the donation was anonymous, so they never did. They were, of course, but they never felt it.

When he reached the cemetery, entering formally for once, not through the railings in the corner but through the gate, he scarcely recognized it. By daylight, on a bright Saturday morning, the cemetery was unmysterious, an open field dotted with stone grave markers and the occasional tree, surrounded with bright Saturday morning traffic. Alec walked briskly up the central path. He could have taken the opportunity to go looking for May's marker, but he didn't. He found the grave that had been freshly dug for Joan Bladon's coffin and waited on the surrounding plastic grass carpet. May's bones had no need of him, nor he of them.

He adjusted his armband. Waiting beside the grave, he suddenly realised how little he knew about Joan Bladon. A holiday snap of a plain, ponderous middle-aged woman in a dirndl dress on an Anglesey beach. A failed marriage, a delinquent son, a departed lover, a Tesco job, rage enough to commit murder, despair enough to commit suicide. It wasn't much. But then, he hadn't asked much. It had been enough that she was, like him, a victim. Which had been, he supposed, although he refused to feel bad about it now, insulting.

Now, in fact, he felt curiously excited.

As the coffin approached, carried by four undertaker's men and accompanied by a tiny group of mourners, Alec noticed that he was trembling. His pulse raced and his underarms sweated. Nervous and dizzy, he took long deep breaths to calm himself. The reaction surprised him. He put it down to superstitious dread at the black clothes and the slow ritual approach, and spoke to himself severely.

There were five mourners. To be precise, there were three – Evie, Trevor, Evie's mum – and two uniformed men Alec identified as warders from Justice City. He was glad to see that Trevor wasn't cuffed and had been supplied with a sober black suit, and they were letting him walk on his own. Evie was on his left, crying, Evie's mum on his right. The occasion was bleak enough without manacles.

How compassionate of him.

How reasonable.

How false.

Seeing Trevor, seeing the coffin, experiencing the passion they raised in him, all at once Alec had understood why he was there. *To do the right thing by the lad?* Who was he fooling? He was neither compassionate nor reasonable, he was consumed by hatred.

He hated Trevor, had hated him, and with good cause, with just cause, for nine long months. For nine long months he'd been without peace, able neither to rest nor to move on. It had been on account of his hatred, finally, that he'd driven out to Justice City, in order to rejoice at the black steel walls, at the suffering within them. He'd needed to reassure himself that the place was as terrible as he remembered. It had been on account of his hatred, too, that he'd agreed to do Trev a favour, turning the other cheek, humiliating him thereby. Helping the man he hated, because he hated him, was a civilized, if cancerous, delight.

He found no pleasure at all, therefore, in seeing Trevor walk free, in a sober black suit, unmanacled, the occasion spared their bleakness. The occasion *ought* to be bleak. Considering the guilt Trevor bore, it could never be bleak enough.

The poor wee sod had a right to the truth . . . Bugger that. Men like Trevor had no rights. The bitter truth about his mother's death would be Alec's just revenge, and it would surely destroy him. He would ram it down Trevor's throat, every bitter word of it, and Trevor would have to live with it for the rest of his life.

Alec shuddered, gritting his teeth to hold himself still. Not that any of this would bring back Trevor's mother, of course . . . or May, or May, or May . . . but it would draw the line that Alec needed. The line under his hate.

He lowered his head and looked down at the ground, unable to endure the sight of Joan Bladon's son. His passion calmed and he breathed more easily.

The undertaker's men approached. He was in the coffin's way and they asked him to move. He stepped back, ended up standing by Evie. She was still crying, and he smiled at her. He felt wonderfully in control. In a minute, he thought, he'd discreetly lend her his handkerchief. He could just see it.

The undertaker's men did professional things with planks and two ropes. The minister began to speak. Alec discreetly lent Evie his handkerchief. The minister had a good sense of the poetry – '. . . *and is cut down, like a flower; he fleeth as it were a shadow, and never continueth in one stay*' – and brought needed solemnity to the edgy, unfocused occasion. Alec forgave him his *Judge eternal* who, for everyone's sins, was *justly displeased.* Mebbe justice, like beauty, was in the eye of the beholder.

Alec folded his hands, interlocking his fingers and playing a tune with them on his knuckles. 'Honeysuckle Rose'. He was distancing himself. Preparing for the moment when he had Trevor's undivided attention. It didn't need the sensibility of a Tolstoy to be able to envision Joan Bladon's life, her death, her wretchedness, but he wanted to be sure Trevor made the effort.

Evie gave him back his handkerchief. One of the undertaker's men had handed her a little shiny trowel and she stooped and threw some earth on the coffin, which was now resting at the bottom of the grave. Trevor did the same, then Evie's mum. Mrs Fairbairn was prettier than her sister Joan had been. Mebbe she'd had a prettier life. Evie, for all her hump, must be a great comfort.

The warders weren't offered the trowel. If Alec was, he didn't notice. '*Forasmuch as it hath pleased Almighty God of his great mercy to take unto himself the soul of our dear sister here departed . . .*' It was a pity, Alec thought, that the mercy hadn't operated a bit sooner, to spare Joan Bladon the need. Operated on her son, mebbe, strangling the little sod at birth.

The words of the prayer book continued. Alec peered sideways at Trevor. He was sobbing wetly, more in need of a friendly handkerchief than Evie. He could fucking do without. Evie's mum was deathly pale, but dry-eyed. She wore a small close-fitting black hat with a little scrap of veil, that was really quite stylish.

'*The grace of our Lord Jesus Christ, and the love of God, and the fellowship of the Holy Ghost. . .*'

Evie's mum said 'Amen' clearly and firmly, and the minister closed his book, and the service was over. Evie's mum went to thank him or whatever, and Evie went with her. Trevor was left alone by the grave, his guards a few paces off, one of them looking at his watch. Alec turned to face him.

Now. The truth. Now.

He touched Trevor's arm. 'Mr Bladon?'

'Wodger want? Come to fucking gloat, have yer?' Trevor wiped his nose on his sleeve. In grief, clearly, Justice City's 'good lad' had forgotten his manners. 'Helped them put me away, didn't yer? Didn't yer? Piss off, I said. Fucking wanker.'

'Mr Bladon, I . . .' Alec's throat constricted and he cleared it. 'Mr Bladon, I think we need to have a talk—'

'Piss off, I said. Didn't yer help them put me away? If I'd been around, yer fucking wanker, none of this'd of happened. I'd of kep' an eye on her. I'd of fucking protected her.'

'Mr Bladon, I think we need . . .' Alec choked again. His control had left him. His hate wasn't strong enough.

He stared at May's killer. Snot was running down Trevor's upper lip. A talk? What words were there? For Christ's sake, after so long, and so much, what words were there? Pity? Shame? Forgiveness?

Shame?

'I'd just like to offer you my sympathy, Mr Bladon,' he said, 'in your sad loss.'

His sympathy – actually, that was the truth too, a truth, though it didn't sound it.

'Liar. Liar. Yer came here to gloat. Wodger know about loss? Fucking liar.'

Taunted like this, Alec hesitated. *What did he know about loss?* Ah, this was the old Trevor, the Trevor he'd loved to hate, the Trevor he'd scraped off the road on the day before May's death, the Trevor who only twenty-four hours later had hacked at her till she died. The old Trevor. Given another chance to set the record straight, another chance to see justice done, another chance to destroy May's killer, to destroy the man who'd dared to ask him what he knew about loss, Alec hesitated. Gave himself time.

'Aye, lad,' he said finally. 'And a happy Christmas to you too.'

He walked away. What words were there? For nine long months he'd chosen hate over grief. He'd hated Trevor and wished him harm, his image of Trevor, hacking at May, hacking at May, his image of Trevor, he'd hated that man, fervently, for nine long months . . . and hate corroded.

It was another of the prices victims paid.

He stopped by a gravestone a short distance off, and sat on it, elbows on his knees. Relief gusted over him, making him dizzy, and he rested his head in his hands. The undertaker's men were gathering up their bits and pieces, filling in time until everyone went away and they could roll up the plastic grass. One of them was arranging wreaths. Alec's wasn't the grandest, but it wasn't the humblest either. Evie and her mum were talking to the minister. Trevor was still on his own, standing by the grave while one of his warders enjoyed a quick puff and a drag and the other muttered furtively into his mobile phone.

What words were there? *Pity* . . . *shame* . . . *forgiveness* . . . Pity was insulting and shame was a vanity, but as for forgiveness . . . had he forgiven Trev? At Tony's, that night last week, he'd asked Morag and Iain, and Rachel Hewson, about forgiveness. He'd claimed he was asking about mothers forgiving their children but he wasn't. He was asking about himself. He was asking about himself forgiving Trevor. The sideways shift had helped him evade Morag's dagger of an answer. When she'd said she thought forgiveness was meaningless unless there'd first been a will to punish, it had been mothers she was referring to. Mothers – not him.

So what words were there? *Forgiveness* . . . *hatred* . . . *a will to punish* . . . such grandiose notions. They needed living up to. Justifying. That was why he'd concocted his mighty image of Trevor as the evil maniac, the drug-crazed hacker. Today's Trevor, the skinny little foul-mouthed inadequate specimen snivelling over there by the grave in his cheap ill-fitting suit, was a poor substitute. He was still pretty loathsome, and he supposed Alec still wished him harm, but he'd never do him any. Certainly not the terrible harm that would come from knowing his responsibility for his mother's death. Joan Bladon had obviously wanted him to know, blowing her brains out in such a public, accusatory fashion, but a mother's forgiveness, hers at least, could only stretch so far, and not every dying wish had to be respected. He understood her position, but the dead were dead.

The dead were dead.

Evie called to him. 'Come over,' she said. 'Meet my mum.'

Alec went. He met Evie's mum and, to find something cheerful to talk about, he told the two of them about the exciting new job he'd been offered at the Everyman. He didn't go on to tell them that the show needed a double bassist, they wouldn't have been interested, but it had just struck him that he should call Rachel Hewson and suggest that she auditioned. The music was mostly fifties ballads and barbershop, not exactly her style, but crossovers between classical and pop were all the rage.

Behind him Trevor stood alone by the grave, still weeping. Poor Trev. Alec didn't suggest that Evie ask her cousin to join them. He'd forgiven Trevor, he really had, but that didn't mean he had to be nice to him.